Vol. 8

Dear Reader,

I hope you enjoy getting to know Anne Gibson and her friends as much as I have. Even more, I hope reading about Anne and Blue Hill Library brings to your mind lovely memories of your own experiences with books or creative endeavors.

Writing *All Sewn Up* brought back memories of my teen years in a small-town library, as my mother was a librarian's assistant. I became a book lover from early childhood, and spending after-school hours surrounded by shelves of every imaginable book was pure heaven for this bibliophile. *All Sewn Up* engaged my interest even more, since I spent many years seated at my old Singer sewing machine, creating clothing for others, as well as for my family. I worked for Singer Sewing Machine Company as a sewing instructor, and as a seamstress at home when my children were little. The act of creating, whether it is lovely garments out of beautiful fabric or engaging stories on paper, gives me a sense of accomplishment and joy.

I wish you many pleasant hours as you visit Anne and the quaint, friendly town of Blue Hill.

Blessings,
Sunni Jeffers
writing as Emily Thomas

Secrets of the Blue Hill Library

Nowhere to Be Found
Shadows of the Past
Unlocking the Truth
Theft and Thanksgiving
The Christmas Key
Off the Shelf
Gone in a Flash

All Sewn Up

Secrets of the
BLUE HILL LIBRARY

EMILY THOMAS

Guideposts

New York

All Sewn Up

Chapter One

Anne Gibson lit a fire in the Nonfiction Room fireplace to take the chill off the room. She hated starting up the furnace to heat the large Victorian home and library so early in the fall, but she might have to if the cold weather persisted. As she looked up, she pushed her large-framed glasses back to the bridge of her nose. A glance at the clock told her she had a few minutes before the members of the Biography Club arrived for their meeting.

The fire caught in several spots, then erupted in a *poof* of flame. She closed the screen as Hershey, her son's chocolate Labrador retriever, began to bark from the back hall, a signal that her children were home from school. She moved to the hallway where she could see Wendy Pyle's car through the front door.

Anne watched Ben and Liddie climb out of Wendy's car and run toward the back staircase that led to their personal quarters. Where was Liddie's coat? She'd left it either in Wendy's car or at the school, which would mean the entire weekend without it, and the weather reports predicted unseasonably low temperatures. Anne reached the front door in time to see Wendy wave as she pulled away.

Anne directed a patron to the Nonfiction Room, then looked in the other rooms on her way up to their living quarters. A man sat reading in one corner of the History Room.

On the second floor, a young mother browsed the shelves with her preschooler in the Children's Room, and Remi, one of her part-time assistants, was shelving returned books in the Fiction Room. Satisfied that everything was under control, Anne went to the back stairs and sprinted up the staircase to the third floor.

"Ben? Liddie?" She knocked on their bedroom doors. Both doors opened.

"Hi, Mommy! Tomorrow's Saturday, so I get to play all day!" Liddie gave her mother a hug. Anne leaned over and kissed her. Liddie loved school, but she also loved unfettered time to play with her dolls.

"Hey, Mom. Can I go outside and play? Please?" Ben asked. Hershey sat beside him, wagging his tail, looking up at her with a "Me too?" expression.

"May I," Anne corrected with a smile. "Do you have homework?"

"A little, but can I do it later? Please?"

"All right, after you change you can go out. But come in if it starts raining. Do you want a snack?"

"Later, thanks." Ben shut his door.

"Mommy, can I have a snack?" Liddie said.

"Sure. But first tell me, where is your coat? Did you leave it in Mrs. Pyle's car?"

"No, Mommy." Liddie shook her head. "I gave it to a girl at school. It was cold outside on the playground, and she didn't have a coat or sweater or anything. I felt sorry for her. Besides, I had my sweater, so I wasn't cold."

"Did she forget her coat, honey? Is she going to bring yours back to you on Monday?"

Liddie shook her head again, sending her light brown hair swinging over her shoulders. "She didn't have one."

"Oh. I see. Well, that was very nice of you, honey." *Except now you don't have a coat either.* "Let's get that snack."

As they went downstairs to their personal kitchen at the back of the second floor, Anne considered what to say to Liddie. Nothing came to mind. Her five-year-old daughter had a soft heart and wanted to help everyone. Anne tried to encourage that, but Liddie also needed to learn the value of things. How could Anne get that message across without discouraging Liddie's compassion?

Oh, Eric, what do I say? How she missed her husband. And never more than when she needed wisdom to guide their children. Eric was one of the most compassionate people she had ever known. And one of the wisest. What would he tell their little girl? Anne would have to replace Liddie's coat, and soon. Winter was coming on faster than usual. Anne sighed as she got out the hot chocolate mix. Liddie watched as she put on a kettle of water to heat and got out two mugs and the graham crackers. September seemed too early to switch from cold milk to hot chocolate.

"Mommy, may I have marshmallows? Please?"

"Sure, sweetie." Anne mixed the cocoa and hot water, adding minimarshmallows to Liddie's cup. She sat across from her daughter and looked into her big brown eyes that reminded her so much of Eric. "Now tell me about your day. How was school?"

Liddie took a bite of a graham cracker and washed it down with the cocoa, leaving a chocolate-marshmallow mustache on her upper lip. She licked it off. "Good." As she told about her day, Liddie's legs swung back and forth under the table. She never stayed still for long.

"I'm going to play in my room now," Liddie announced, wiping her mouth on a napkin and getting up from the table.

"All right. I'll be downstairs for a little while." Anne felt relief that her daughter had chosen to stay inside.

Liddie started toward her room, then darted back to give Anne a hug. "Thank you for the hot chocolate."

Anne smiled as she made her way downstairs to the library.

* * *

The wind howled all night, making the Queen Anne Victorian house creak and groan eerily, which sent Liddie and Ben to Anne's bedroom seeking comfort. It hadn't rained, but the wind whistled through the trees and around the eaves, keeping them all awake. At midnight they went to the kitchen, where Anne warmed milk and got out vanilla wafers to dip in it.

After the cozy snack, they'd all settled down and were able to sleep through the rest of the night, but Anne felt bleary eyed in the morning. The hardwood floor chilled her bare feet as she got out of bed. She would have to use the library fireplaces this morning and see if that warmed the rooms enough to delay using the furnace. Thankfully, Alex and the boys were gathering wood today. She hoped they got enough for the season. Starting this early, it could be a long, cold winter.

Alex Ochs and his nephew, Ryan, came by after breakfast to pick up Ben for their woodcutting expedition.

"Be careful and do as Alex says," Anne told Ben.

"I will, Mom."

"He'll be fine," Alex said, accepting a cup of coffee while the boys went to Ben's room to get his boots and some extra clothes, just in case he got muddy. Alex had on jeans, a plaid flannel shirt, work boots, and a stocking hat. With a day's growth of beard, he looked rugged, like a logger. He smiled at her and his blue eyes sparkled. "I'll take good care of the boys, Anne. Don't worry."

* * *

On Sunday morning, Anne bundled Liddie up in several layers against the cold, and the family headed out to church. As Anne pulled into the church parking lot, she noticed a flash of color that she recognized. Liddie's coat. The young girl wearing it walked toward the church entrance with her mother, who wore a tattered flannel shirt for warmth. The fuzzy white kittens on the girl's pink jacket confirmed it was the one Anne had bought for Liddie from a department store catalog. In that moment, Anne's heart swelled with pride and gratitude for her daughter's tender heart.

They found their favorite pew and sat down just as the organ played the introduction to one of Anne's favorite hymns. "Great is Thy faithfulness, Lord unto me!" the congregation sang with enthusiasm. Next to Anne, Liddie held onto one side of the hymnal, although she couldn't read most of the words. The sunlight shining through the stained-glass windows cast a rainbow glow over them like a sweet reminder of God's presence.

"Please be seated," Reverend Tom said, then called the children up front for the children's sermon. Ben and Liddie went to sit on the steps going up to the platform with the other children. Reverend Tom sat on the top step and told them that the hymn they just sang was about God's compassion that never fails. He asked them what *compassion* meant. Several children spoke up with answers about being nice to other people. Ben suggested it meant feeling sorry for people.

Reverend Tom explained that compassion included recognizing people's suffering and helping them. He told a story about a school bully who picked on one small, shy boy. The boy had a new video game, and the bully stopped him on the way home from school and demanded his video game. When the boy resisted, the bully punched him in the nose, making it bleed. Then the bully took the boy's backpack with the game and turned to the other kids and laughed, daring them to try to stop him. The other kids ran off, except for a small boy named Sammy, who went to help the injured boy. He took him to his house, and his mother helped stop the nosebleed and cleaned him up. She gave the boys milk and cookies and then took the injured boy home.

"Why did the other kids run away?" Reverend Tom asked the children.

"Because they were afraid," a child answered.

"Yes, but Sammy showed compassion when he stopped to help, even though it could have caused him trouble—just like the story Jesus tells about the good Samaritan in the Bible. The Samaritan, who helped a stranger, was a true neighbor to that man because he showed mercy and kindness. Jesus said, 'Go and do likewise.'"

Anne couldn't help thinking about Liddie's kindness to the little girl she had just seen coming to church. She glanced around the room and spotted the fuzzy pink coat in the back corner. She heard Reverend Tom challenge the children to look for ways to help others.

"For instance," he said, "we have a donation box in the foyer for winter coats and other warm clothing. Have you seen it? Look on your way out this morning. I believe the new stove in the church kitchen came in it. Some of our ladies covered it in bright red, yellow, and blue striped wallpaper. It's beautiful. But it's empty. With winter arriving early, it is sadly in need of warm items."

Reverend Tom invited the children to go downstairs for junior church. Liddie retrieved the new coat that they'd bought the day before after the library closed, and then she followed her brother and Ryan and the other children downstairs.

The main service continued with a message from Reverend Tom that dug deeper into the story of the good Samaritan. Afterward, Anne chatted with a few friends before gathering the children and heading for the car.

On the way home, Liddie squirmed in her seat. "I'm going to look through my room for things I can give to the poor," she announced.

"We can all do that," Anne said. "But, remember, we gave away lots of things you'd outgrown when we moved from New York, so we may not find a lot."

"I want to give too, but I can't think of anything I have that I don't need," Ben said, looking thoughtful.

"I'll help you look," Anne said. "Right after lunch."

* * *

Late Sunday afternoon, Anne stared at the stack of clothing on the kitchen table, amazed at how much she and the kids had gathered: sweaters and warm pants the children had already outgrown since last season. Wardrobe items she hadn't worn in several years. Ben had also found an extra jacket and gloves. Even though they'd given away much before their move, they still had more than they needed.

"I'm going to ask my friends for clothes too," Liddie said, her eyes shining "I'm going to fill up the box at church all by myself! Mommy, can we go shopping and buy some more coats?"

"Sweetheart, having me buy coats for the clothing box wouldn't be the same as your collecting coats to give away. Reverend Tom didn't mean we have to go out and buy a lot of clothing, although we will watch for sales and pick up a few things. I imagine some of our friends have gently used clothing they can donate if you ask them. And what about Mrs. Farley? You could call her and ask."

"Oh." Liddie's animated expression disappeared. She looked up at her mother. "But I want to fill the box by myself."

"You both helped children in New York when we donated your outgrown and extra clothing before we moved."

"Oh yeah. I forgot about that!" Ben said, smiling.

"That's good, isn't it, Mommy?" Liddie asked, perking up.

"Yes, sweetheart. It's very good. But it means we don't have that many extra coats left. This pile is it. When you involve other people, it gives them a chance to be generous, and you can collect a lot more."

"I'm going to ask my friends at school," Liddie declared.

"Now you're getting the idea," Ben said.

Just then, Anne's cell phone rang. It was Wendy. "Hey, Anne, I have a great idea."

Anne wasn't sure whether to smile or grimace. Wendy did have great ideas with enthusiasm to match, but her great ideas often meant extra work for Anne. "What's that?"

"Reverend Tom said we need to fill the clothing box, right? I thought about crocheting scarves, but it would take time to make enough to help. Then I thought, what if we held a crochet class at the library and taught everyone how to make a scarf, and we donated them to the box? It would teach people a skill, give the library an activity, and fill the box, all at the same time. What do you think?"

"I...think I like it. Aunt Edie loved to crochet and knit, and she left lots of supplies. We can even use her yarn."

"Super! Then we don't have to buy any. I can come over tomorrow so we can go through it. We can put up signs and flyers and start next week."

"So soon?"

"It's already getting cold. The sooner, the better, I say."

"I suppose you're right." Anne could barely think as fast as Wendy could act. At the moment, though, she couldn't think of any reason not to start right away. The clothing box needed the warm items.

After she ended the call, Anne thought about all the supplies and old clothing of Aunt Edie's in the attic. She might not have time to go through it tomorrow with the library open, but she could look now.

"I'm going to the attic to look for yarn. Anyone want to come with me?" she asked Ben and Liddie.

"Cool! I love going up there," Ben said.

"Not me. It's dark." Liddie shook her head.

"You can stay down here," Anne said.

Liddie frowned. "All by myself?" Her voice quavered. "I guess I'll come with you."

"All right. Put on your jackets. It'll be chilly up there."

After they bundled up, Anne unlocked the attic door and turned on the light. The light that came through the small windows was muted and gray, and the overhead bulb barely illuminated the large room, filled with Aunt Edie's possessions and Anne's extra furniture and belongings.

"Let's look for yarn first. Then we'll see if we can find any coats or sweaters in Aunt Edie's boxes. I put the crochet and knitting supplies back in the corner." She led the way along aisles between stacks of boxes and unused furniture. She intended to sort and catalog the attic's contents, but there hadn't been time. Taking care of the library and the children filled her days.

They reached the back corner. Anne found the stack of clear plastic bins. "Here they are." She opened the top one.

"Wow, look at all that yarn," Liddie said. "Can I have some for Cleopatra? Maybe I can make something."

"Sure, honey." Cleopatra was Liddie's favorite doll. Anne pulled out a thick pink yarn. There was only one skein. "How about this one?"

"Oh yes. She'll love it!" Liddie took it and held it against her face to feel its softness.

Anne pulled out several knitting and crochet pattern books. "Ben, would you hold these? Wendy might want them."

"Okay."

Anne handed him the stack, then looked through the contents of the bin. "This has a lot of sewing supplies." She sorted the contents of the second bin, leaving yarn and crochet hooks in it. Anne removed the lid on the last bin. *Eureka!* Skeins of yarn in every possible color filled the container.

"Wow," Ben said. "I bet that could make lots of sweaters."

"Wendy is going to teach a class on how to make winter scarves. You can take the class if you'd like. Aunt Edie loved to make things to give away. She'd be pleased that we're using her yarn for scarves."

"Isn't that a girl thing?" he asked.

"Not necessarily. Some men like to knit and crochet."

The doubtful look on his face made Anne chuckle.

"I want to make a scarf," Liddie said. "Can I take the class, Mommy?"

"Yes, dear. I'd like to take it too."

Anne took out several multicolored skeins. Below them, she found fine yarn suitable for babies. "Maybe we can do some other winter project too, later on. There's plenty of yarn."

Anne pulled out a shiny trifold brochure. She started to set it aside, but it felt thick and had a staple in the top. Curious, she held it up. It showed a picture of a sewing machine with the word *Bernina* across the top. Anne opened the brochure. Inside, a receipt was stapled to the top. She held it up to the light so she could read it.

"What's that?" Ben asked.

"It's a receipt for—" Anne gasped. "It looks like twenty-four sewing machines. It must be a mistake."

"Wow. That's a lot of sewing machines," Ben said.

"Yes, it is. It has Aunt Edie's name on it."

"There's a sewing machine in the craft room," Liddie pointed out.

"That belonged to Aunt Edie. But this can't be right. Aunt Edie only had one sewing machine, and it isn't a Bernina."

CHAPTER TWO

W hat a morning," Remi Miller said, putting her backpack behind the checkout desk at noon on Monday. "I can't get my mind around biology. Good thing I'm going to be a librarian and not a nurse."

"You'll be surprised at how much you'll use classes like that." Anne enjoyed mentoring the younger woman, whose chosen career mirrored her own. "If you don't mind, I'll leave the library in your capable hands while I do some work upstairs. I'll be up in the attic if you need me."

Remi smiled. "Sounds spooky."

Anne laughed. "It doesn't seem that way to me. The light isn't very bright, but the only ghostly critters up there are dust bunnies."

"Funny."

Upstairs, Anne put on a sweatshirt, grabbed a flashlight, and made her way to the attic. At times it seemed almost bigger than the house, and the cavernous space was filled with stored items. Anne made some intriguing find every time she went up there. As she entered it now, she thought about how Alex and his workers—under her supervision—had moved the furniture and heavy boxes into the corners of the attic. This had freed up a lot of room downstairs while the house was being converted into the library and their apartment. Still, she didn't remember seeing any boxes that would have held sewing machines... though she had to admit she hadn't been supervising every single minute.

Anne started at the front corner and moved boxes to see what was buried beneath and behind them. She found boxes that she had packed and marked *Kitchen*, *Bedroom*, *Parlor*, and *Knickknacks*. Next, she pulled out a box that she had packed and marked *Edie's Winter Clothes*. Anne had donated most of Edie's clothing and household items to charity, but she'd saved some, unable to part with them yet. She'd meant to sort through them yesterday, but the receipt had made her forget.

Beneath a stack of boxes, she spotted her great-aunt's cedar chest. It was a lovely antique cherry chest, with stacked bun feet and carved roses around the edges. Anne recalled seeing it in Aunt Edie's bedroom and now decided it would make a wonderful piece in her own bedroom. But she would definitely need help getting it down the attic stairs. She removed the boxes on top of it and opened the lid. The rich scent of cedar wafted up. Inside were layers of clothing wrapped in tissue paper. She recognized Aunt Edie's special Christmas dress and lifted it up. The soft red-and-green, wool and silk, plaid dress had black velvet-covered buttons all the way down the front and a white, lace-trimmed collar, with matching cuffs on the long sleeves. Somewhere, there was a wool hat that went with it. Anne's mother had inherited the delicate cameo brooch and earrings that Aunt Edie had worn with the dress.

Beneath the dress were more layers of garments, which Aunt Edie had taken great care to preserve. Anne was eager to unpack them and see what treasures lay in between the sheets of tissue paper. She got a box and carefully lifted out the layers and laid them in it. Then she set the box aside to go through later. For now she must continue her search for the sewing machines.

For an hour, Anne worked her way around the attic. She saw intriguing boxes and bins to examine another day, when warmer weather raised the temperature inside, but found no sign of even one sewing machine.

Having no luck in the attic, Anne carried the boxes of Aunt Edie's winter clothes downstairs and set them in her bedroom to go through later. Then she headed for the basement. She didn't want anyone in the library to see her in her dusty condition, so she went down the back stairs. She flipped on the light and descended to the basement, the musty scent of dampness growing stronger with each step.

Dim light filtered in through small windows set about twelve feet apart around the stone foundation. A sizable, well-lit laundry room occupied the right corner next to the stairway. A chute from the upper floors emptied into a large laundry bin next to the washing machine. Shelves held laundry soap, bleach, and various supplies. A worktable covered in white oilcloth dotted with tiny yellow flowers occupied the center of the three-sided room. Anne rarely ventured beyond the laundry area, but she did so now, carefully scanning all the wooden shelves — which extended around the outer walls and divided the basement into makeshift rooms — for anything resembling a sewing machine or even a box that might have held one of the elusive Bernina machines.

One room held old gardening implements and plant food. Another area held jars of home-canned goods that were labeled in Aunt Edie's bold script: applesauce, peaches, plums, stewed tomatoes, piccalilli relish, rhubarb chutney, pickled beets, green beans, and various jams. Anne still hadn't had time to sort through the basement contents, but it appeared some of the dates were recent. She could still use the canned good that were only a year or two old. Thoughts of Aunt Edie's peaches and cream pie or some fresh marinara sauce made Anne's mouth water. Aunt Edie had loved to preserve her own fruits and vegetables, and Anne had loved partaking of the bounty. The home-canned produce was the next best thing to fresh out of the garden.

Finally, Anne accepted the fact that her basement search yielded the makings for dinner but no sewing machines. Anne hoped she had better luck finding the recipe for Aunt Edie's marinara sauce than she had finding the missing sewing machines.

Back upstairs, Anne changed out of her dusty clothes and puzzled over the missing machines. Maybe Aunt Edie had fallen victim to a scam. Anne knew that con artists often targeted elderly people. Her great-aunt had been mentally sharp, but some older people became vulnerable as they aged. Had Aunt Edie's mind begun to slip? Or... It seemed an unlikely thought, but could her aunt have developed a shopping addiction? Anne had heard of people getting caught up in lotteries or purchasing things from telemarketers or TV shopping networks or even becoming hoarders. But where were the two dozen sewing machines? Had Edie paid for the machines and never received them? Had she been too embarrassed to admit it? It made no sense, but it shouldn't really surprise her. She'd already discovered that Aunt Edie was good at keeping secrets.

* * *

"This yarn is perfect." Wendy held up a skein of royal blue wool yarn Monday afternoon. "There must be enough here for dozens of scarves." She and Anne were sorting through the bin of yarn Anne had carried downstairs from the attic.

"I wasn't sure what kind of yarn to include. You don't think it would be too scratchy?" Anne asked.

"Not at all. It's part lamb's wool and part synthetic blend. It'll make a great scarf. Are you going to take my class?"

"I'd like to, if the library isn't too busy. Liddie said she wants to take the class. Do you think she could pick it up at her age?"

"Oh yes. She's a good age to start learning. My girls can help her."

"I asked Ben if he wanted to take the class, but he didn't seem too excited about it."

Wendy laughed. "I tried to teach my boys. They just wanted to make knots and ropes."

"Ben would rather be reading. Or outside playing," Anne said.

"My boys too." Wendy held up a skein of soft lavender merino wool. "This would make a gorgeous scarf. A long, loopy one."

"With all this yarn, I'm sure there will be plenty, and believe it or not, there's more in the attic. I left most of the fancy yarn and baby-fine yarn up there. You can pick some out for yourself."

"I might do that after the class. So, how is Liddie's coat drive going?" Wendy asked.

"We cleaned out our closets and got a pretty good pile but not that much. I have a couple of boxes of Aunt Edie's things to go through. Liddie told me she's going to ask her friends at school. I hope she won't be disappointed if she can't fill the box. It's huge."

"It is. I'd give you some things from my closets, but I also want my kids to participate in giving." Wendy set aside piles of suitable yarn. "We need to weigh the yarn balls. I think the equivalent of two skeins per scarf should be enough. Do you have rubber bands or plastic bags we can put the yarn in for each scarf?"

"I have plastic bags. We can put a crochet hook and pattern in with the yarn to make individual kits." Anne opened a drawer and took out a box of plastic bags. She set them on the counter and began filling bags with the skeins Wendy had set aside. "I agree, it's important for all the kids to get involved. Liddie will have to learn that this isn't her exclusive project. She'll find some coats. There are plenty of people she can ask."

* * *

Anne kept the car running with the heater on as she waited for Ben and Liddie outside the school later that afternoon. The school bell sounded, then the doors opened and dozens of children poured out of the front doors.

"Mommy! I got to talk to the principal today!" Liddie said as she climbed into the backseat and buckled herself into her booster seat.

"Did you get in trouble?" Ben asked as he fastened himself in.

"No, silly. Miss Reed took me so I could ask about the Lost and Found."

Anne glanced at Liddie in the rearview mirror. She was wearing her new coat.

"What did you lose?" Ben asked.

Liddie let out a big sigh. "I didn't lose anything. Mr. Bailey said I can have coats and hats and stuff from the Lost and Found if no one comes to get them. But I have to wait a couple of weeks."

"That's very nice. Although I would hope children check there for their lost items."

"Oh, they will," she said. "Mr. Bailey is going to tell everyone that lost-and-found things will be donated if they're not picked up. And Miss Reed is going to tell parents so they can bring in warm clothes too."

"That's wonderful, Liddie. You're doing a great job of getting people involved."

"Do we have a Lost and Found at the library, Mommy?"

"Not yet, but I'm sure we will need one eventually."

"When we do, can we donate the clothes people leave?"

"We could have a policy like the school. If people don't claim items within a couple of weeks, we can donate them. We'll have to put up a sign."

"I know!" Ben said, getting into the spirit of the discussion. "Can we put up a sign at the library and have people drop off coats and stuff there?"

"That's a good idea, Ben. If you and Liddie will make the sign, we'll put it up."

"Yay! Will you help me, Ben?" Liddie asked.

"Sure."

Anne was pleased to see Ben's interest. As soon as they got home, Ben asked for paper and markers.

"Be sure to say that the items will go to the Blue Hill Community Church for distribution to local people in need," Anne said.

"Okay. Can we do it now?" Ben asked.

"Do you have homework?"

"A few math problems and words for a spelling test."

"Not me," Liddie said.

Ben frowned. "Lucky you."

"Do your homework first, Ben. I'll quiz you on the spelling words after you do the math problems. Liddie, you forgot to make your bed this morning, so you do that and straighten your room."

"Okay. Hurry, Ben. Do your homework so we can make the sign." Liddie rushed off to her room.

Nothing like a little incentive, Anne thought as she started a pot of spaghetti sauce while the children worked.

When Ben finished his homework, Anne got out a large sheet of yellow construction paper and colored marking pens. "Let me know if you need help."

"We can do it," Ben said. "Can't we, Liddie?"

Liddie gave a firm nod. "Yep!" They disappeared into Ben's room with their supplies.

An hour later, Anne was ready to call the children for dinner when they came out of Ben's room.

"Here's our sign." Ben held it up. *KEEP A KID WARM* crossed the top in block letters, outlined in black and filled in with bright colors. Hand-drawn pictures of balloons, hearts, coats, hats, and mittens dotted the poster, and instructions said to bring warm clothes for needy children to the library for the donation box. At the bottom was a picture of a large red, yellow, and blue striped box with an arrow pointing inside the top.

"That's beautiful." The care Ben and Liddie had put into their poster impressed Anne. It was clear and readable yet showed their originality and youth.

"Yay!" Liddie yelled, jumping up and down. "Can we put a big box under it?"

"How about one of the clear plastic storage tubs?"

"Can we put two of them? One won't be big enough."

"We'll start with one and see. We can empty it when it's full and take the clothes to the church."

"Okay!"

"I hope people like it and bring clothes," Ben said. He had caught Liddie's excitement, and Anne was pleased that he was willing to help his little sister.

"I'm sure they will."

As they hung the sign on the wall near the checkout desk, Ben noticed a stack of printed flyers on the counter advertising the crochet class.

"Mom, can we make some flyers too? Then people can take them home and we can take some to school."

"I think that's a good idea."

"Can I do it on your computer?"

Anne glanced at her watch. "You have an hour before bedtime. Can you do it in that time?"

"Sure."

"Me too! I want to help," Liddie exclaimed.

"You can tell me what to say," Ben said. "Come on."

* * *

After Ben and Liddie went to bed, Anne went to her room to look through her aunt's winter clothes. She pulled out sweaters, turtleneck shirts, flannel slacks, and a jacket and coat, all items her aunt had worn recently and that Anne had saved out of sentimentality. Anne held one scarf up to her face and breathed deeply, letting the faint scent of Aunt Edie's favorite perfume evoke many warm and precious memories. Anne nearly decided to pack up all the clothes again to keep, but she forced herself not to. Aunt Edie wouldn't want her clothes just sitting around without use. She'd want someone to have them who needed them. With determination, Anne set the entire box aside to donate to the warm clothing drive.

Anne turned to the second box, which held the items from Aunt Edie's cedar chest. She took out one tissue-wrapped garment and set it on the bed. Peeling back the tissue, she found a black angora sweater with rhinestones around the collar. Aunt Edie had worn the sweater to the theater when she had made a trip to New

York City to visit Anne a few years earlier. Somewhere there was a black satin skirt to go with it. Aunt Edie's faux mink coat still hung in the closet. They had dressed to the nines that night. Aunt Edie was so elegant, people had stared at them as they entered the theater. Aunt Edie had paused, smiling, and someone took her picture. Then another camera flashed. Anne had teased Edie, telling her that people would think she was some star of the silver screen whose identity was a mystery. At that, Aunt Edie had raised her chin, affected a regal air, and strolled into the theater. After the play, over hot chocolate back at the Belvedere Hotel, where Edie had stayed, they had laughed about their moment of stardom and wondered what the photographer would think when he reviewed the picture he had taken of them.

Anne set the sweater aside and took out another garment. She unwrapped another lovely sweater, then a delicate shawl that smelled of lavender, and then a pair of long white evening gloves. Anne remembered many of these extra special pieces and set them aside to save. Someday she would share them with Liddie.

Anne lifted an item that felt heavier than the others. Setting it on the bed, she peeled back the tissue. A soft royal-blue wool blazer appeared, and it looked new. Anne was sure she'd never seen it before. She picked it up to examine it. Tailored details set it apart from an off-the-rack garment. The jacket had bound buttonholes with ornate silver buttons, flat felled seams, facing, interfacing, and a hand-finished lining. Had Aunt Edie made the jacket? She'd been a talented seamstress.

Anne tried it on. It fit as if made just for her. She had a feeling Aunt Edie would be pleased if she saved and used the clothing in the cedar chest. Anne found a padded hanger and hung the blazer in her closet.

Anne looked through the rest of the clothing from the cedar chest. She found a couple of vintage dresses, a beaded handbag, and several decorative tops. None of them were good candidates for the clothing drive. She found one more sweater to include with the clothing for donation, but she would keep the other items in the old chest for future use. Sometime in the future there would be special occasions to wear them.

Chapter Three

Tuesday after lunch, Anne left the library in the hands of a volunteer and drove to Mildred's house, thinking that if anyone could answer the puzzle of the missing sewing machines, Mildred could. Anne knocked on the door, and a few minutes later Mildred answered. A tape measure was hanging around her neck, and a pincushion adorned her wrist.

"Anne, what a pleasant surprise. I was just thinking about you. Your daughter called me last night, you know. She asked me if I have any 'gently used' winter clothing. I thought that was so cute. I bet she heard that phrase from you."

Anne chuckled. "That does sound like me."

"Please come in. I'm making jackets out of polar fleece that I found in a box of fabric Edie gave me last April." Mildred's lips pressed together as she paused for a few seconds. "It was just days before she passed away. She told me she didn't have time to use it. I never thought she meant time left to live." Mildred blinked several times. "She couldn't have known, could she?"

Anne didn't know how to answer that question. She waited for Mildred to continue.

"I haven't wanted to look at that fabric. Then Reverend Tom mentioned the need for donations of warm clothing.

I knew Edie would want me to make jackets for the donation box. Come on back to my sewing room. I'll show you." Mildred started walking down the hall toward the bedrooms.

She led Anne into a room that held an ironing board and a worktable, plus a sewing machine. A Bernina sewing machine. Anne stared at it, trying to determine if it was the same model as the ones on the receipt. Had Edie given Mildred a sewing machine? Anne didn't want to ask outright.

Mildred picked up a pile of green polar fleece off her worktable. "I thought I could give the jackets to Liddie to put in the box, instead of doing it myself. After all, she did ask, and it's Edie's fabric." She held up a fleece jacket that was almost finished.

Seeing the jacket gave Anne a lump in her throat. Even now, Aunt Edie's legacy reached out to help others. "Oh yes. Thank you, Mildred. Liddie will be thrilled. She and Ben are working so hard to collect items. I've been praying they'll have some success."

"I agree. We need to encourage our young people to be generous."

"Wendy is going to teach a crochet class at the library and have everyone crochet a scarf for the donation box. We're using some of Aunt Edie's yarn. Would you believe she left two tubs full? So there's plenty to go around."

"She'd like that." Mildred sighed.

"I know Aunt Edie sewed, knitted, and crocheted a lot of items to help with fund-raisers. I remember seeing some of the beautiful aprons and pillows she made for the rummage sale at church and the hospital auxiliary. I imagine you worked on some of those projects together."

"We did. Before I got my Bernina, I had a little Singer Featherweight sewing machine that was easy to carry, so I would take it over to Edie's. We'd set up an assembly line, cutting out patterns, then stitching them together. We would sew on bits and pieces of trim to add a touch of sparkle. You know how Edie was. She could see the humor in any situation, and sometimes we'd spend more time laughing than working, but we always got a lot accomplished. We had such fun." Mildred turned away and surreptitiously dabbed at the corner of her eye before continuing. "So many memories. Those were good times. And working with someone else makes the time go more quickly."

"I've been using Aunt Edie's old sewing machine. I'm puzzled that she was still using the old Singer."

"She loved that machine," Mildred said. "I can't imagine she would ever replace it unless it was irreparably broken."

"The odd thing is that I found a receipt among Aunt Edie's sewing supplies for Bernina sewing machines. Why would she buy new machines, then not use one? Do you remember her buying some Berninas?"

Mildred gave Anne a sharp look and shook her head. "No. I always told her that she should get a Bernina. I love mine. But she told me her Singer was perfectly good." Mildred stopped and stared at Anne. "You said *machines*? As in more than one? That doesn't make sense. What would she do with more than one sewing machine? It must be a mistake." She shook her head. "Oh, and while we're speaking of sewing...I almost forgot. I found something odd in the box of fabric."

Mildred dug into a large box of fabric on the floor. She pulled out a catalog of patterns. A piece of paper stuck out of the top like a bookmark. Mildred opened to the page and pulled out the paper. "This is just the way I found it. It's a receipt for rolls and rolls of fabric." Mildred handed Anne the receipt. "Great prices, but what in the world would Edie do with all that fabric? Open a store?"

A Able Surplus Sales. Five lots of fabric rolls. Cartons of patterns. A carton of assorted sewing supplies. *Lot* sounded like a description from an auction. It must have been a large amount.

"Strange. Do you know what A Able Surplus Sales is?"

"No. And she didn't mention it to me," Mildred said. "You know Edie loved a bargain. She'd often call and invite me to go with her so I could get in on a big sale of some sort. But she didn't tell me about this. I don't understand, unless..." She paused, frowning. Then she shook her head, leaving her thought unfinished.

"Unless what, Mildred?"

"Nothing. I just think she must have had some kind of project in mind. But I just don't know what."

Mildred seemed distressed by Edie's secretive behavior, and Anne didn't know what to think either. How did Aunt Edie get involved in such odd, large purchases? Why?

Mildred neatly folded the jacket she'd shown Anne and set it on the worktable. She looked up and blinked, as if shifting mental gears. "Anyway, I should have the jackets ready by the end of the week. In addition to Wendy's crochet class, I could teach a class at the library on knitting stocking hats for the donation box if there is enough yarn left. I used to teach, you know."

"Really? No, I didn't know. You taught knitting?"

"Knitting, crochet, sewing, cooking. All the important household activities."

"That's wonderful. There's a lot of yarn, but let's wait and see how the crochet class goes. I don't know how much interest we'll have. If it works out, I'd love to have the library offer more classes."

"You might want to talk to the high school domestic arts teacher," Mildred suggested. "That's what they call home ec now. Maybe she'll give the students extra credit if they take the class."

"That's a great idea. Thanks. I'll do that." Anne glanced at the clock on the wall. "Speaking of students, I'd better go get mine. School will be out soon."

Mildred walked her to the door. "I'll let you know when the jackets are ready, but drop in anytime. I love having company when I'm at home."

While Anne drove to the school, she thought about Mildred and the sewing machines. She said she'd told Aunt Edie that she should get a Bernina for herself, so had Mildred somehow been instrumental in Aunt Edie's purchase? But she claimed she didn't know anything about it, and her bewilderment seemed genuine.

And what about the huge quantity of fabric Aunt Edie had evidently purchased? Had Mildred, in her enthusiasm for her sewing hobby, inadvertently encouraged her best friend's crazy purchases? What had Mildred been thinking when she'd said, "unless…?" She'd passed it off as nothing, but was Mildred holding back information?

Anne wondered where she should look next. Someone had to know about the mysterious sewing machines. But who?

As Anne waited outside the elementary school, her cell phone rang. She didn't recognize the number. "Hello?"

"Hello, is this Anne Gibson?"

"Yes it is." Anne frowned, trying to place the voice, which seemed familiar.

"Oh, good. This is Miss Latham, from the high school. Your favorite English teacher."

Anne laughed. "Oh, Miss Latham, how are you? It's wonderful to hear your voice. What can I do for you?"

"I'm doing well, thank you for asking. I can't tell you how delighted I am that you are back in town and have made our dreams come true for a local library. Along those lines, I have a proposition for you. Could you come by the high school at lunchtime on Wednesday?"

"Yes, I'm sure I can."

"Good. I'll be in the lunchroom on duty. We can talk then."

Miss Latham said good-bye and hung up. Anne hadn't seen her former English teacher in years. She'd loved English, especially when she had Miss Latham for her junior and senior honors English classes. Miss Latham was a no-nonsense teacher who drilled the basics of grammar and syntax into her students and assigned the classics for reading and book reports. Though she required a great deal from her students, she had a passion for reading, and she encouraged creative thinking and writing. Miss Latham had been a major influence in Anne's love of words and her decision to major in library science. Anne couldn't wait to see Miss Latham and discover what her proposition might be.

* * *

That night, after the children went to bed, Anne settled into an easy chair in the cozy living room of their upstairs apartment. She'd set aside a new novel by one of her favorite authors that had arrived at the library earlier in the day. She often took advantage of her position as librarian to preview books before putting them out for the public. It was her job but also a guilty pleasure. She got to be the first to read new books. But it helped her suggest titles to the townspeople who used the library, and many had come to rely on her recommendations.

She opened the book's cover and gently smoothed open the first pages to chapter one.

To the untrained eye, everything looked normal, but Detective O'Brien knew better. A bit of dust disturbed on the mantel. Faded paint showing where different sized artwork had hung. A missing heiress. No doubt. This was a crime scene.

Anne stared at the words. Did she herself have a crime scene? All she had to indicate anything out of the ordinary were two old receipts. Had Aunt Edie purchased two dozen sewing machines? And had she also purchased five lots of fabric? If so, where were the machines and fabric now? Had they been stolen? Or had some con artist swindled her out of the money? *Unless*...Mildred had said, leaving her thought unfinished. Unless what? What did Mildred know? Or suspect?

Anne set aside the book and got the brochure and the sewing machines' receipt that she'd put in the desk. The receipt looked like a form from a pad that anyone could buy at an office supply store. It had a phone number, but no address. The area code and prefix were local, and the handwritten receipt didn't come from a store register. It was marked simply *"24 Bernina sewing machines. Paid in cash"* with no dollar amount given. Unprofessional at best. Fraudulent at worst?

Anne punched in the phone number on her cell phone. She heard a click and three rising tones before a voice said, "The number you have reached is no longer in service."

Anne checked the number she'd entered. It matched the number on the receipt. Whoever sold Aunt Edie the machines was no longer in business. Or at least not at the phone number provided. Had her aunt even received the sewing machines? How could Anne find out?

Anne then took a look at the receipt for the five lots of fabric. She booted up her laptop and searched the Internet for A Able Surplus Sales, which was the name of the business on the receipt. She found similar names but nothing that seemed to fit. Why would Aunt Edie purchase anything from such a seemingly fly-by-night source? If Mildred knew, she wasn't saying.

Anne thought of Reverend Tom. He kept close tabs on his congregation and the town and had known Aunt Edie very well. Maybe he could shine some light on the strange receipt. It was too late to call him now, but she determined to see him as soon as possible.

* * *

Wednesday morning, Ann heard the front door open as she replaced a heavy volume of Pennsylvania history on the shelf. Looking behind her, she saw Wendy coming toward her from the library entry hall with a book under her arm.

"Good morning," Wendy said in a quiet but cheerful voice. She came over to stand next to Anne. "I wanted to show you the scarf patterns I found." She opened the book and turned to a tabbed page. "I've found three great patterns. They are all simple to make. I could teach all three and let the students pick which one to make."

Anne studied the patterns on the tabbed pages. "Three might be a bit much. What if you pick one and then show the different stitches so they can do the others at home? That way everyone is doing the same thing."

Wendy thought for a moment. "You might be right. One is a basic stitch. It's not as attractive. I love these two. This fancy scarf is simple. The ribbed scarf uses a half double stitch."

"I love the fancy scarf, but it is so feminine. We need scarves for boys too," Anne pointed out. "The ribbed one would work for anyone."

"True. My boys wouldn't wear this one." Wendy removed the tab from the fancy pattern page. "I can teach the various stitches so people can use them at home."

"Great idea."

"I put flyers up at Thrifty Drug Store and Benkelman's. I'll take flyers to Blue Hill Elementary and to the junior high when I pick up the kids. Maybe that will get some attention. Do you want me to pick up Liddie and Ben?"

"Yes. If you don't mind. I can take a flyer to the high school. I'm going over there this afternoon. Miss Latham, the English teacher, asked me to come by. Something about the library, I'm sure. I had one call this morning about the crochet class—a mother who homeschools and her two daughters."

"Good. My girls will be there. I'll ask them to sit by Liddie so they can help her, but I bet she'll pick it up without much trouble. It's amazing what the little ones can do."

"And me. I plan to come. Aunt Edie taught me basic crochet years ago, but I've forgotten. With all that yarn, I'd better learn again."

"Good. At least we'll have a few people."

* * *

When Bella Miller entered the library for her shift at ten thirty, she noticed Ben and Liddie's coat drive sign right away.

"What a great idea!" she said. "I bet I have some sweatshirts I can donate. I need to put an announcement about it on the library Web site. We're getting lots of hits on our calendar, so the more events we schedule, the better." Bella had a special passion and talent for social media and the Internet. She had developed a Web site for the library and kept the calendar current.

"Good. Would you post that we'll be collecting coats and warm new or gently used clothing for the next couple of months? Could you also put Wendy's crochet class on the calendar? It's this Saturday." Anne handed Bella a flyer. "Here are the details."

"I'll do it right away."

"Thanks. I'm going to take a flyer out to the high school. I need to see Miss Latham too. She wants to talk to me, and I imagine it has to do with the library."

"I had her for honor's English. I got college credit for her class too. Everyone loves Miss Latham, even if they're a little in awe of her."

"I was in Miss Latham's class when I was in high school, and she was my favorite teacher." Anne almost laughed at Bella's look of disbelief. Bella was only about fifteen years younger than Anne, but it probably seemed like eons to the college girl. Miss Latham must seem ancient. She'd seemed old to Anne, and that was years ago.

At eleven o'clock, Anne put one of the flyers for the crochet class in her purse and headed for the high school, but she made a detour and stopped at the church. Reverend Tom's car was parked in back of the building. She parked next to it and went inside. When she tapped on the open door of his office, he looked up from his desk and smiled.

"Anne. Come on in." He stood and offered her a chair.

"Good morning," she said, sitting across from him.

"I heard your daughter wants to fill our donation box all by herself."

"That's what she said. She seems pretty determined to follow through."

"Good for her. It's a big box. Perhaps she'll accept help from the rest of the congregation."

"I think so. She accepted Ben's help in making signs for the library for drop-offs. Wendy is going to teach a crochet class at the library next Saturday to make scarves for the donation box. And I'm on my way to the high school to take a flyer to the domestic arts teacher for her students."

"Perhaps I need to offer some other suggestions on Sunday and challenge people to be creative, like Wendy."

"I'm not sure anyone is as creative as Wendy." Anne smiled. "But that's a great idea."

"So what can I do for you today?"

"You knew my aunt well. Do you remember if she seem confused or distracted in the last couple years of her life?"

"Not at all." Reverend Tom's brow furrowed, and he leaned forward on his elbows. "Why do you ask?"

"I just wondered. She seemed fine when I talked to her and when we visited her, but could she have gone through some kind of imbalance from medications or stress about a year and a half ago? I found a receipt in her sewing and knitting supplies, and Mildred found one too, in a box of fabric Edie gave her. They were made out to her and one indicates she purchased twenty-four expensive sewing machines, but I can't find one of the machines, much less twenty-four. The other receipt, the one Mildred found, lists several lots of fabric rolls and assorted sewing supplies. She has bins of sewing supplies but nothing in the huge quantities indicated on the receipt." She passed the receipts to him.

He looked at them in surprise. "Twenty-four? She never mentioned anything to me. What did Mildred say?"

"She doesn't know either. The receipt says Aunt Edie paid cash, but I couldn't find proof of delivery. It doesn't seem to be from a store. A physical store anyway. Not one that I can find. There's no address, and the phone number has been disconnected. The other receipt, for the fabric, has the name of a business stamped on it. Have you ever heard of A Able Surplus Sales?"

The pastor shook his head. "I haven't heard of A Able Surplus Sales before. I usually hear if someone is contacting people in Blue Hill with fraudulent schemes—either from church members or in the *Gazette*. Still, I can't imagine Edie falling for a scam. She seemed sharp and clear witted up until the day she died."

"I'd sure like to find out who's behind A Able and what happened to all these sewing machines and fabric. I'd also like to find out why Aunt Edie wanted them in the first place?"

"Knowing your aunt, I'm sure there's a logical explanation. He looked thoughtful, then added, "Though I can't imagine what it could be."

Anne stood. "Thank you. I'm stumped right now too. But if someone took advantage of my aunt, chances are they swindled other people around here as well."

"I wish I could be more help. If I hear of anything, I'll let you know."

CHAPTER FOUR

It was lunchtime when Anne pulled up to the high school. The parking lot was nearly full, but she found an empty visitor's spot at the front near the modern single-story building.

Anne stood in line at the long counter in the office behind several students waiting their turn. Watching the lively chatter and the activity of a busy school day took Anne back to her own high school years, although she'd been at the old high school, which had been remodeled and now served as the elementary school.

When Anne's turn came, Shelby Truman, the office secretary, looked up and smiled. Anne had gone to school with Shelby's older sister, Nancy. "Hi, Anne. What can I do for you today?"

"I'm here to see Miss Latham. She asked me to stop by. I believe she's in the lunchroom? But I want to talk to the domestic arts teacher too. Would she be in her classroom?"

Shelby checked her schedule. "Yes. Please just sign the visitor's log." She handed Anne a visitor's badge. Anne signed in and clipped the white badge to her collar.

Teenagers filled the hallway, clustered in groups, laughing and talking. The noise level drew Anne to the lunchroom. She spotted Miss Latham near the front, her watchful eye observing the activity. Anne knew from experience that Miss Latham didn't miss a thing.

When Anne approached her, Miss Latham looked at her and smiled.

"Anne, it's so nice to see you. You haven't changed a bit."

"Thank you, Miss Latham. Neither have you." And she hadn't. Her former English teacher seemed ageless. Her dark pixie-cut hair had grayed, but her skin was unlined and her posture unbent by the passing years. She was mature and stately, but her lively brown eyes still had the same laserlike alertness that Anne remembered so well.

"Thank you for coming out to the school. It's so good to have you back in Blue Hill, Anne. I suppose it seems pretty quiet here after living and working in New York, especially when you work in a library."

"It's different, but I wouldn't call it quiet." Anne chuckled, looking around the noisy room full of animated teenagers. "It's never this noisy though. The library and my children keep me busy. So, what is this proposition you have for me? You've stirred my curiosity. You mentioned on the phone that it involves the library?"

"It does. I've been wondering would you be willing to have an intern from one of my classes? I have an advanced student who needs a challenge. I think the library would be the perfect place for him."

Anne's mind churned with the possibility and the extra time it would involve. With the Library Guild, plus the Miller twins as part-time employees, she had enough help, and an intern would require her personal oversight. But she didn't want to say no to Miss Latham. Besides, she wanted to encourage interest in libraries, especially in the younger generation with their effortless access to the Internet. "I assume this would be one of your extracredit projects. How much time would you want this internship to involve, and how much instruction would I need to give?"

"I would like the intern to spend a couple of hours a week at the library, helping out, for a couple of months. I'll take care of the assignment. The student will keep a journal of his time there, and I'll give him a research project to do at the library on his own time. He's very self-motivated. You wouldn't need to do more than give directions."

"I can do that. Who knows? Maybe we'll inspire a future librarian."

"At least a future library advocate. I know libraries struggle to keep current in our changing technological world."

"All the encouragement and love for literature that I received from you and my aunt pointed me down my career path. I'd love to pass that on to the next generation."

"Good. Your aunt did a great service to this town with her gift. It's about time we had our own library so we don't have to go to Deshler. Edie Summers had a heart for young people and education. She volunteered around the school, even though she didn't have children of her own."

"I remember her helping my mother with PTA projects."

"She worked with a few students on reading comprehension up until a couple of years ago. They often turned out to be my best readers. She also helped in the home economics department. Of course, it's called domestic arts now. She and Mildred Farley spent a lot of time there."

"Really?"

"Oh yes. Mildred taught home ec for some years."

"I don't remember that." Anne remembered Mildred saying she'd taught, but Anne assumed she had volunteered with 4-H or Girl Scouts or some community program. She hadn't realized Mildred had meant high school.

"It happened before your time, when her children were little. In fact she gave up teaching to be home with them but came out of retirement temporarily a few years back, when the school needed a teacher to fill in until they hired a new one. Mildred said she was relieved when the school board hired a young teacher right out of college, but I'm not so sure. She is only a few years older than I am, you know. I've been encouraged to retire this year, but I'm resisting. Mildred stayed involved and came back to give a few demonstrations. I think she mentored the new teacher."

"That's very interesting," she said. "I need to go see the domestic arts teacher about a library project. Is the classroom in the back wing?"

"Yes. Next to the shop class."

"Thanks. It sure is nice to see you, Miss Latham."

"You too. I'll come by the library to see you. And I'll send you the intern."

"I'll look forward to meeting him."

Anne tried to picture Mildred teaching high school. It made sense. She loved to cook and sew and knit. She also made her own clothing, and her home decor included lots of handmade doilies and pillows and needlepoint pictures. Anne pushed open the door to the large domestic arts classroom and peeked in. The room was empty except for the teacher, who bent over her desk, working intently.

"Excuse me. I'm Anne Gibson, the librarian at Blue Hill Library. Do you have a minute?"

"Come in." The teacher rose. Was this the teacher who replaced Mildred? Anne had pictured a woman in her twenties when Miss Latham said she'd been hired right out of college. She didn't look young enough to be a recent college graduate, unless she'd gone to college later in life. This woman was tall and stocky and middle-aged. But then, lots of people went back to college for second careers.

The teacher held out her hand. "I'm Darlynn Jamison. I'm so glad to meet you. What can I do for you?"

"We're holding a crochet class at the library Saturday, and the scarves made will be donated to the needy in the area." She handed her a flyer. "Wendy Pyle, Coach Pyle's wife, is teaching the class. We'd love to have some of your students attend."

"Wonderful. I'll tell my students and encourage attendance. I'm interested in any programs that they could attend. Does the library have a kitchen? I could set up demonstrations with local chefs or the hospital dietician, if you'd like."

"Oh, that's a great idea. The old kitchen might be suitable. We use it for meetings and as a workroom. I've cooked in there, but the appliances are old. It has the basics but nothing electronic. And we'd have to limit enrollment, due to space."

"Of course. While people do want to learn to utilize the microwave and convection ovens and make health food concoctions, there are plenty of classes we could offer using standard appliances," Darlynn said. "Holiday foods, gifts from the kitchen, breads, ethnic foods or ways to use various ingredients. I can think of lots of great projects."

"Let me think about it. Perhaps after the first of the year, when we need some indoor diversions." With the combined talents of Wendy, Mildred, and the domestic arts teacher, it seemed the library could offer a special activity monthly with no problem. That would provide great ways to serve the community.

"Yes. Excellent," Darlynn said. "I'll be happy to handle the details."

Anne looked around. "I took a home ecclass in high school many years ago."

"It couldn't have been that long ago," Darlynn said, chuckling. "I imagine the course curriculum and the equipment has changed some since then though."

"Your cooking area is state of the art, and we only had three old sewing machines. Looks like you got lots of new machines."

"Yes. I'm fortunate to have top-notch machines to teach all kinds of sewing techniques." She walked over and took the cover off of a machine. "You can't get much better than Berninas, although these are some of their more basic machines."

Ann blinked. It was a Bernina just like the picture in the brochure. She looked closer. The model number was the same as the machines on the receipt. Could Aunt Edie have donated sewing machines to the school? The same machines her best friend had recommended? That would explain everything. No one had swindled Aunt Edie. She saw a need and filled it. And that sounded just like something her aunt would do. "I admit I don't know much about sewing machines."

"These are electronic. Students love anything computerized."

"It looks new. When did you get them?"

"They were here when I came. I believe someone donated them to the school in the spring a year or two ago."

"Are there twenty-four new machines, by chance?"

"No. Goodness, I wish. We have twelve. Why do you ask?"

"I found a receipt for twenty-four Bernina sewing machines in a box at the library, which of course was my great-aunt's home. I'm trying to discover what happened to the machines. It looks like the school—your classroom—has twelve of them. Also, did you find boxes of fabric and sewing supplies?"

"No. The students have to supply their own."

"*Hmm*. That's perplexing." Only twelve machines. If these were among those that Edie had purchased, then what happened to the other twelve and all the extra supplies? At least she had half an answer. Or she believed she did. But what did Aunt Edie do with the other twelve machines and a great deal of fabric?

* * *

Anne had just gotten home when she heard the back door open and what sounded like dozens of feet running up the stairs.

"Knock, knock," she heard from the stairwell. It was Wendy's voice. The children—Anne's and Wendy's—were out of school.

"Come on up. I was just fixing some tea."

"Great. I could use a cup. *Brr!* It's cold out there! Kids, we won't be here long."

The children had already disappeared into Ben's and Liddie's rooms. Wendy removed a pair of gloves and her coat, which she hung on the back of a chair. "I passed out the flyers. The junior high school's secretary promised to post it on the bulletin board, and I talked to several teachers. I hope we attract some people, but I'm not overly optimistic." She sat down at the dining room table.

"We might get some from the high school. I talked to the domestic arts teacher earlier today. She sounded very interested." Anne set cups and tea bags on the table as the teakettle whistled. She poured steaming water into the cups, then handed one to Wendy and sat down across from her.

"The teacher and I had a good visit. Did you know someone donated a dozen new sewing machines to the school?"

"I remember Chad mentioning that. Seems like it was a couple of years ago. It was an anonymous donation."

Anne hesitated a moment. Aunt Edie had wanted her gift to remain anonymous, she felt sure. But twelve of the machines were missing.

"I found a receipt when I sorted through Aunt Edie's sewing supplies. I'm pretty certain she was the one who donated the sewing machines."

"Really? I'm not surprised. That sounds like something she would do. I remember she and Mildred were friends with the domestic arts teacher."

"I didn't know that. But wasn't she young?"

"Oh yes. I think they kind of took her under their wings. Edie probably felt sorry for her, having to teach with old equipment. The school couldn't afford new machines and wouldn't have bought them if they had extra money. They need new gym equipment and band music and all kinds of other things."

"Most schools do. But there's a discrepancy between the donated machines and the receipt. Aunt Edie bought twenty-four machines. The school only has twelve. I can't account for the other twelve."

Wendy whistled. "That's a lot of sewing machines. They'd be pretty hard to misplace."

"That's what I thought. I searched the attic and the basement here at the house. Nothing. They aren't here."

Wendy frowned. "What do you think happened to them?"

"I don't know. I asked Mildred, and she doesn't know anything about the machines. I can't help wondering if Aunt Edie was swindled." Anne got up and took the receipt out of her purse. She laid it in front of Wendy. "Doesn't this look fishy to you?"

Wendy picked up the receipt and studied it. She looked up at Anne. "There's no name and address."

"I know. And the phone number has been disconnected."

Wendy shook her head. "Not good. You think they only delivered half the machines and kept the rest?"

"I don't know what to think. But I intend to find out."

* * *

Wendy was the first person to come into the library Thursday morning. Anne had turned on the computer and was checking in a stack of returned books.

"Good morning." Wendy gave Anne an energetic smile as she came up to the desk. Wendy always looked bright eyed, no matter what time of day it was. Anne envied her energy, though she thought so much vitality must be exhausting. "What is with this weather? It looks like it could snow," Wendy said.

"I hope not. It's way too early for that." Anne shivered just thinking about it. "What brings you in here so early?"

"I wanted to show you the scarf I made with our pattern last night after dinner." Wendy took a bright blue, green, and red scarf out of her purse and held it out to Anne.

"That was fast. It's beautiful. Did you use variegated yarn?"

"Yes. I think it came out well. I thought we could put it up with the sign. It might attract more attention."

Wendy went around the checkout desk and found some tacks in the drawer and put the scarf up on the bulletin board.

"I hope you don't mind, but I mentioned the sewing machine receipt to Chad."

"That's all right. What did he say?"

"He said he helped move a bunch of new sewing machines into the domestic arts class a couple of years ago. In the spring, he thought."

Anne stopped entering returns and looked up at Wendy. "Really? Did he say how many there were?"

"He couldn't remember. But one of the boys from the football team helped him with the machines."

"Wow. So Chad was there when the machines were delivered. Did he know if they were from my aunt?"

"No. He was helping the domestic arts teacher. She had them take the machines to her classroom and set them up on the tables. Then they took the old machines and put them in a storage building."

"I wonder if the rest of the sewing machines ended up in storage too? I'll have to ask."

"Of course. It's not like it would be easy to hide twelve sewing machines," Wendy said. "They'll show up."

After Wendy left, Anne kept on musing. Surely someone would know if there were more sewing machines at the school. She made a mental note to contact the school principal. But why had Aunt Edie purchased so many if the school only needed twelve?

* * *

Sunshine and warmer temperatures brought the residents of Blue Hill outdoors on Friday. Many visited the library. Even with Bella working, Anne was busy most of the morning processing interlibrary loans, tracking down reference books, and offering book recommendations.

At lunchtime, Anne made a quick trip downtown to talk to the administrator of Edie's estate.

"Anne, it's good to see you." Mr. Merill rose from behind his desk to shake her hand when his assistant showed her in. "I hope everything is going well at the library."

"The library is doing wonderfully. I have a question about Aunt Edie's estate though. I hope you can clear something up for me."

"I hope so too. What is it?" He waited for her to sit down before he resumed his seat. He leaned back in his imposing leather chair as he waited for her to speak.

Anne took the receipts out of her purse and passed them to him. "I found this receipt in the attic. It's for twenty-four Bernina sewing machines. Mildred Farley found the other receipt for fabric and sewing supplies in a box of material my great-aunt gave her. These are dated a year before Aunt Edie died. Do you know anything about these transactions?"

Mr. Merill studied the receipts, frowning. He looked up at Anne. "No. I don't know anything about these. Edie certainly didn't discuss them with me. What did she do with all these sewing machines and fabric?"

"Well, that's what I'm trying to find out. I've discovered she donated a dozen of the machines to the high school. At least I believe she did. The donation was made anonymously. But the other twelve sewing machines and the huge amount of fabric seem to have disappeared. I don't recall any mention of them in her will. They weren't listed as part of her estate, were they?"

"No. She must have disposed of them before she gave me an inventory of her estate. The list she gave me was very detailed."

"I remember. She was a stickler for detail," Anne said. "I was hoping she had discussed such a large purchase with you or someone."

"Not with me," the administrator said. "Of course, she was free to make whatever purchases she wished. Your aunt was a very independent woman."

"I know," Anne said. "It just seems odd."

"Odd, indeed," Mr. Merill said, handing the receipts back to Anne. "If I had to guess, I'd say it looks like inventory someone would purchase to start up a business."

"I suppose that's possible. But wouldn't she have drawn up some kind of agreement if she made a loan to someone or if she became a partner with someone?" Anne asked.

"I would expect so. Unless it was an outright gift."

"Suppose she did set someone up in business? Would she be liable if the business incurred debts?"

He rubbed his chin. "That would depend. If there was any written agreement, then she could be liable—or rather, her estate could be liable. I don't have any record of such an arrangement. I think she would have told me. I wouldn't worry about it, unless we hear from someone making a claim on the estate."

Mr. Merill's assistant buzzed him that his next client had arrived.

"I'm sorry." Mr. Merill stood. "I'm afraid I wasn't much help. Is there anything else I can do for you?"

Anne rose to leave. "No. I appreciate your time."

"Please let me know if you discover what happened to the missing sewing machines and fabric. I admit, I'm very curious."

"I will."

Anne's own curiosity had certainly increased. Could Aunt Edie have set some unknown person up in business somewhere? But who and where? It made no sense.

When Anne got back to the library, she went upstairs for a late lunch. First she placed a call to the high school principal. He was on another call, so the secretary took a message. Anne had just made a cup of tea and sat down with a strawberry yogurt and half of a toasted bagel with cream cheese when her cell phone rang. "Hello, this is Anne."

"Anne, this is Jim Beckett, the principal at Blue Hill High School. I'm returning your call."

"Oh yes. Thank you for calling back so quickly. I just learned that your domestic arts department received a donation of sewing machines about a year and a half ago. I believe my great-aunt might have been the donor. I found a receipt for the machines among her things."

"Really? Perhaps there is some way to recognize her generosity."

"Oh no. That's not why I called. She wanted to remain anonymous, I'm sure. I noticed there were twelve sewing machines in the classroom, but, you see, my aunt purchased twenty-four machines. I'm trying to trace the remaining twelve, and I wondered if they could be in a district warehouse somewhere."

"*Hmm.* I'm not aware of any machines in storage, but I can ask our maintenance staff. We do have a district warehouse, and I'll have the maintenance supervisor contact you. He should have an inventory of everything in storage. His records might help if we aren't able to locate them right away."

"Thank you. That would be very helpful. If they're not being used, I'd like to figure out a way that they could be put to use as my aunt intended."

"If we do have the machines, I'm sure we can figure something out," Mr. Beckett said.

"What is the supervisor's name?"

"Frank Evans. Since it's Friday afternoon, I doubt you'll hear from him until Monday."

"That's fine. Thanks. I hope he can help me solve this puzzle."

CHAPTER FIVE

Wendy and her brood came inside when she brought Ben and Liddie home from school.

"Are you getting any more interest in the crochet class?" Wendy asked Anne, who was looking through the latest *Library Journal*.

Anne set the journal aside for later. "Yes. I had two more sign ups today. One of them said she liked that she could learn something new and help the community at the same time."

"Good. I plan to come early to set up and make coffee and hot water for cocoa or tea. I'm making cookies tonight."

"Don't feel that you have to provide refreshments. People are coming to learn crochet."

"Oh, it's no problem."

"No, Wendy," Anne said with a chuckle. "You're setting a dangerous precedent. I don't want people thinking they will get refreshments at *every* event we hold."

Wendy chuckled. "People know I get carried away. Don't worry about it."

Liddie ran up to the checkout desk. "Mommy, can I go ask the neighbors for coats? I can hand out the flyers we made. Can I?" She stopped and looked over at Wendy. "Oops. 'Scuse me, Mrs. Pyle. I'm not supposed to interrupt."

"You're excused," Wendy said.

"Honey, I can't leave right now," Anne said. "Did you ask Ben to go with you?"

"He's got homework."

"One of my girls can go with her." Wendy turned around to look for her children. They had all scattered. "Liddie, go find Sarah. See if she will go with you. Tell her I said it was all right."

"Okay." She started to run off, then turned back to her mother. "Can I, Mommy?"

"Yes, if Sarah can go with you."

"She's sure going all out with this coat drive idea," Wendy said, watching Liddie disappear down the hallway.

A moment later, Liddie and Sarah came back to the desk, wearing their coats. "Can I have some flyers, Mommy?"

"There are only ten flyers left. You can take all of them." Anne handed Liddie the flyers. "Don't go too far. It'll be getting dark soon."

The two girls rushed out the front door. "I'll have to print off some more flyers tonight. Quite a few people have taken them, so maybe we'll start getting some donations. Mildred promised three jackets that she's making, plus we'll have the scarves from your class tomorrow, so at least we'll have something to take to the church Sunday."

"I'd better get home and make my cookies," Wendy said, hooking her purse straps over her shoulder.

After Wendy and her children left, and while Bella was minding the checkout desk, Anne cleaned up the kitchen workroom, getting it ready for Wendy's crochet class. She moved the worktable to one end so Wendy could use it for her demonstration and supplies. Then she set up folding chairs in rows facing the table. She didn't know how many to arrange but decided to be optimistic, so she set up fifteen chairs, which filled the large kitchen.

By the time she finished setting up, it was closing time and Bella came in to get her backpack.

"I locked the front door and picked up all the books left lying around. Do you want me to stay and shelve them?"

"No, you go on home. We'll do it tomorrow."

"All right. I'm going to come back for the crochet class. I can come early if you want help."

"Thanks. That would be great."

Anne let Bella out and locked up after her, then went upstairs. She found Ben printing flyers on their personal printer and Sarah and Liddie cutting them.

"Hey, Mom, we're doing flyers so we'll have some for the desk tomorrow," Ben said.

"Great! Now I won't have to do them." Anne went to look at the flyers. They were printed two to a page, so the kids had to cut them in half. Liddie's were crooked, but it didn't matter. It pleased Anne that the children had taken the initiative to make more flyers by themselves.

"Did you hand out all the flyers?" Anne asked.

"Yes. Every single one," Liddie said. "People were really nice and said they would look for clothes to bring to the library. And look, Mommy!" Liddie ran over and picked up a navy blue garment off of a chair. She grinned as she held it up high like a trophy she'd won. "We brought back a jacket and a hat! Can I take them downstairs now?"

"That's wonderful, Liddie. Let me check them." Anne looked over the quilted windbreaker. "It looks new." The dark blue knit ski hat was in good shape.

"They're from the lady at the end of the street," Sarah said. "She told us her husband never wore the jacket before he died. She was sad, but she wanted to give it to someone, so she gave it to us. I told her that I thought her husband would be happy that his jacket will help someone."

"That was kind, Sarah. I'm sure it made her feel better."

"I hope so, Mrs. Gibson."

"Liddie, you can take these downstairs. Then when you kids are finished with the flyers, I told Sarah's mother we would take her home." Anne handed the coat and hat to Liddie, who went out to the grand staircase and flipped on the light, then went down to the foyer to deposit the garments.

"I printed twenty pages. Do you think that's enough?" Ben said.

"That makes forty flyers. I think that's plenty for now. We can always make more later," Anne said.

"Two more to go," Sarah said as she cut through a page.

Liddie came back up the stairs and turned off the stairwell light.

Anne got her purse and put on her coat while they finished. Ben stacked the cut flyers and put on his jacket. Sarah helped Liddie, then put on her own coat and gathered her schoolbooks.

"All set?" Anne asked.

Ben was already bounding down the stairs while Anne and the girls followed him.

When they got to the Pyles' house, they all went inside. Ben and Liddie went off to find their friends. Wendy was in the kitchen with Chad, who was at the table, drinking coffee and eating a cookie.

"I thought I'd stop to see if you need a taste tester, but it looks like you've got that covered," Anne said with a smile.

"Here." Chad pushed a plateful of cookies in Anne's direction. "You can spoil your dinner too. Have a seat. Want some warmed-over coffee?"

"No, thanks." Anne sat at the end of the table, so she could see both Wendy and Chad. She took a cookie and bit into it. "*Mmm.* This is delicious. What is it?"

Wendy grinned. She'd just taken a pan out of the oven and held it up toward them. Anne could smell chocolate and pecans. "It's my variation on ranger cookies. I add a bit of this and that."

"I taste chocolate and cranberries and pecans. You need to rename them — Wendy's This-and-That Cookies or something."

"I get mobbed when I take them to school," Chad said.

"I can see why." Anne finished her cookie.

"Another one?" Wendy asked.

"Much as I'd like one, I'd better pass, or I won't be able to eat any dinner."

"I'm not concerned about that," Chad said, taking another cookie.

"Chad, can I ask you a question?" Anne said.

"Sure."

"Wendy told me you helped unload a bunch of sewing machines at the high school about a year and a half ago. Can you remember how many you unloaded?"

"*Hmm.*" He gazed off toward the corner as he finished chewing his cookie. "If I remember right, I only carried five or six, and Vince carried about the same number. We put them all in the classroom."

"Could there have been two dozen machines? I talked to Darlynn Jamison, the domestic arts teacher, and she said there are only twelve machines, but there should be twenty-four," Anne said. "Could half of them have gone into storage?"

"I don't think so. It seemed like a lot of boxes, but I doubt it was that many."

"You mentioned Vince. Who is he?"

"Vince Parker. He was one of my football players, although he only lasted one season before he dropped out. Sad," Chad said, popping another cookie into his mouth. Anne wondered if there would be any left at the rate he was eating them. "He could have been a starter. The kid was fast and big for his age. He'd played football back in West Virginia. No interest though. He got in with the wrong crowd."

"That's too bad. Darlynn said the machines were there when she started teaching. Do you remember who was teaching when the machines arrived?"

"Yes. It was Victoria Parker. Young teacher, just out of college. Vince was her younger brother."

"Really?" Anne perked up. "Were the sewing machines delivered by a store?"

"It's been so long ago. But I don't think so. We unloaded the machines from the back of a pickup truck." Chad frowned thoughtfully. "I can't remember for sure, but I don't think it had a name or logo on it."

"Could the truck have belonged to Vince?"

"No. Vince didn't have a vehicle. I'm sure of that, because I gave him a ride home a few times after practice. It might have belonged to his uncle. I didn't think to ask. Victoria was there and we moved the boxes into the school. She was very excited."

"I'd think so. You said Vince got in with a bad crowd. Were they involved with drugs or what?"

"Mostly petty things. They loitered behind the stores after school and the owners complained, but the kids didn't steal anything that I know of. They disrupted classes and activities and violated curfew. That sort of thing. They hung out with some older boys too. That concerned me. Vince got caught with a stolen bike. He claimed he didn't know it was stolen, but he wouldn't tell where he got it. He was arrested. The judge gave him probation and community service. I tried to talk to him, but he wouldn't listen to me either. They moved away soon after that."

"Do you know where they went? Could they have taken the missing machines?"

Chad shook his head. "I don't know where they moved to. But I seriously doubt if Vince took the extra machines. Victoria wouldn't have allowed him to steal from Edie or anyone. She tried to steer her brother in good directions, which wasn't easy, I'm sure. He had a giant chip on his shoulder and he wouldn't listen to anyone. His arrest for that theft really upset her."

"I can imagine. She must have been at least five or six years older than her brother since he was still in high school. You mentioned an uncle, so do they have family here? Did Vince and Victoria grow up around here? Do you know if they have other family here?"

Chad laughed. "You're sure full of questions today. I'm pretty sure they didn't come from here, but I couldn't swear to it, since we aren't originally from here either. I remember that Vince was living with his aunt and uncle though. I suppose Victoria took a job in Blue Hill so they could be close to their relatives. I don't know about their parents, but I got the impression they had a rough life before coming to Blue Hill."

Chad's answers didn't help Anne figure out the mystery of the missing sewing machines. If anything, she had more questions. She wanted to find out more about Vince and Victoria Parker. Where did they come from? Why did Vince have a chip on his shoulder? And who were his friends in the wrong crowd?

Chapter Six

Anne watched out the window as the sky brightened Saturday morning, washing the scattered clouds in a lovely pink hue. The sun rose above the horizon, promising beautiful weather. Anne closed her Bible and gave thanks for the day, then went to prepare to meet it. Liddie and Ben were up by the time she'd dressed. As she and the children finished breakfast, the back door buzzer chimed.

"I'll get it," Ben said, rushing to the intercom that they'd had installed when they converted Aunt Edie's old house into the library and their home. "Hello? Who's there?" he asked.

Anne heard Mildred's voice responding. "Ben, invite her up and go open the door for her, in case she has something to carry."

"Okay, Mom." He punched the intercom button. "I'm coming down to let you in," he called out. Then he tromped heavily down the stairs.

A few minutes later he reappeared, carrying a large plastic bag. Mildred was right behind him. He put the bag on the table.

"Good morning," Mildred said. "I hope you don't mind my coming so early."

"Not at all. Would you like a cup of coffee?"

"Yes, thank you, but first I want to talk to this young lady." She turned to Liddie.

Liddie's eyes grew big. "Me?"

"Yes. I brought you something." Mildred picked up the large plastic bag and held it out to Liddie. "For your clothing drive."

Liddie took the bag from Mildred and peeked inside.

"Go ahead and open it," Anne said. "I want to see too."

Liddie pulled out a soft bundle of fleece. She dropped the bag on a chair and held up the object. Her eyes got wider. "It's a coat!"

"You asked me if I had any gently used warm clothing. I decided to give you something new. There are more. I made them."

"It's so soft," Liddie said, rubbing the soft green pile against her cheek. "Like my teddy bear." She reached back into the bag and pulled out two more.

Mildred's eyes twinkled. "Do you think that will work for the donation box?"

"Oh yes! Thank you!" Liddie reached up and gave Mildred a hug. "Mommy, can I put them in the box downstairs?"

"Yes, but be careful carrying them. You can use the elevator this once."

"I'll help." Ben hurried out the door that separated their living quarters from the library before his mother changed her mind. As a rule, she didn't let them use the elevator. It was not a play area, and besides, the stairs were good exercise.

Anne poured two cups of coffee and gave one to Mildred. "Sit down and visit for a moment."

"I won't stay long. I know you're busy."

"I have time. Thank you for bringing the coats for Liddie."

"You're welcome. I'm glad I could encourage her."

"I visited the high school this week and met Darlynn Jamison, the domestic arts teacher," Anne said.

"That's nice. I haven't met her. And I still can't figure out why they changed the name. It's home economics. Plain and simple."

"That's how I think of it too, but you have to admit, your sewing is a type of art."

Mildred grunted. "I suppose. I'm glad to hear they still offer it. With the budget cuts every year, I keep expecting them to drop the program."

"It seems to be doing well. Did you know the school got a dozen new Bernina sewing machines?"

"I did hear about them getting machines, but I assumed they were used. Stores sometimes donate their floor models to schools or charities. It's odd that the school kept it so low-key." Her eyebrows rose in realization. "That receipt you found. You said Edie bought some Berninas. She donated them to the school, didn't she? That sly fox. I can't believe she didn't tell me."

"I don't know for sure, but it seems likely. They are the same model as the ones on the receipt. Are you sure she didn't mention them?"

"Positive. Did the teacher know who donated them?"

"No. She said the machines were there when she started."

"Victoria Parker was there before this teacher. Edie must have given them to the school so Victoria would have decent machines to work with." Mildred frowned as she took a sip of coffee. "While I substituted for a few months, the school's old machines constantly broke down. They needed new machines. Still, I can't believe Victoria didn't tell me either."

From Mildred's bewildered expression, Anne thought she might feel hurt or slighted by her friends' omission. "According to Wendy, it was an anonymous donation, and if Aunt Edie was the donor, like I suspect, she probably swore Victoria to secrecy. Sometimes she could be so private."

"That's true, but she usually confided in me." Mildred shrugged, as if to shake off her thoughts.

"I didn't realize you taught home ec at the high school. Miss Latham told me you went back to teach a few years ago, and then you helped when the school hired a young teacher. Was that Victoria? Did you know her well?"

"Yes, it was. I got to know her very well. Such a dear girl. It was her first teaching position. I suppose you could say I mentored her. I gave demonstrations to her classes on several occasions, and sometimes Edie helped me. We both took her under our wings. Victoria sewed beautifully, but we taught her to crochet and knit." Mildred smiled.

"You liked her a lot."

"Like a niece. She had such a sweet disposition. She could have been bitter, considering what a hard childhood she had in the Appalachian backwoods, but she never let her past tarnish her sunny outlook. Her brother—now that was a different matter." Mildred shook her head. "Took after their father, I suppose." She set down her cup. "I'd best be going and let you get on with your day. It's almost time for the library to open." She stood.

Anne glanced at her watch. She needed to hurry and get downstairs. She hadn't told Mildred there were still twelve sewing machines unaccounted for, and she wanted to ask more about Victoria and Vince, but it was getting late. "You're right. Wendy is holding her crochet class this afternoon, so we'll be busy."

Anne followed Mildred downstairs, then went to check on the library. The three jackets nearly filled the plastic bin. Anne found another empty bin to go next to it, just in case they needed the space.

* * *

Even with extra help, the library kept Anne busy. An hour before the class, Bella and Remi came in. They dived in to work, shelving books that had been returned or left lying around. A half hour before the class, Wendy came in with her girls. She and Sarah carried trays of cookies to the kitchen.

A total of fifteen children and adults filed into the kitchen to take the crochet class. Many of the adults had brought their younger kids and took them upstairs to the Children's Room, where Hannah Pyle read stories to them. Ben took it upon himself to act as a one-man welcome committee, spending most of the time during the class greeting people at the door and showing donors where to deposit their clothing items.

In spite of the class and Story Time going on, Anne stayed busy checking out books. The crowd seemed to draw others who wanted to see why the library had so many cars out front. Some neighbors came by with coats and winter clothing to donate. One woman from down the hill told Anne she hadn't known about the coat drive until Liddie and Sarah came to her house with a flyer. By the end of the day, the bins overflowed with clothing. Anne was delighted, even though she'd missed the crochet class.

"Wonderful program," Darlynn Jamison said as she put a blue and gray scarf in the basket by the checkout counter.

"You're fast," Anne said.

Darlynn laughed. "I made this one before the class. Monday after school I'll bring in the one I started today. I think I'll continue the project. Four of my students came. They can finish in class and maybe we'll interest a few more students. Remember, I'll be happy to help set up other programs."

"I'm sure I'll take you up on your offer."

Two other people left their completed scarves, while others promised to finish them at home and bring them in. Anne knew some of the attendees could crochet already, and she wondered why they'd come to the class. She asked Nellie Brown about it.

"It was the free yarn," Nellie told her in a quiet voice, leaning over the counter so others wouldn't hear. "My sister and I want to help the community, but we can't afford to buy supplies. Besides, I'd heard Wendy was making cookies and I knew you'd have coffee. We don't get a lot of social activities during the daytime, and we don't get out at night anymore."

"Would you like to take home some yarn to make a couple more scarves?"

Nellie's eyes lit up. "Oh yes. We can make as many scarves as you like."

"If you can wait a few minutes until the crowd is gone, I'll get some for you."

"All right. Betty went to the Nonfiction Room to look for a new biography. I'll wait in there with her."

Anne spoke to several others and checked out stacks of books as parents collected their children and storybooks to take home.

"Mommy!" Liddie whispered excitedly next to her, tugging on Anne's sweater. "Look at the boxes. They're full!"

Anne looked down. Liddie's eyes sparkled and her face glowed. "I know. Isn't it wonderful?"

"Yes! Ben said it was because of the flyers me and Sarah passed out. Can we take them to church now?"

Anne refrained from correcting Liddie's grammar. "We'll take them with us in the morning."

"Aww. Okay."

Alex and Ryan came by to get Ben, who was spending the night with Ryan.

"Busy place," Alex said, leaning an elbow on the checkout desk.

"It's been a zoo. And I couldn't be happier. Wendy's crochet class drew a crowd."

"That's great."

"I've had offers from Mildred and the domestic arts teacher to put on other classes. *Hmm.* We need something to attract the men. I don't suppose you want to give a class?" Anne gave him a look of speculation. Alex laughed.

"I don't know what I could teach. Woodworking would be a little noisy and very dusty."

"Yes, I suppose it would. All right. You're off the hook."

"Good. I'll get the boys and scoot out of here before you come up with another bright idea."

Anne chuckled as he walked away. Then Wendy caught her attention.

"Did you see Liddie's scarf?" Wendy asked, coming up to the desk.

"No. Did you make one?" Anne asked her daughter.

"I started. See?" She held up the start of a scarf in multicolored yarn, with reds and yellows and purples. It was four inches long. "Sarah helped me. Mommy, can you help me finish it?"

"I knew I should have taken your class," Anne said, smiling at Wendy. "I'll try, honey. It's been a while since I crocheted, but Aunt Edie taught me how years ago."

"You'll remember," Wendy encouraged. "And I'll leave the patterns with you. Liddie, why don't you come home with us, and you can work on your scarf with Sara and Emily?"

"Can I, Mom?"

"Yes. Thanks, Wendy."

"No problem. I'll bring her home in time for dinner. Maybe by then we'll have a few more scarves to add to the pile. Did you find out anything more about the sewing machines?"

"Not yet. I'll do some more checking this afternoon."

Anne gave the elderly sisters several skeins of yarn, then she locked up the library after Wendy and her gang left, taking Liddie with them.

Before she shut down the computer, she typed Victoria's name into the search engine to see if she could find any information about her. She found a tennis player and a doctor, but neither fit the age or what little she knew of the young domestic arts teacher. Despite her lack of success with finding Victoria on the Internet,

Anne utilized her research skills and decided to pull out several high school yearbooks from the local history section. She had managed to procure most of the recent years. Victoria would have joined the high school staff three years ago so Anne turned to that volume first and opened it to the staff pictures.

There she was, looking like she'd been misfiled. She appeared as young as her students with dark hair pulled back in a ponytail, no jewelry, and no obvious makeup. She could have been fourteen. Her eyes looked straight at the camera, even though her head was at a slight angle. There was nothing beguiling or secretive about her appearance. Ann flipped over to the class pictures. She couldn't find Vince in any of them, though his name was listed as a junior.

Anne picked up the next yearbook. Victoria's picture was the same. Again, Vince was not pictured with his class. She looked for the football team and found his name under a team photo. Counting through the rows, she picked him out. He was taller and larger than most of his team members. Dark, longish hair. Dark eyes. Menacing scowl. Was that a pose for the picture or his normal demeanor? He appeared older and more experienced, though not in a good way, than his sister — as if he'd seen the darker side of life and he carried it on his broad shoulders. Anne could imagine him as a troubled youth but not his sister. Was her innocent appearance misleading?

Anne went upstairs to the small desk in the little hidden room they'd discovered when they'd remodeled the old house. She had put her great-aunt's address book in a desk along with some of her personal writings. The tattered red leather book was stuffed with notes and held closed with a rubber band. Anne had written to a few of the friends and distant relatives in the old address book to let them know Aunt Edie had passed away. She didn't recall writing to Victoria.

Anne sat at the desk and went through it. Entries went back to the days when the town had party lines and four-digit phone numbers. They'd been crossed out and new numbers penciled in. Some names were crossed out too. Friends who had moved or passed away before Edie. Names, addresses, and phone numbers filled small pieces of paper. Anne read every one, checking the front and back for any information that might be helpful. She finally found Victoria's phone number. It wasn't a local prefix, so Anne was sure it was a cellular phone. She got her phone and punched in the number. A man answered.

"Hello, is Victoria there?"

"Who?"

"I'm looking for Victoria Parker. I have this number written down." She repeated the number from the note.

"That's my number. I don't know no Victoria whatever," the male voice said.

"Could this have been her number two years ago?"

"Don't know. I've had it over a year."

"Sorry to have bothered you." Anne disconnected the call and sighed, frustrated by the dead end. There was no address so evidently Aunt Edie had lost track of Victoria. That struck Anne as odd. Wouldn't Victoria have wanted to keep in touch with her benefactress?

* * *

After Wendy brought Liddie back home, Anne and Liddie went downstairs to check the clothing collected for the church donation box.

"Wow, look at all the clothes," Liddie said, eyeing the two bins overflowing with garments. "I can't wait to take them to church." Liddie bounced up and down, clapping her hands. "Reverend Tom will be surprised when we fill up the box."

"Indeed he will," Anne said.

People had been generous. One piece at a time, Anne and Liddie looked over the coats, hats, gloves, sweaters, and assorted warm clothing. Anne was surprised and impressed that everything looked clean. She set aside a couple of pieces with seams that needed repairing and others that had missing buttons. Fortunately, Aunt Edie's supplies included a jar filled with assorted buttons.

"Let's take these upstairs to repair after dinner," Anne said, handing a light coat and a flannel shirt to Liddie. "You can put them in the sewing room." She picked up a shirt and two jackets and followed Liddie upstairs.

Anne gave Liddie the task of finding buttons to match the ones missing on a jacket and shirt while she put a black bobbin and thread in the old Singer sewing machine. She sat at the machine and placed the sleeve hole of the jacket under the presser foot, ready to fix the seam. The machine started, sewed three stitches, made a horrible grinding noise, and stopped. She tried to resume, flipping the lever to reverse, then forward. A telltale odor of hot metal came from the machine but no sound. She raised the presser foot and manually turned the wheel to lift the needle out of the fabric, expecting to find a knotted mess of thread underneath where it bound up. The jacket wasn't caught. The bobbin wasn't bound. The machine had just stopped.

Anne tried the plug, making sure it was firmly in the receptor. The cords weren't loose and everything looked fine. The machine just would not start. Great. What a time for it to decide to quit. Anne got out a needle and thread and stitched the seam by hand. She didn't do a lot of sewing, but she needed a machine for mending. She wished she had found one of the Berninas in the attic. It would sure come in handy right now.

CHAPTER SEVEN

W hen Anne pulled into the church parking lot, Ben and
Ryan came running to the car.

"We came to help carry in the coats and stuff," Ben said.

"Thank you, boys." Anne opened the trunk and piled coats,
sweaters, crocheted scarves, and hats into their arms.

"I can help too," Alex said, coming up to the car, reaching out
his arms.

"Great. We have a lot of donations." Anne gave Liddie a
jacket and sweater, then gave Alex half of what remained and
took the rest herself. They made quite a procession, carrying full
armfuls into the church. Reverend Tom saw them coming and
held the door open for them.

"That's quite a load of clothing," he said.

"Yeah. Liddie's been collecting them," Ben said.

"Ben helped," Liddie said.

"They've both worked hard to spread the word," Anne said.
"Plus we have scarves crocheted at the library class."

"Impressive. That's going to help a lot of families," Reverend
Tom said.

The clothing nearly filled the large box.

"We have to get some more, Mommy," Liddie said.

"We will. I'm sure your advertising will bring more into the library. I'm proud of you for taking this so seriously and working so hard on it."

Liddie smiled at the praise.

"Thanks for your help, guys," Anne told the boys and Alex.

"Happy to do it," Alex said, smiling at her. They found seats in the sanctuary as the music began.

After the singing, Reverend Tom got up to give announcements. "Some of you may have noticed that the donation box is full. Thank you to all who have brought items. I saw several of our young people carrying in most of what you see. One of our youngsters has made a commitment to fill the box on her own. I know she had help, but she is working hard to get the word out. We will empty it this week and distribute the clothing to needy families. Let's see if we can fill it up again next week. The children are doing their part. Go through your closets and ask your neighbors. Let's all help."

After church, as they finished lunch, Liddie gave her mom a look of deep concern.

"Reverend Tom said we have to fill the box again. That's a lot of coats and hats. I don't know if I can do it again."

"Sweetheart, you don't have to do it all on your own. That's why he asked everyone to help. We might collect some more at the library."

"I certainly hope so," she said, sounding so grown up, Anne had to smile.

* * *

On Monday morning, after taking Ben and Liddie to school and helping Remi Miller open the library, Anne stopped at the fabric store around the corner from Main Street. According to the phone book, the Stitching Post did sewing machine repair. She took the machine out of the trunk and carried it to the store.

Colorful fabrics in fall colors were draped in the store window along with leaves and pumpkins. Several homemade Halloween costumes and a denim outfit were arranged on display.

A bell rang when Anne opened the door and stepped inside. A middle-aged woman stood behind a worktable measuring fabric. A tape measure was draped around her neck, and she had a pincushion on her wrist. A customer stood across from her. The saleswoman glanced up at the sound of the bell. "I'll be with you in a few minutes. You can set the machine on the back counter."

"Thanks." Anne carried the machine to the back and set it down. She looked around while she waited. Rows and rows of low tables held bolts of fabric in every imaginable color and type. Anne looked for blue wool but didn't see anything like the blazer she'd found in the cedar chest. Near the front of the store were several sewing machines. Anne wandered up to look at them. They were brands she hadn't heard of. No Berninas.

The customer paid for her fabric and left. The saleswoman came to Anne. "Are you here for a sewing machine repair?"

"Yes, I hope so. I have an old Singer. I don't know if it's repairable. It just quit on me."

"We can take a look. Let me write up a repair tag. Our repairman works on the weekends, so it will be a while before he gets back to you."

"That's fine. I don't do a lot of sewing. Mending, mainly."

The saleswoman wrote up a repair ticket. "I'll have the repairman call you with an estimate before he does anything," she told Anne. Then she carried the machine to the back room.

Anne waited for her to return.

"Can I help you with something else? Did you want some fabric or anything else?"

"No, thank you, but I do have a question. Do you ever buy fabric from warehouse overstock or auctions?"

"No. We have a regular supplier who comes in twice a month with new selections. He checks our stock and makes a note of what's low, so he can bring more the next time."

"Have you worked here a long time?" Anne asked.

"Since we opened, four years ago."

"Did you know Edie Summers, by chance?"

The woman shook her head. "Name doesn't sound familiar."

"How about Victoria Parker?"

The saleswoman thought for a moment. "Wasn't she the home ec teacher out at the high school? She came in a few times looking for fabric that she could tell her students to buy. Nice young woman, always polite and pleasant. I haven't seen her in a long time. I've met the new teacher. She's been in a few times."

"Did Victoria or perhaps an older woman bring in a bunch of bolts of fabric to see if you would buy them about eighteen months ago?"

"No. No one has ever approached us to sell us fabric. Sorry."

"That's all right. I just wondered. Thank you. I'll wait to hear from your repairman on my Singer."

Anne left the fabric store and returned to the library.

She was drinking a cup of coffee and looking through a catalog of new releases at her library desk when her cell phone rang. She didn't recognize the number.

"Hello?"

"Hello, this is Frank Evans. Is this Anne Gibson?"

"Yes it is."

"The high school principal asked me to call you," he said. "Something about sewing machines?"

"Oh yes. Thank you for calling me. The high school's domestic arts department received some new Bernina sewing machines about a year and a half ago."

"Yeah. I remember that. We still got the old ones in the warehouse."

"That's what I want to talk to you about. The classroom has twelve new machines, but there were actually twenty-four. Are the other twelve in storage?"

"Not that I know of. Just the old ones."

"Is there any way I could come look to make sure they aren't there? They'd probably still be in the original boxes."

"Well…" There was a pause on the phone.

"I won't take up too much of your time," Anne said.

"I suppose I could look this morning."

"Oh, good. I can be there in fifteen minutes or so."

"You don't need to. But I guess it's all right. Come to the warehouse in back of the bus barn," Frank said.

"I'll be there. Thanks!" Anne disconnected and finished her coffee as she marked a few books to order. Then she put away the catalog and went upstairs to get her coat and purse.

On her way out the door, she paused at the checkout desk where Remi Miller was logging returned books into the computer system. "I'll be gone for an hour or so," Anne said.

"No problem. I'll be here," Remi said.

Anne drove to the school bus barn and parked in back, next to a long buff-colored steel building with a green metal roof. She'd never been here before, though it had existed all the years she was growing up. It had no windows. No sign to identify it. There were two doors on the side of the building. One at each end. Anne went to the closest door and knocked, but no one answered. She stood there for a couple of minutes looking around. Her car was the only vehicle there. The bus barn entrance was around the front of another building. Steely gray clouds obscured the sun. Though the early morning fog had lifted, the air held an opaque quality from the chilled humidity. She shivered and pulled her collar up around her neck.

A pickup truck pulled up next to her car. Blue Hill School District was printed on the door. A short, stocky man got out and walked toward her. He carried a clipboard with a stack of papers in his left hand.

"Frank Evans," he said, offering his hand. "You must be Anne."

She shook his hand. "Yes, I am. Nice to meet you, Frank."

He gave her a nod, then pulled a set of keys on a retractable cord from his belt and opened the door. A wall of black greeted them. He stepped inside and flipped on the lights. The blackness turned to yellowish gray as a long column of overhead lights came on.

"Come on in, but watch your step. The fluorescent lights aren't very bright. They'll get brighter though."

Anne stepped inside. Frank closed the door behind them. Narrow aisles cut between tall rows of metal shelving.

"I've got an inventory list here. It should be correct, but it's hard to keep up. People from the schools can come get supplies or borrow chairs and tables. They're supposed to fill out requisitions, but it doesn't always happen. And there's attrition. Things get broken… Anyway, I don't have any Bernina sewing machines on the warehouse inventory, but we'll look just to be sure. I talked to the high school maintenance manager. They don't have much storage space there, but he confirmed that they aren't storing any sewing machines."

"Thanks for checking. They have to be somewhere," Anne said. As they walked along, Anne saw stacks of folding tables, chairs, desks, boxes of books, paper, and office supplies. A row of large metal lockers lined the walls.

"What are in those cabinets?" Anne asked.

"Flammable materials, like paints, oils, and chemicals."

They came to an overhead door, then two large lawn tractors, several weed eaters and trimmers, and two metal trailers. Past that were tubular structures that looked like scaffolding frames. Across from the equipment, the shelves held large cartons of paper goods for the school lunchrooms and the bathrooms. The next set of shelves held cartons of lightbulbs, boxes of door hardware, and plumbing fittings.

"It certainly takes a lot of supplies to run the schools," Anne commented.

"Yup. We order in bulk, but we go through these supplies every year and have to order more. Here's the extra electronic equipment," Frank said, pointing to the next set of shelves. The labels on the boxes indicated computer equipment and biology laboratory equipment. Next to them, three plain cardboard boxes were marked *Old Sewing Machines* with hand-printed lettering.

"Those are the old machines from domestic arts," Frank said. "I'll open them to be sure." He lifted one down and used a key to cut through the tape.

Anne peered inside the box. Not new. Not a Bernina. "Definitely not the type of machine I'm looking for. But thank you for checking. You don't need to open the other two. The new machines would be in Bernina boxes." Her eyes had adjusted to the dim lighting. Even so, as she peered behind the boxes, she couldn't make out the labels on the boxes facing the next aisle.

Anne's hands were getting numb and the cold was penetrating her bones by the time they reached the end of the aisle and started up the next. It hadn't occurred to her that the metal building would feel as cold inside as the weather outside. She couldn't imagine working in here. She doubted anyone stayed inside for very long.

They walked the entire building, checking every shelf. Anne saw sports equipment, stage sets, and wardrobe containers, lumber and various building materials but no Bernina sewing machines.

"Well, that was a wild-goose chase. I'm sorry I put you to so much trouble," Anne told Frank when they finally stepped outside and he locked the warehouse.

"No problem. Gave me a chance to look over our supplies. Sorry you didn't find your missing sewing machines. I remember when we got the new ones. They didn't come through normal deliveries. One day, they just showed up and we had to remove the old ones. I'm thinking we need to get rid of them. We don't have lots of room to store surplus."

"I can see that. Thanks for letting me look."

Anne considered her next step as she drove back to the library. She'd hoped the extra machines would have turned up at the school warehouse. Where could they be? Who would know if anyone else in town had received an anonymous gift of twelve sewing machines?

* * *

After lunch, Anne worked in the library searching for all of the local organizations that might have benefited from a gift of Aunt Edie's sewing machines, thinking she might have donated the rest of them to a charity.

Remi came over to where Anne was working.

"I've finished shelving all the returned books," Remi said. "Are you working on a research project? Is there something I can help you with?"

Anne looked up and smiled. "It's research for myself. I'm making a list of all the possible organizations in our area who might benefit from a donation of sewing machines." She tapped her pen against the notepad. "I've got the usual groups. Hospital auxiliary, women's shelter, 4-H, Girl Scouts—that sort of group. Can you think of any I might have missed?"

Remi looked at Anne's list. "Is there a quilting group out at the retirement home? Or maybe a sewing class at Stonebridge Elementary? Although they're probably too young. I remember someone donated a bunch of sewing machines to the high school a couple of years ago."

"Yes, I saw them when I was out there talking to Miss Latham. I met the domestic arts teacher, Darlynn Jamison. She showed me one of the machines. I'll add your suggestions to my list. It won't hurt to ask. If you think of any more, let me know."

"Do you want me to ask around?"

"Sure. I'm looking for a group who already received a donation of machines, like the high school. It would have been about the same time. Twelve machines."

"Really? Wow. I think we would have heard about it if some group got such a large donation."

"Perhaps, but it was anonymous. That's why I'm having so much trouble tracking it."

Anne went upstairs to call the groups on her list. In each case, the answer was the same. No one had received any sewing machines. Everyone wanted to be on the list if the missing machines were found. Running out of places where Aunt Edie might have donated the machines, Anne switched directions. She got out the phone book and looked up the Chamber of Commerce. Then she punched in the number.

"Chamber of Commerce. How can I help you?" a woman answered.

"Hello, this is Anne Gibson, from the Blue Hill Library. I'm trying to trace a local company called A Able Surplus Sales. Do you have a record of that company?"

"It doesn't ring a bell. Let me look in our business directory."

"I appreciate it. Thank you." Anne listened to scratchy music while she was on hold for several minutes.

"Could you give me that name again, please?" the woman asked.

"It is A Able Surplus," Anne repeated.

"That's what I thought you said. I don't find any record of that company or even any name close to it. I looked in our current directory and our previous one. Are you sure it is a local company?"

"It had a local post office box, but I'm wondering if the company may have closed."

"Could be. People start businesses that never get off the ground. That's why the Chamber is so important. We help the community and our member businesses."

"Yes. Well, thank you for looking for me."

"You could call the Better Business Bureau. They might have a record of the company." The woman rattled off a phone number. Anne wrote it down.

"Is the library a member of the Chamber of Commerce?" the woman asked.

"Oh yes. We joined as soon as we opened," Anne said.

"Good. It's important to support our local businesses."

"Yes. Thank you." Anne said good-bye and disconnected, then punched in the number for the Better Business Bureau.

"Pittsburgh Branch, Better Business Bureau," a man's voice answered.

"Hello, I'm calling from the Blue Hill Library, trying to trace a company named A Able Surplus Sales from Blue Hill, Pennsylvania. Do you have any record of this company? Any ratings or complaints?"

"Let me check."

Anne waited again while music played in the background. This time it was lovely piano music. The music stopped.

"I don't have any record of such a company," the man said. "Could it be under a different name?"

"That's the only name I have. Thank you for checking for me."

"You're welcome."

Anne disconnected the call, then frowned at her cell phone. Had A Able Surplus ever existed? Aunt Edie purchased and received at least twelve sewing machines. *Somewhere* there was a company that sold them to her plus twelve more. Despite all these dead ends, Anne was still determined to get to the bottom of this.

Chapter Eight

Tuesday morning, Anne stood on a stepstool, dusting the top shelf of the early-American history books. She removed a book that had been put back in the wrong place and added it to a stack on a rolling cart. No matter how often she checked the shelves, she found misplaced books. The library door opened and Anne saw Mildred come in carrying several books. She set all but one of the books on the library checkout desk, then turned, looking around. She spotted Anne and came into the Nonfiction Room.

"Good morning, Mildred," Anne said, stepping down from the stool.

"Good morning, Anne. Are you busy? Can you talk?"

"I can take a break." Anne moved the cart of books out of the way. "How can I help you?"

Mildred held up the book in her hands. "I brought something to show you."

Anne glanced around. The library wasn't busy, and the few visitors were occupied. This was her chance to ask Mildred some questions. "Let's go back to the workroom where we can talk."

Mildred nodded and led the way back to the old kitchen. "I can't come in here without thinking about all the meals I shared with Edie in here," she said.

"I know. I feel the same way. Would you like a cup of coffee or tea?"

"No, thank you. I've had mine this morning." Mildred sat at the kitchen table. "You go ahead."

Ignoring the coffeepot, Anne sat down across from Mildred.

"I talked to a couple of people at church who attended the crochet class on Saturday. They all said it went very well and they would come to another class," Mildred said.

"Yes. We were pleased by the turnout, and so far we've collected ten finished scarves. We should get a few more this week from those who took them home to finish."

"I saw some of the scarves in the donation box at church. They looked wonderful. I expect the same success from my knitting class, but we will need a second class to finish it up. Here is the hat pattern I plan to use." Mildred handed Anne the book, open to a picture of a boy wearing a stocking cap. "We need three ounces of four-ply yarn for each hat. Is there enough yarn left in Edie's supplies, or should I get some?"

Anne hadn't agreed to hold another event so soon when Mildred had broached the subject on Saturday morning, but the crochet class had been well attended, and the donation box could certainly use more warm hats. Besides, she knew Aunt Edie would be pleased that her house was being used to help others and that her best friend was involved. "There's plenty of yarn left. Knitting needles too. When were you thinking of holding the class?"

"Oh, the sooner, the better."

"I considered holding an event each month, so what if we schedule your class for a month from Wendy's class?" Anne got up and retrieved the calendar Bella had tacked up on the wall. "That would be the last Saturday in October and the first Saturday in November. Would that work for you?"

Mildred's brow furrowed. "Do you think we should wait that long?"

"We threw Wendy's class together in a hurry, and it went all right, but we need time to promote our events if we want community participation. We'll still be early enough that the hats will be in big demand."

"I suppose you're right. Those dates are fine with me. What do we need to do to promote it? What shall I do?"

Anne thought about it for a moment. Wendy had done all the planning and flyers for her class, which had been a spur-of-the-moment event. Regular functions would be good for the library, but she needed to figure out a policy to cover these volunteer events. "I will make a room available and set it up. Could you work with Bella Miller to put an announcement on our Web site and Facebook page and to make up a flyer? She works tomorrow. I can run off copies and put them at the checkout counter. Maybe you could put up a few flyers as announcements around town."

"I'll come in tomorrow to work with Bella. Perhaps I can get Wendy to help me distribute flyers. She's good at that sort of thing."

"Yes, she is, and I'm sure she'll be happy to help. We can talk about ideas at our next Library Guild meeting too. Now I need your help if you have time."

"I'll be happy to help you, if I can."

"Aunt Edie's old Singer sewing machine just died. I was trying to repair the sleeve on a donated jacket, when the machine literally ground to a halt and wouldn't move. I took it in to be repaired, but some of the clothes that come into the library need minor repairs. Would you be able to do the mending for me?"

"Of course. That won't take much time. Just bring them over or call me and I can come get them." Mildred shook her head. "I told Edie she should replace that old machine a long time ago. Sentimentality won't get things done."

"I know." Anne nodded. Watching Mildred for a reaction, she said, "I wish I had one of those Berninas like yours that she purchased. I still can't figure out what happened to them."

"But you said you found them at the school."

"Well... Not all of them. Aunt Edie bought twenty-four sewing machines. The school only has twelve. I've looked everywhere, but I can't find the rest. Can you think of anywhere they might be?"

Mildred looked shocked. "Why, I have no idea. That's... extraordinary."

"Is it possible Aunt Edie fell victim to a scam?"

"Oh no. Edie was too sharp for that. What makes you think that?"

"The receipt. Like the one you found. It's handwritten on a generic receipt form. There's no company name and no address and the phone number is out of service."

Mildred's brow furrowed. "But you saw the sewing machines."

"Half of them. The other half disappeared into thin air, if they even existed. If Aunt Edie fell for a scam, she might have been too embarrassed to admit it."

"I can't believe that. She would demand justice."

"Yes. But what if it was someone she trusted? Someone she cared about?"

Mildred's eyes narrowed. "Like who?"

"I don't know. Perhaps Vince and Victoria Parker. Chad told me that Vince helped him unload the machines and put them in the domestic arts room but only the dozen machines. Victoria was there. As far as I can determine, Vince and Victoria are the only ones who might have known that Aunt Edie bought the machines."

"Impossible. Victoria couldn't be involved in anything fraudulent. How do you know they knew the machines came from Edie?"

Anne stared at Mildred. "I assume they knew. Vince unloaded them and Victoria was there to receive them. Someone had to know. What about Victoria's brother? Did you know him?"

"Vince worked during the summer for me and for Edie doing yard work. He worked hard and did a good job, but he didn't talk much." Mildred paused, frowning. "He always seemed as if he was brooding about something. Victoria didn't go into any detail, but I know their family was poor and they'd endured a lot of hardships. Her father was a hard man. I got the impression alcohol was involved. Victoria hoped living in Blue Hill would be good for her brother. We all tried to help. He hung out with some no-account friends and they got him into trouble, but I can't believe he would steal from Edie."

Mildred shook her head several times, as if dismissing the possibility. Her frown disappeared. "You'd understand if you knew Victoria. I remember when Edie and I took her to a craft fair in Deshler. We had such fun. Victoria made lots of notes. She couldn't wait to take some of the ideas back to her class. She was a born teacher, always looking for ways to improve her teaching and help her students. I promise you, Victoria did not—*could not*—take advantage of your aunt. Absolutely not."

"Do you know where they moved to?"

"Victoria had applied for a teaching position in Philadelphia. I don't know what school district. I…" Mildred's frown was back. "I don't have her address. Last time I saw her aunt in town, she hadn't heard from her either, but you could ask."

Mildred didn't offer any more information, and her pursed lips made Anne hesitate to ask any more questions.

As Mildred got up to leave, she said, "If I were you, I'd ask about those friends of Vince's. They were trouble."

"Do you know any of their names?"

"No," Mildred said in a curt voice. She gathered her purse and book. "I hope you find the other machines."

"I hope so too. Thank you, Mildred."

Mildred left without a nod or a good-bye. Obviously, Anne had upset Mildred. She'd been defensive when Anne asked her about Victoria. Anne understood that Mildred didn't want to believe Victoria could have betrayed their friendship, but how could she be so certain that the young teacher from a hard background hadn't taken advantage of Aunt Edie's generosity?

If only she could talk to Victoria and ask her about the sewing machines, but no one seemed to know for sure where she'd gone. Why hadn't she kept in touch with Aunt Edie or Mildred? That seemed odd to Anne, since they'd been so kind to the young teacher. She had a feeling she'd opened a wound asking Mildred where Victoria had gone. After the friendship she and Aunt Edie had given so freely, it must hurt to have been forgotten.

* * *

Mildred arrived at the library a few minutes after Anne opened the door on Wednesday morning. She didn't smile. Was she still upset at Anne's questions about Victoria?

"Is Bella here yet?" Mildred asked. "I want to get the advertising for my knitting class online right away."

"Yes, she is. She's just putting her lunch in the refrigerator. Come on in. This is a good time to work on the announcement, before we get busy."

Bella came out from the workroom.

"Hi, Mrs. Farley. How are you today?"

"I'm fine, Bella. Anne suggested I work with you to advertise the knitting class I'm going to teach here at the library on Saturday, four weeks from now. It will run along the lines of Wendy Pyle's crochet class, only we'll hold two classes. I'll be teaching the community to knit stocking hats, and they will be donated to the warm clothing drive."

"That's a great idea. Maybe I can come in and take your class. I learned to knit when I was in Miss Parker's domestic arts class, but I don't remember very well."

Mildred beamed. "Since I taught Miss Parker to knit, I'm sure I can help you brush up on your skills. This will be a refresher course for you."

"I'll tell Remi too. It'll be fun. So what do you want to put on the library calendar?"

Mildred went behind the desk with Bella and they worked together for an hour. When they finished, Anne heard the printer chunking away, printing out flyers. As Bella went to get them, Mildred sought out Anne at her desk.

"Bella is quite talented," Mildred said. She didn't smile, but she didn't frown either. Her mood seemed lighter. "She made short work of designing the flyers. They look professional."

"Yes, she does a wonderful job for the library. Did you talk to Wendy about putting the flyers up around town?"

"Yes. She agreed to distribute half of them, and she gave me a list of places I can take the rest. I'm looking forward to teaching this class."

"Do you miss teaching? I imagine it's hard, as a teacher, not to be involved in teaching or mentoring."

"I didn't teach while my children were growing up. Although I helped with their activities and I taught Sunday school, so I suppose I kept my hands in. When the children graduated from high school and went off to college, I'd been away from teaching for so long, I didn't even try to go back. Then the school needed a temporary teacher. I was happy to help out, and I rediscovered the joy of teaching. Even mentoring Victoria kept me involved. I do miss it, now more than ever."

"Well, this will give you an opportunity to teach again. You might want to consider volunteering to teach at the retirement home and with other civic organizations."

"I might do that. We'll see. I don't have the stamina I once had, but the occasional class would be good." Mildred gathered her purse, said good-bye to Anne, and went to get some of the flyers that Bella had made so that she could start distributing them.

"This is becoming a busy place," Bella commented to Anne after Mildred left. She placed a stack of flyers on the checkout desk and tacked a flyer up on the bulletin board. "Now if we could just get my professor to come give a class on the fundamental theorem of calculus, I'd be all set."

"Oh dear. I'm afraid that wouldn't attract too many patrons."

Bella laughed. "I guess you're right. I don't know if I'd attend."

"Bella, you said you were in Miss Parker's class. Did you know her brother, Vince?"

"I knew who he was. He didn't socialize much. I felt sorry for him, coming into a small school during his junior year. It must have been hard adjusting, being the new kid. I mean, most of us had known each other all our lives. I tried to be friendly to him, but he didn't seem to be interested. Besides, I didn't care for his friends."

"Really? Who were his friends?"

"He hung out with older guys. Most of them were from out of town. From Deshler, I think. They didn't have jobs and they weren't going to college. A bunch of deadbeats."

"I don't imagine that helped his popularity."

"For sure. Too bad too. He was cute, in a sad sort of way that made you want to cheer him up. I think he could have made friends if he'd tried. I don't know. Maybe he liked being kind of wild."

"Wild? Like what?"

"Like hanging out, harassing the girls as we left school. Nothing dangerous, just repulsive. Whistling and catcalls. That sort of thing. I noticed he didn't do it so much, but his friends did. They hung out at the convenience store and at the pool hall just outside Blue Hill. One of the oldest guys was over twenty-one and would often buy cigarettes and drinks for them. Then they'd get loud and more obnoxious."

"Do you know who some of his friends were?"

"Not really. There was a guy named Rocky, but I don't think that was his real name. He was the one who got the alcohol for them. Then there was Danny something. Goodman, I think, 'cause I remember he asked Remi out, and she turned him down. She told me she wouldn't date him because there was nothing good about him."

"Danny Goodman and Rocky. Do you remember anyone else?"

Bella shook her head. "I didn't really know Vince that well. He wasn't easy to get to know. I think he only moved here because of his sister, Miss Parker. I saw him arguing with her after class a couple of times. He acted like he hated being in Blue Hill and couldn't wait to leave. One time I heard her tell him he could go back home, and he said 'no way' and stomped off. So I guess he thought home was worse than Blue Hill. Did you ever meet Vince or Miss Parker?"

"No, but I don't know that I came to visit Aunt Edie in the time they lived here, other than maybe a day or two, so it's not all that likely I would have met them."

Anne wished she had met the brother and sister. Maybe she would have a better idea of their character and their relationship with Aunt Edie. Her aunt had been a good judge of character. But what about Vince's friends? Anne jotted down their names. Danny Goodman and Rocky. Poor companions for a disgruntled, friendless young man.

* * *

Thursday morning, Betty Bultman came in to help out for a few hours. Her flowery perfume drifted over to Anne as she walked by to put her purse and coat in the workroom. She came out and approached Anne at the desk, high heels clicking on the floor.

"Good morning, Anne. Any specific projects for me this morning?"

"If you could keep an eye on the checkout desk, that will be a big help. I need to run a few errands in town. Will you be all right here alone for a couple of hours?"

"Sure. You go on and don't worry about the library. In fact, if you have time, you should go get a manicure or a pedicure. Between the library and raising your children alone, you don't have much time for yourself," Betty said, tapping her long, perfectly manicured nails on the desk.

"Thank you. I really appreciate your help. One of these days I'll make an appointment to get my hair trimmed, but not today. I've built up the fires in the fireplaces, so you don't need to add any logs. I'll be back by noon at the latest."

"Oh, that's good," Betty said, looking relieved.

"If you have time, you can look through the new fiction books. I'd love to have your reviews of the recent ones you've read too. You can type them into the computer and I'll have Bella put them on our Web site." The mayor's wife was one of Blue Hill's most avid readers.

"I'll be delighted to write some reviews. Now you just take your time."

Anne grabbed her purse, a notebook, and her grocery list and headed out the door. It was a gray day, and the weatherman had predicted rain later.

She parked in front of the red Victorian building that housed the *Blue Hill Gazette*, then climbed the steps to the covered porch and front door.

"Good morning," the young receptionist greeted her. "How can I help you?"

"Good morning. I'd like to go through your archives from two years ago."

Grace Hawkins came out of her office at the sound of their voices.

"Anne. Nice to see your cheerful smile on such a drab day. I heard you held a crochet class at the library last Saturday. We could have listed it under community events. Do you have anything else coming up?"

"The crochet class was a last-minute thing. But we do have another event, as a matter of fact. Mildred Farley will be teaching a two-week class on consecutive Saturdays on how to knit a stocking hat. The hats will be donated to the Blue Hill Community Church clothing drive. Did you know we are collecting coats and warm clothing for those in need this winter? Liddie is spearheading it. We have a collection bin at the library."

"Liddie, your daughter?"

"Yes. We take the clothing from the library to the church. She is determined to fill the clothing collection box at church."

"What a wonderful project. I can make a note of that too. How long will you be collecting coats?"

"Through this month and next."

Grace jotted down some notes on a small pad. "I'll call you if I need more information. Children collecting coats and warm clothes for the needy would make a great local interest story for the paper. Is that why you came in?"

"No. Actually, I'm trying to hunt down some information. About a year and a half ago, the high school domestic arts classroom received a dozen new sewing machines from an anonymous donor. Do you remember anything about that?"

"Yes. I interviewed Victoria Parker about that. She was thrilled to receive the state-of-the-art machines. A pretty generous gift."

"Do you have any idea who donated them?" Anne asked.

Grace shook her head. "Not a clue. Whoever did wanted to remain anonymous. The benefactor missed out on a nice tax deduction."

"That's true. Maybe she, or he, didn't need it. On a different subject, do you know anything about a kid named Vince Parker? He was Victoria's brother."

"The name rings a bell. Can't think why though."

"He played football for a season. Coach Pyle said he'd gotten into some kind of trouble."

"That's possible. There might be something in one of the police reports."

"I'd like to look through the *Gazettes* from a couple of years ago, around the time someone donated the sewing machines."

"Be our guest. Is there something specific you're looking for?"

"I'm not sure. Anything about Vince Parker or Victoria. Do you happen to know where they went when they left Blue Hill?"

Grace shook her head. "No idea."

"No one seems to know. They were friends of my aunt, and I'd like to find them."

"I don't recall reporting anything about the Parkers, but you're welcome to go through the papers." Grace turned to the receptionist. "Could you get the newspapers for Anne, so she can take them with her, please? Get the entire year."

"That'd be great," Anne said.

The receptionist went back to the newspaper morgue and returned a few minutes later with a carton of newspapers. Anne signed for them and carried them out to her car. She loved being in a small town that allowed such freedom to utilize its resources. She wondered if she would have the same good fortune at the high school. It couldn't hurt to try. She took out her cell phone and called.

"This is Shelby Truman. Can I help you?" the secretary said.

"Shelby, it's Anne Gibson. I was wondering if you have a forwarding address for Victoria Parker, the previous domestic arts teacher, or for Vince Parker, who would have been a student there when his sister was teaching? Victoria was a good friend of my aunt's."

"Hi, Anne. Hold on a minute. Let me see what I can do."

Anne heard music, then a male voice.

"Hello, Anne. This is Jim Beckett. Were you able to find the missing sewing machines?"

"I'm afraid not. But thank you for connecting me with Frank Evans. He was very helpful. He took me through the school warehouse. It appears that the school does not have the missing machines."

"I'm sorry we couldn't clear that up for you. We don't give out addresses of teachers, or former teachers, in the case of Miss Parker. We also don't give out information on students."

"Oh. I was hoping to contact her. She was a good friend of my great-aunt, and she was the teacher who accepted the sewing machines. I don't believe she has been informed of my aunt's passing. Also, she might know what happened to the other twelve sewing machines."

"Yes. I was going to say that in this instance, I believe we can make an exception. I'm sure she would want to know about your aunt. I will pass you back to Shelby. She can provide the information."

"Thank you so much. I appreciate your help."

"You're welcome. If you'll hold for a moment, Shelby should pick up the line." The music came back on.

"Anne, are you there?"

"Yes. Mr. Beckett said you could give me Victoria's address?"

"Yes. Here it is." Shelby read off a post office box address in Philadelphia and a telephone number. Anne wrote them on the back of her grocery list. "That's the only contact information we have for her and for Vince Parker. I hope it helps."

"Thanks, Shelby. I hope so too."

Anne ended the call and looked at what she'd written. She couldn't be positive, but she thought the phone number was the same as the one she'd found in Aunt Edie's address book. If that was the case, she could write a letter. Maybe Victoria would write her back and clear up the mystery.

CHAPTER NINE

Anne strolled every aisle at the Newlands' cozy grocery store, thinking ahead to doing more baking and cooking cold-weather meals. She picked up a pot roast and potatoes and carrots for the Crock-Pot and apples and pears to make a crisp for dessert.

Anne knew Betty Bultman meant it when she told her to take her time. Betty enjoyed helping out at the library and being involved in the community. She felt it was her civic duty as the mayor's wife, but it helped that she had a passion for books. It gave Anne a little extra personal time, which was invaluable for a single parent.

Betty stayed at the library until after lunch, giving Anne time to work at her desk. She answered several e-mails related to the library. With nothing urgent requiring her attention, Anne took the grocery list with the scribbled address and phone number out of her purse. She compared the phone number to the one in Aunt Edie's address book. It matched. Anne already knew the number wasn't Victoria's anymore. Anne got a sheet of paper with the library logo out of her desk and started a handwritten letter.

Dear Victoria and Vince,

We haven't met, but perhaps my great-aunt, Edie Summers, may have mentioned me. It is with great sorrow that I share the news that my aunt is no longer with us. She went to bed in her beloved home one night last April and woke up in heaven. She wasn't ill and did not suffer.

It was Aunt Edie's wish to leave behind a legacy for the town of Blue Hill, and so, as you can see on the letterhead, her lovely home has become Blue Hill Library. My children and I live in the upper floors, and I am serving as the library director. (It was due to her encouragement that I majored in library science in college.)

I've discovered that you were both close to Aunt Edie, especially Victoria. I found a receipt among her things that indicated she purchased twenty-four Bernina sewing machines and that she may have anonymously donated a dozen of them to the high school domestic arts department while you were here in Blue Hill. I've seen them, and they are greatly appreciated by the new teacher and students. I'm hoping that you may be able to tell me what happened to the remaining twelve sewing machines, as well as a considerable amount of fabric and sewing supplies that Aunt Edie also purchased. I haven't been able to locate them here in Blue Hill. I pray they are being used to honor her life, although I know she wanted no recognition. I'd appreciate it if you would call me or respond to me at this address.

I hope this letter finds you both in good health and well-being. If you are ever in Blue Hill, I would love to meet you.

Sincerely, Anne Gibson

She reread the letter. It would do. She took out a library envelope, addressed it to Victoria and Vince Parker, and put a stamp on it. Then she wrote, *Request Forwarding Address* on the envelope.

"Has the mail come yet?" she asked Betty.

"Not yet."

"Good. I have a letter to go out."

"There are a couple of books for the mailman that I packed up to go out on interlibrary requests. I'll be happy to drop them off at the post office on my way home," Betty said.

"Would you? That would be wonderful. Thank you." Anne handed the letter to Betty. She glanced at the address and looked over at Anne.

"Victoria Parker. Wasn't she a teacher at the high school for a couple of years? I didn't think she was married."

"She was my Aunt Edie's friend, and I just discovered her address. I was writing to let her know about Edie's passing." Anne had no reason to share her personal correspondence with Betty, but she didn't want the mayor's wife speculating either. "Vince is her brother, not her husband. He did yard work for my aunt."

Betty reached out and put her hand on Anne's shoulder and gave her a look of sympathy. "I'm sorry. It must be hard to have to tell people that your aunt died."

"Yes, it is. But I think Aunt Edie would want them to know."

Betty took the letter and put it with the two book packages. She retrieved her coat and purse and three new hardback novels from the kitchen, her high heels clicking across the floor.

"I'll read these over the weekend and get them back, along with reviews," Betty said. "I hope you have a good weekend."

"Thank you, Betty. I hope you have a good weekend too."

Betty smiled. "I will. I have three new books to read."

* * *

Anne didn't have an opportunity to look through the newspapers until evening. She waited until Ben and Liddie had gone to bed, then she took the carton of newspapers to the living room.

Starting with June of the previous year—the year before Aunt Edie died—she worked backward, utilizing her speed-reading skills, looking for articles that might give her information. She scanned the papers for any mention of the high school, any police reports of thefts that might have implicated a teenage boy, any complaints about traveling salesmen or unwanted marketing calls. She found police reports of lost dogs, car accidents, minor vandalism, and a few domestic disturbances. A couple of police reports mentioned Manny's Pawn Shop. The shop seemed to attract shoplifters but nothing that might incriminate Vince Parker. A warrant was listed for Clinton Rockford for failure to appear in court. She wondered if the name Rocky, for Vince's friend, could be a nickname for Rockford. She made a note to check on Clinton Rockford. She found the small article about the new sewing machines on the community page in March. That coincided with the timing of the sewing machine order. In one of the January newspapers, a small ad in the classified section caught her attention.

We buy and sell household equipment, tools, and small machinery. Call A Able Surplus Sales.

Excited, Anne got out the receipt and compared it to the advertisement. The phone number matched. Anne wrote the information on her notepad. So someone had been soliciting business in the area. Had Aunt Edie called them or did they call her? Who initiated the purchase? Did the company still exist somewhere? Had it ever existed? They delivered at least twelve sewing machines. Had they cheated Aunt Edie out of the other twelve machines?

Anne made a copy of the ad and returned the newspaper to the carton. She hadn't discovered much, but she had a few notes to investigate — more than she'd had before.

* * *

On Friday the sun came out and the temperature warmed up. The weather report promised a beautiful, warm weekend. As she went about her library work that morning, Anne kept thinking about the snippets of information she'd found the night before in the newspaper archives. The brief police reports didn't reveal anything. She checked the telephone book for the last name Able but found no matches.

Remi came in at two. She stashed her backpack and books in the workroom and came out to the desk. "How's it going? Have you been busy?"

"Not really. Sometimes the warm weather brings people to the library, and sometimes they go elsewhere. Today it's elsewhere."

"I guess I can't blame them. It's beautiful outside. Have you been out?"

"No, but I do have some errands to run. I'll do them now, while you're here."

"Sure. I'll be here until closing," Remi said.

Anne stopped first at the *Gazette* office to return the newspapers.

"Good afternoon, Anne. I'll take those." The receptionist came around and reached for the carton.

"Thank you. Is there a chance I could find out the address of an advertiser?"

"I'm not sure. Let me ask Grace."

The receptionist set the newspapers aside and went to Grace's office. She came back after a minute. "Grace said you can go on back."

"Thanks." Anne went to the editor's office. The door was open.

Grace sat at her desk, typing on her keyboard. She looked up from her work and smiled. "Come on in. Did you find anything helpful in the archives?"

"Possibly. Got a minute?"

"Sure. Have a seat." Grace indicated the chair across from her desk.

Anne sat down and handed Grace the photocopy of the advertisement. "Is there some way to find out who placed this ad? I found an old receipt that indicated my aunt made a large purchase from them, but their phone number is no longer in service."

"Let me look it up." Grace typed a search into her computer. She looked for a few minutes. "There's a Blue Hill post office box number. That's it. Looks like they paid cash for the ad."

"May I have the address? I need to get in touch with them."

"Sure." Grace printed a copy and gave it to Anne. "If the number is out of service, they might have moved or gone out of business."

"Good possibility, but maybe they have a forwarding address. Thanks."

As Anne drove to her next stop, she thought about the address from the classified ad. Why would Aunt Edie have bought sewing machines from a seller with only a post office box, when there was a fabric store in Blue Hill and a sewing machine store in Deshler? It made no sense, unless her aunt got such a great deal on surplus fabric that she'd bought twice as many as she needed and gave them away or sold the rest slowly.

Anne parked at the south end of town hall and entered through the door leading to the police department.

"Hi, Anne, what brings you in here?" a cheerful voice said from behind the counter. The petite woman in uniform had her blonde hair pulled back and rolled into a neat bun at the nape of her neck.

"Josie? Joselyn Bolling? I hardly recognized you. I didn't know you worked for the police department." Josie had been two years behind Anne in school.

Josie grinned. "Yeah, it's me. I've been working for Blue Hill's finest since I graduated. So what can I do for you?"

"Is it possible to find out if my great-aunt, Edie Summers, ever filed a theft report for a dozen missing Bernina sewing machines or a complaint against a company called A Able Surplus Sales? It could have been any time from March on, two years ago."

"Let me look." She typed a search into the computer and tapped her fingers while she waited for the results.

"No search results. Sorry. Are you certain she was robbed?"

"No. Not at all. I found a receipt for twenty-four sewing machines. I've found twelve of them, but twelve are missing."

"They must be somewhere. What was the company name again?" She started typing as Anne repeated it. "*Hmm*. No complaints against the company. Is it local? I don't recall hearing the name before."

"It had a local post office box, but the phone has been disconnected."

Josie frowned. "Odd. Any other names you want to check?"

"Yes. Do you have an arrest record for Vince Parker? I believe he moved away in June two years ago."

Josie typed in the name and tapped her fingers for a moment. "Nothing." She verified the spelling.

"He might have been a minor at the time," Anne said.

"That explains it. We wouldn't show him, even if he was arrested. I can't give out information on a minor."

"Thanks, Josie. That's a big help." Then Anne remembered the names Bella mentioned. She pulled her notepad out of her purse. "What about Clinton Rockford or Danny Goodman? I believe they were older."

"Now, *those* are names I recognize." Josie started typing again. "The two were convicted of stealing cars and running a chop shop where they dismantled the cars and sold off the parts. They're both serving time in the state penitentiary."

"Really? How long ago were their convictions?"

"Last year. I don't see any arrests on them the year before, but they may have been stealing and chopping cars then. Wait. There was a Failure to Appear warrant for Clinton Rockford. Looks like it was dismissed. Do you think Vince Parker was connected with them?"

"I heard that he knew them, but I don't know if he was involved in their illegal activity. I hope not."

"If he was, he's probably still involved in some kind of crime." She typed in some more data and waited a couple of minutes. "I don't see his name coming up. Would he be an adult now? Do you know where he is?"

"I'm sure he's over eighteen. I'm not sure where he lives. Possibly Philadelphia. Perhaps leaving Blue Hill was good for him. His sister was trying to get him to straighten out. Maybe she succeeded."

"Maybe." Josie looked doubtful. "Sorry I can't be more help."

"That's all right. Thanks for checking. It's good to see you again."

"You too. Take care."

Anne turned to go but stopped when Josie called to her. "I think there was an incident at Manny's Pawn Shop. Something about stolen property. You might go talk to Manny."

Anne jotted down the name, thanked Josie again, then hastened out the door. She walked the short distance to the post office. After waiting for a while in the line, she showed the clerk the copy of the ad receipt. "I wonder if I could find out who rented this post office box?"

"Oh no. We can't give out that information. Best I can do is tell you if it is rented or available."

"All right. I'd appreciate it if you'd check for me."

"Just a minute." The clerk typed a search into his computer. "I show that box is available. There's no forwarding address order. Do you want to rent it?"

"No, thank you. But thanks for checking."

"Sure. Anything else? Stamps?"

"Not today. Thanks." There was a line behind her now. There hadn't been when she came in. She smiled at the woman behind her, then exited the post office.

Anne felt a bit disappointed as she got into her car. Nothing she learned from the police department or the post office helped. Whoever used the post office box as his address had let it go.

She started her car and backed out, trying to remember where Manny's was located. Manny's Pawn Shop had been around for years, but she'd never been there. She thought it was south of town, so she headed that way. She found a ministorage and an old garage with go-carts and off-road all-terrain vehicles scattered around the parking lot. There were also a couple of small warehouse-type buildings with no signs on them. But no pawn shop. Giving up, she turned in the direction of the elementary school. She was a little early, but she would wait there for the kids to get out of school. She'd gone half a mile when she saw a faded sign on an old gas station that had been converted into a store.

Manny's Pawn Shop.

There were no cars in front. She parked and walked up to the door. A closed sign hung in the door. She would have to come back when Manny's was open. A small sign in the corner that listed regular hours didn't help. Evidently Manny didn't stick to his own schedule.

An eclectic collection of merchandise filled the display window. A drum kit, a drill press, a bowling ball in a colorful bag, a vacuum cleaner. Behind a microwave oven, she spotted a sewing machine. It looked like a Bernina. Could it be one of the missing machines? And did the shop have more of them tucked away somewhere?

CHAPTER TEN

A nne could see something was bothering Liddie as soon as she got into the car. She handed her mother a paper. "The school is collecting coats, Mommy."

"That's nice. They will reach people who don't come to the library or the church."

"But, Mommy, I have to take a coat to school. So does Ben. I already gave mine away. Should I give my new coat to the school too?"

"No, Liddie. They don't expect every student to take in a coat, certainly not your only coat. You don't have to participate in the school coat drive, since you've already given yours and collected so many for the church. All the coats go to help others in need."

"But I want to."

Anne waited until Liddie and Ben fastened themselves in their seats. "Honey, we'll talk about it at home. Okay?"

"Okay, Mommy." She could hear the sigh in her daughter's voice.

"Hey, Mom, can Ryan spend the night?" Ben asked.

"Do you have homework?"

"Yeah. We have to do maps of Pennsylvania and fill in lots of stuff. I thought we could study in the library. You have lots of cool maps."

"That's a good idea. Yes, he can come over. Why don't you invite both him and Alex over for dinner? I'm making Grandma's goulash recipe. We can have French bread too." The simple pasta dish had been a favorite comfort food when Anne was growing up. Sometimes her mother spiced it with a Mexican flair, while other times she used Italian seasonings. Tonight Anne was making it Italian.

"Okay! Thanks, Mom."

Evidently Ben wasn't too concerned about the school coat drive.

Later at home, after the library had closed, Liddie and Ben set the table while Anne boiled the macaroni and cooked the ground beef and tomato sauce for the goulash. When Anne opened a can of pitted ripe olives, Liddie begged for some for her fingertips. Anne indulged her with three olives. Liddie stuck them on her fingers and grinned as she ate them one by one. She helped her mother stir the mixture of ingredients together with Italian spices, the rest of the olives, and grated cheese.

Anne had just put the goulash in the oven to bake when the door buzzer sounded. Ben ran to the intercom. He clicked the door open, then ran down the stairs to greet Alex and Ryan.

The boys clattered up the stairs to Ben's bedroom, and Alex appeared in the kitchen doorway.

"Hi. How are you doing?"

Anne looked up and smiled. Alex had on clean jeans and a clean shirt, and his hair was still damp from a shower. "I'm fine. How was your week?"

"Busy. We're trying to get as many outside projects done as possible before the snow starts flying."

"Good idea." Anne put down the knife that she'd been using to dice cucumbers into the salad bowl. "Can I get you to do me a favor?"

"Sure. What do you need?" Alex pushed up his sleeves as if preparing for work.

"I want to bring Aunt Edie's cedar chest down from the attic and put it in my room. If you can take one end, I can get the other."

"Do you want to do it now or after dinner?"

"Dinner needs to stay in the oven about thirty minutes, so let's do it now."

Anne started up the stairs as Alex followed.

"I found the chest when I was looking for winter clothes for the donation box. I'd forgotten it was up there. I took the contents out, but the chest was more than I could handle." On the third floor, Anne opened the attic door and turned on the light. They climbed the attic stairs and stepped into the huge, dimly lit room.

Alex looked around. "There's still a lot up here. Do you want to move anything else down?"

"Not right now." She led the way along the narrow aisle to the chest and removed a box that sat on top of it.

Alex removed another box, then lifted one end of the chest. "It's not too heavy, just a little awkward. Let me go first, so I can take the weight going down the stairs."

Anne picked up the other end, and they maneuvered their way through the stacks of boxes and furniture to the attic stairs.

Alex started down. "Can you raise your end up?" he asked.

"Yes, I think so." Anne held it by the bottom and gingerly stepped down one step at a time until they reached the door, which they'd left open. Alex went through.

"Stop a minute while I turn off the light and shut the door." She set down her end. A few seconds later, she picked it up again.

"Okay. I'm ready to go."

"We're just taking it to your room, right?" Alex looked down the hall.

"Yep. We're almost there."

They carried the chest to her room.

"I think it will fit right at the end of the bed," Anne said, picturing it there with a quilt folded on top.

They set it down in place, then stepped back. Anne looked at it with satisfaction. "Perfect. Just as I pictured it." She turned to Alex. "Thank you for doing that. And it's just about time for dinner to come out of the oven."

Alex followed her downstairs. She handed the salad bowl to him to put on the table, then she took the goulash out of the oven and slid the French bread in to warm.

"Ben, Ryan, Liddie," she called up the stairs. "Time for dinner."

Six feet stampeded down the stairs, and the kids took their places at the table with Alex. Anne carried the hot bread to the table, sat down, and asked a blessing over their meal. After everyone else had filled their plates, she filled hers, then looked over at Alex.

"Did you get the notice from the school about the coat drive?"

"Yes, among all the other papers Ryan dumped on the kitchen counter. Seems like every organization in town has jumped on this bandwagon."

"What kind of wagon?" Liddie asked.

"A bandwagon. It was a wagon used to carry a band in a parade," Anne explained. "People who wanted to be part of the band would try to jump on the bandwagon. Now it just means an idea or a project that becomes popular and everyone wants to be part of it. Like the coat drive. Reverend Tom mentioned it as a need in church, and people started trying to fill the need. When you talked to the school, your teacher and principal thought it was a good idea, so they are trying to help as well, just like we're trying to help through the library."

"Oh. So is it our wagon or the church's wagon?" Liddie asked.

"It's the church's wagon," Ben said. "You...we jumped on it."

"I think it's everyone's wagon now," Ryan chimed in.

"Liddie, there's no wagon. It's just an expression," Anne offered. "It just means that everyone is trying to help, but it's the same project. If we help with one part of the project, we're helping all of the various parts."

"Like...what we get at the library helps fill the church box?" Liddie asked.

"Exactly." Anne was relieved that Liddie understood the concept.

"Mommy, I know!" Liddie's eyes lit up in a lightbulb moment. "I could take one of the coats from the donations downstairs to school."

So much for Liddie understanding the concept of community giving. "Now think about that. Someone already donated it to take to the church. Would it be fair for you to take it out and take it to the school?"

Liddie frowned. "No. But I need a coat to take to *schoo-ool*," she said, dragging out the word.

"But you've already collected enough to fill the box at church," Anne explained.

"But, Mommy," she said, "everyone will take a coat to school 'cept me!"

"Honey, not everyone will be able to take a coat. Remember you already gave your coat to the girl who didn't have one. If everyone had to take a coat, those children who only have one or don't have any would feel left out."

Liddie's face registered dismay. "That's not fair."

Liddie toyed with her food in silence through the rest of the meal. When the boys finished and excused themselves to go downstairs to work on their project, Liddie excused herself too and carried her plate to the sink. She followed the boys to the Reference Room.

After she'd left, Alex chuckled. "Good try, but I doubt you won that round."

"I'm afraid you're right. How about a cup of coffee?"

"Sure. Thanks for dinner, by the way. It hit the spot."

"You're welcome." Her mother's super-easy comfort food was always a hit. She took the rest of the dishes to the sink, then carried two cups of coffee to the table.

"I don't want to stifle her desire to help others, but we've already gone through our clothes and Aunt Edie's clothes, and I bought a couple of coats and sweatshirts on sale. She's also canvased the neighborhood. I don't have anything else to send with her."

"Then don't."

"*Hmmph*. Easy for you to say."

"True. Ryan won't even ask. I had to prod him to go through our closets."

Anne chuckled. "Ben caught Liddie's interest. Otherwise, I doubt he'd have gotten so involved." Anne took a sip of coffee, then set her cup down. "Alex, do you remember meeting a young high school teacher named Victoria Parker or her brother, Vince Parker, a couple of years ago?"

Alex thought for a minute, then slowly shook his head. "It doesn't ring a bell. Should I know them?"

"I don't know. They lived in Blue Hill for about two years. Victoria taught domestic arts and became friends with Aunt Edie and Mildred. She attended church with them. Her brother was still in high school, and he did yard work for both of them."

"I might have seen him working in the yard, but I never met him or his sister."

"How about A Able Surplus Sales? Ever heard of them?"

Alex pressed his lips together, then shook his head. "Nope. Sorry."

Anne told him about the sewing machines and the company that didn't seem to exist, and that Vince and Victoria were the only ones she knew of who might have seen all of the machines. "That's how I found the cedar chest. I was up in the attic looking for sewing machines."

"That's crazy. I can't imagine your aunt buying all those sewing machines. Especially from some bogus company. I suppose you've looked everywhere."

"Everywhere and then some. Twelve of them just disappeared."

"That's a shame. If I can help you find them, let me know. If anyone can figure it out, though, you will." Alex stood and picked up his empty coffee cup. "Let me help with the dishes, then I'd better get going."

"No need. I'm going to load them in the dishwasher but thanks."

"No problem."

On his way out, Alex offered to take them all out for breakfast the next morning. Since she had to open the library, Anne accepted for the children. They would love it, and she would have some time to herself without Liddie's begging—a win-win situation. After Alex left and Ben and Ryan were done with their maps, the boys took sleeping bags to the living room and settled in with a video documentary on tropical bugs and frogs that Ben had brought home from school. Liddie thought the subject matter was gross, so she happily went to her own bedroom. Anne read her a story, then tucked her into bed. Liddie closed her eyes and prayed out loud, listing everyone she knew and asking God to bless them.

"And please, God, help us get coats to take to school to keep people warm. Amen." Liddie reached up and gave her mother a hug and kiss. Then she turned over and closed her eyes.

Anne took the book she'd been reading and went to her room where it was quiet. She put Aunt Edie's tissue-wrapped clothing back into the cedar chest, then got into her pajamas and settled in bed to read. She'd barely read two pages when her cell phone rang. She was tempted to ignore it. She glanced at the incoming name, then answered it. "Hi, Mom! How are you?"

"I'm fine. We're fine. I just wanted to hear your voice. Are you busy?"

"No. Ben is watching a video with Ryan in the living room. They're having a sleepover. Liddie is in bed. I was just reading a book."

"Of course you are. What is it? Is it good?"

"Really good so far, though I'm only on chapter two. It's a cozy mystery set in Maine, called *The Lighthouse Goes Dark*. It's by a new author named Diane Spencer."

"*Ooh!* Sounds great. I'll have to look for that one. So what's happening in your life?" her mother asked.

"The usual. Working in the library and keeping up with the children." She told her mother about the church's clothing drive and Liddie's vow to fill the donation box and how the library had gotten involved.

"Good for her. I'm glad Ben has taken an interest too. Collecting warm clothing at the library is a great idea. Helps your patrons connect with the library on a more personal level."

"Yes. We've had a great response. The school has also joined in to collect winter clothing. The children brought home announcements to take in coats to donate. Liddie wants to take in a coat, but we've gone through everything here, even Aunt Edie's clothing in the attic. Liddie gave away her own coat, so I had to buy her a new one. Now she wants me to buy another one. I'm trying to impress on her that going to the store and buying things isn't the answer to every problem. I'm not making much headway, I'm afraid."

"Yes, that's tricky. You want her to be generous, and yet she needs to understand there is a cost involved. Good luck with that."

"Right, and there's another problem. Well, not exactly a problem, but a puzzle. Do you know anything about Aunt Edie purchasing two dozen Bernina sewing machines about a year before she died?"

"What? No. Seriously? Why would she make a huge purchase like that? Did she plan to open a dress factory or something?"

"I wish I knew. She also bought cases of fabric and sewing notions. I've discovered that she donated a dozen to the high school domestic arts class anonymously, or at least I'm pretty sure she did, but the other twelve seem to have disappeared into thin air. There's no trace of them, and no one knows she bought them. Not even Mildred."

"Honestly, I don't even pretend to understand Edie's thinking. She was a bit eccentric, but this seems strange even for her. You say she donated twelve. I can see her doing that. Are you certain she didn't donate all two dozen and they aren't using them all?"

"If she did, no one knows where they are. The domestic arts teacher wasn't working at the high school then, so she only knows about the ones in her classroom. I've talked to the principal, and the maintenance supervisor took me through the school warehouse. We didn't find any more new sewing machines. There was a young teacher then, Victoria Parker. Evidently she'd become friends with Aunt Edie and Mildred. But she moved away soon after that."

"I believe Edie mentioned her to me. Edie and Mildred were teaching her to knit."

"That's right. Mildred told me Victoria spent a lot of time with her and Aunt Edie. Wendy's husband remembers helping unload the sewing machines and putting them in the domestic arts classroom. He doesn't think there were more than twelve. What would Aunt Edie have done with the other twelve?"

"Do you think she was cheated?"

"That's what I'm wondering. Could she have been confused?" Anne asked. "It seems so irrational. I don't know the company that sold them to her. I've called around, and she didn't donate them to any other charity that I can find."

"You don't suppose—no, that's preposterous," her mother said.

"What?"

"Well, you know Edie was an avid user of the Internet. She used to e-mail articles and pictures to me all the time. What if she met someone online who talked her into buying all those sewing machines?"

"That's what I was wondering too," Anne said. "Though Reverend Tom says he never saw any sign of that."

"There isn't any money missing from the trust fund she set up for the library, is there?"

"No. I met with Mr. Merill and asked him if he had any record of the sewing machine purchase. He didn't know anything about them. I think this all took place before Aunt Edie set up the trust. He wondered if she might have helped someone start a business. That's possible, but if so, it didn't happen in Blue Hill as far as I can discover. Since she didn't mention it in her will, he doesn't think there is any liability to the estate."

"That's good. I'm afraid there's no law against buying things, even if the purchase makes no sense. Edie had the right to purchase anything she wished. I just hope she wasn't cheated. If you happen to find the other dozen machines, though, I wouldn't mind having one." Anne's mom laughed.

"Me too. Aunt Edie's old Singer just died, so I need a new machine. But I'm about to give up. I can't find the Berninas anywhere."

"I suppose not all puzzles are meant to be solved. I need to scoot. Love you, honey. Give the children hugs from me."

"Love you too, Mom. Give my love to Dad. And thanks for calling."

Anne hung up. She picked up her book again and tried to read, but the only mystery on her mind was what had happened to the other twelve sewing machines.

CHAPTER ELEVEN

The last patrons had left Saturday afternoon when a teenager came in and approached the desk.

"Mrs. Gibson?"

"Yes. I'm sorry, but I was just closing the library. Do you need something you can find quickly?"

"Oh no. I'm here because Miss Latham sent me. She said she talked to you about my being an intern at the library. I'm Jason Fisher," he said, as he reached out his hand. She remembered seeing him at the library on several occasions.

"Nice to meet you, Jason. Why do you want to help at the library?" she asked, as she shook his hand.

"Honestly?" He gave her a serious, straightforward look. "The extra credit. But I love to read. Anything. I really like history. Miss Latham gave me a research assignment to learn about the railroad era in Blue Hill and how it affected the town and what happened when it left."

"That's an ambitious project." Anne recalled Miss Latham giving her a similar assignment for extra credit. She had researched the railroad era and the impact it had on education in Blue Hill.

"I know. I plan to use it to help me get into the history department at Harvard."

"I'm impressed. Do you know the library system?"

"Yes, ma'am. The Dewey Decimal System. Miss Latham made us learn it, but it's all mathematical, so it's easy."

Anne smiled. She'd learned it early, thanks to her mother and Aunt Edie taking her to the Deshler library every week, but Miss Latham had taught it and tested her students when Anne was in her class. "Excellent. That will help you in your work here. Thursdays we're open until 8:00 p.m. Could you come in on Thursday afternoons?"

Jason's eyes lit up. "Yeah! I mean, yes, ma'am. That's cool. I'll be here Thursday right after school. Thanks!"

"You're welcome. I usually pick up my children after school, so make it four o'clock. I'll see you then."

Jason ran out and bounded down the steps, down to a car parked at the curb out front. He pumped his hand in the air, then he opened the car door and plopped in. Anne could see a woman, probably his mother, in the driver's seat. She hadn't asked how old Jason was. Since Miss Latham taught honors English to juniors and seniors, she guessed he was a junior.

It would be interesting to follow Jason's discoveries about Blue Hill and the railroad. The town had flourished during the railroad's peak, but when it closed down, the town nearly died. Anne knew that was still happening to many towns all over the country. When an industry failed or mining shut down, towns floundered. If enough people stayed and persevered, the town might survive and even revive, as Blue Hill had done. But not until many had suffered through hard times.

She thought about Victoria and Vince Parker. Chad had said they'd come from West Virginia. Mildred said they'd had a hard life. Anne knew many Appalachian areas had suffered from shutdowns in mining and timber and steel manufacturing. Is that what had brought the Parkers to Blue Hill? Anne locked up the library doors as her cell phone started to vibrate in her pocket.

She didn't recognize the number, but it was local.

"Hello, Anne speaking. How may I help you?"

"This is Paul Simmons, the repairman at the Stitching Post. You left your Singer sewing machine here for repairs?"

"Oh yes. Thanks for calling. Can it be repaired?"

"I'm afraid not. At least I wouldn't recommend it, unless the machine has special sentimental value. It needs a new motor. You can get a new machine with a lot more capability for not much more than the repair would cost."

"I don't think I want to spend the money to repair it." The machine was indeed sentimental because Edie had taught her to sew on it. But it had served its purpose. When it was time for Liddie to learn, Anne wanted it to be on a more modern machine.

"I figured that'd be your answer. You can come pick up the machine on Monday. No charge for looking at it."

"Thank you. Could you use it for parts?"

"Sure could, if you don't want it back."

"Please keep it. I'd prefer to see someone get some good out of it."

Anne felt a little sad as she ended the call. Though she didn't have quite an attachment to the old machine, Aunt Edie had really loved it. And now she had one more thing to add to her to-do list:

buy a sewing machine. Preferably used and inexpensive since she didn't need a fancy machine. Although, she thought, she might do more sewing if she had a nice machine, like the missing Berninas.

Suddenly Hershey started barking loudly from the back door. Anne was glad she'd already closed and locked the library for the day.

"Hey, Mom, we'll be outside, okay?" Ben shouted from the back door. Ben and Ryan, with Hershey close on their heels, let the back door bang shut as they went back outside. She heard deep chuckling.

"I guess you know Ben is home," Alex said, coming down the hall from the back door to the library desk, where Anne was straightening books and Liddie was coloring.

"Can I go play too?" Liddie asked.

"Put on your jacket."

"Okay," Liddie yelled as she bounded up the stairs.

Anne laughed. "I didn't realize how quiet it's been all afternoon until just this minute."

"You'd think they'd already run out of steam. They've been outside for a couple of hours, helping me clean up a construction site."

"But that was work, not play."

"True. Hey, I talked to my uncle this afternoon. He invited me to go listen to a piano concert at the retirement residence tomorrow afternoon. Would you like to go along? He hinted that I might bring you to see him."

"He did, did he?" Anne smiled. Alex's Uncle Walter was quite a dapper gentleman. "What about the kids?"

"I doubt they'd enjoy it. Wendy's oldest girl said she'd be happy to babysit. Either here or at my house."

"In that case, how can I refuse?"

"Uncle Walter will be thrilled."

* * *

Before church the next day, Anne looked at her closet, trying to decide what to wear that would be appropriate for an afternoon concert at the retirement center. They'd be going right after church. She didn't want to be too dressy, but she wanted to look nice. Alex's uncle would be in a suit and tie, which seemed to be his standard attire. Alex would be casual. But she had a feeling this was a big occasion for the residents of the retirement home. Anne saw Aunt Edie's blue wool blazer hanging next to her gray wool slacks. She reached up and pulled the two hangers down and added a soft gray mock-turtleneck sweater that matched her slacks A pair of blue lapis lazuli earrings went well with the blue jacket, she thought, as she checked her appearance in the mirror. She left her hair down, and because it was a somewhat special occasion, she put in her contact lenses. Then she went to help Liddie get ready.

When Alex came out to the car at church to help them carry clothing in from the car, she knew she'd chosen well. He stopped and stared at her, and a big grin spread across his face.

"You look great," he said, taking an armload of clothes from her.

"Thanks. You look pretty sharp yourself."

He grinned. "I'll look sloppy next to Uncle Walter, but it's the best I could do." He had on good jeans, an open-collar shirt, and a brown tweed jacket with leather patch elbows. She thought his best looked very nice.

She gave Ben, Liddie, and Ryan some clothes to carry, and then she picked up the last of the donations from the library and followed the children into the church. She added her armful to the box, then turned around and heard a gasp.

"Anne. Where did you get that jacket?" It was Mildred. She looked like she'd seen a ghost.

"I found it in Aunt Edie's cedar chest. I'm sorry, I never thought it would upset you. Did you make it for her?"

"No, but I have one that is identical, only mine's emerald green. Victoria made it."

"Oh." Now it was Anne's turn to be stunned. "I didn't know. Should I not wear it?"

Mildred shook her head. "Oh no, it's perfect on you. Edie would love for you to wear it. I was just surprised. I didn't know Edie had received it. Victoria brought mine to me the night before she left. She told me she was working on one for Edie, but she hadn't finished it yet. It was a thank-you gift for all we'd done for her." Mildred took a hankie out of her pocket and dabbed at her eyes. "You see how thoughtful she was?"

"Yes. That means she must have sent it to Aunt Edie after she moved."

"I suppose you're right. As far as I know, Edie never wore it."

"It was wrapped carefully in tissue. I thought Aunt Edie had made it. She must have been saving it, perhaps for something special."

"Well, I'm glad you found it," Mildred said. "And I'm glad Victoria was able to finish it before Edie died." Mildred sniffed and wiped her eyes. "I'd better get inside." She turned and hurried away.

Anne stared after her aunt's friend, shaken. How sad that Aunt Edie hadn't worn the beautiful jacket. But how lovely that Victoria had honored the two women who'd befriended her in such a special way. Anne had seen the loving stitches in the jacket. It was obvious she had truly cared for them.

* * *

On the way out of church, Anne caught up with Wendy and Chad.

"You look gorgeous. Where did you get that jacket?" Wendy touched Anne's sleeve.

"I found it in Aunt Edie's things. It was hers."

"She'd be happy to see you wearing it. I hear you're going to a concert with Alex today." Wendy wriggled her eyebrows.

Anne gave a dismissive wave. "We're going to see his Uncle Walter. Do you remember him? He's a charming gentleman."

"Alex takes after him, I think."

Anne laughed. "I was hoping to ask Chad something."

Wendy tapped her husband on the shoulder. He was talking to someone, but he turned around.

"I don't want to interrupt you, but I have a question when you have time."

"Just a sec." Chad finished his conversation, then turned back to Anne.

"You said you tried to help Vince Parker. Did you ever meet his relatives?" Anne asked.

"I didn't meet them, but I dropped him off at their house a couple of times after football practice. It was an older two-story brick house on Elm Street. I can't remember his relatives' name, but it's some kind of tree or something. I remember that because I thought it was ironic that they lived on a street with a tree name. Not much help, I'm afraid."

"That's all right. It's more than I knew before. Thanks, Chad."

"No problem."

Chad and Wendy's oldest daughter appeared beside them. "Hi, Mrs. Gibson, I'm ready to go whenever you are."

Anne looked toward the wing where the kids were coming out of junior church and saw Ben and Liddie.

"Hannah!" Liddie said, running to hug Hannah around the waist.

Ben was talking with Ryan and two other boys.

Anne laughed. "Looks like I don't have to worry about my children missing me this afternoon."

"I'll take good care of them," Hannah said.

"I know you will. Shall we go?" Anne turned toward her son. "Come on, Ben."

"Can Ryan come now?"

"He'll be over as soon as he goes home and changes, so let's get going."

Ben pumped his fist in the air. "Yes!" He led the way, fast-walking to the car.

* * *

Tall maples, decked out in brilliant red, gold, oranges, and purples framed the Blue Hill Retirement Center. Border beds of chrysanthemums in every imaginable color filled planter boxes, giving the center a festive air. As they entered the building, Anne could hear the lively tune of "The Entertainer" pouring from a room off the back of the reception area. Walter Ochs waited by the door, waving to them, looking handsome in a gray suit with a blue tie to match his eyes, his thick gray hair neatly combed back.

"Hello, Uncle Walter." Alex shook the old man's hand with both of his.

"Good to see you, my boy." Walter's eyes twinkled as he turned to Anne. She reached out both hands and he squeezed them warmly. "Welcome, Anne. So glad you could come. I've saved us the best seats in the house."

As the music ended, he offered Anne his arm and ushered them into the large lounge, where tables and comfortable seating areas filled the room. A grand piano sat in one corner. The pianist wore a long red gown and a sparkly necklace and earrings, which glittered as she began to play a new piece, moving her hands across the keys, her head swaying to the rhythm of a Chopin waltz. Walter led them to a love seat near the piano with chairs on either side forming a cozy U-shaped arrangement. A woman with curly ash blonde hair and dimples in her plump rosy cheeks smiled up at them from one of the chairs. When she stood, she barely came to the top of Anne's shoulders.

"I'm Ruby. I've been looking forward to meeting you," she said in an overly loud voice. "Walter has told me all about you both. Come sit down." Someone nearby shushed her. She pressed her lips together, accenting the red lipstick bleeding into the wrinkles around her mouth. She waved toward the love seat, then sat down.

Anne took the side closest to Ruby. She guessed Ruby's age at maybe fifteen years younger than Walter, who at ninety-three seemed young for his age. As they listened to the music, she caught glances between the older pair. Ruby would blush and glance quickly away if their eyes met, then his mouth would curve up just slightly. She thought his gaze looked more tender than flirtatious. Anne glanced over at Alex. He was watching the interaction between his uncle and Ruby too. He grinned and gave Anne a wink. It wasn't just her imagination.

When the concert ended, after the pianist played several encores, the staff brought out punch and coffee and a large sheet cake. Walter explained that the event was a monthly celebration for everyone having a birthday that month. He and Alex got up to bring them each a drink and a piece of cake.

"What a lovely concert," Anne said to Ruby. "Do you have entertainment here often?"

"I don't know. I've only lived here three weeks. I have my own home in town," she said. "I'll be moving home when my daughter gets up here from Texas."

"Really? So this is temporary for you?"

"Yes. As soon as my daughter convinces my son that I'm not crazy, I'll go back home, although I'll miss seeing Walter. He has plenty of friends though. And I can come visit him. I still have my car. That is, if my son hasn't sold it. He doesn't think I should drive anymore."

Oh dear, Anne thought. Ruby seemed all right, but her son must have reasons for wanting to protect her. Anne didn't know how to respond to the woman, so she was glad to see Walter and Alex returning.

"Did Anne tell you she is a librarian?" Walter asked Ruby as they ate cake. Then he turned to Anne. "Ruby is an author. She's written several cookbooks. You might have them in the library."

"Really? That's wonderful," Anne said. "What are the titles?"

Anne made note of Ruby's full name and book titles, promising to check and make sure they carried her books. Local authors were always popular.

"I won't be writing any more books until I move back home," Ruby said. "My kitchen here is too small to experiment. Such irony. I finally remodeled so I have all state-of-the-art appliances and filtration systems, and my son decides I've been robbed. He insisted I move here to protect my estate. I tried to tell him the changes I made were to protect my health, but he says I didn't need them. I have the results of the water and air pollution tests to prove I'd been living with dangerous health hazards. Stanley showed me the poisons in my water. No wonder I'd been feeling weak and tired all the time."

"Stanley?" Anne said.

"Yes. He was the nice young man who tested my water. He came to my door because he'd found polluted water at my neighbor's house. He might have saved my life. He found coliform bacteria and heavy metals and traces of medications in my water. That wasn't all. I had him test my air, and it was five times more polluted than the outside air. I noticed the difference as soon as he installed the water and air filtration systems. And it wasn't that expensive. Not compared to the thousands it would cost for nursing home care. That's where I was headed before, you know."

"Do you know the name of Stanley's company?" Anne asked. "Could it be A Able Surplus Sales?"

"That doesn't sound familiar. I don't remember. Just Stanley. He was so helpful."

"I'm sure your son is just trying to protect you," Alex said.

"I know," Ruby said, shaking her head sadly. "I can't convince him that I'm capable of handling my own life."

After an awkward pause, Alex stood. "It's been nice visiting with you, Uncle Walter, and a pleasure to meet you, Ruby, but we need to get going. We left Anne's children and Ryan with a sitter, and I expect they'll be wanting dinner soon."

Anne took his cue and stood. "I didn't realize it was getting so late. Thank you for inviting us, Walter. I enjoyed the piano concert and our visit. So nice to meet you, Ruby. I'll look for your cookbooks." She took Ruby's hand and squeezed it gently.

"Come back and visit soon," Walter said.

"I probably won't be here much longer," Ruby said.

As they walked to the car, Anne couldn't help thinking about Ruby's encounter with Stanley.

"Do you think she was scammed?"

"Hard to say," Alex said. "Evidently her son thinks so. If Stanley is who I think he is, he has a reputation with contractors for shoddy work and padding his invoices. I doubt if this guy did anything out-and-out illegal. Unethical, perhaps. That's the scam."

"That's a shame. I feel sorry for her."

"Me too."

"Do me a favor and go home by way of Elm Street."

"Sure. What's on Elm?"

"That's where Vince Parker was living when he was going to high school here."

"Do you have an address?"

"No, but Chad Pyle said it was a red brick two-story house and his relatives had a last name that had something to do with a tree."

"All right then. Let's go see what we can find." Alex turned east for a quarter mile, then turned onto Elm Street, headed back toward town. They passed several red brick homes, but none of the names on the mailboxes had anything to do with trees.

"We're almost to the end of the street," Alex said. Half a block up, the road ended at a T.

Anne looked right and left. "There. Pull over." She pointed to the right. Behind a large evergreen tree was a two-story red brick house. "Can you see the mailbox?"

A bush nearly hid the metal mail receptacle. "It looks like D GLAS. Could it be Douglas?" Alex said.

"Douglas is a type of fir tree. Maybe that's it." The yard was full of leaves. The blinds were all pulled. A package sat on the front porch by the door. No car in sight. "It looks deserted."

"Yes, it does. Do you think it's the house you're looking for?"

Anne jotted down the address. "I don't know." Another dead end.

CHAPTER TWELVE

Monday morning, as Anne reached home after taking the children to school, her cell phone rang.

"Good morning, Anne," Reverend Tom's hearty voice boomed in her ear. "I hope I didn't call too early this morning."

"Oh no. I was driving, on my way back from dropping off the kids."

"Ah. I'd hoped to talk to you yesterday after church, but I missed you. I've been thinking about your question about your great-aunt Edie, about her state of mind her last couple of years. I'm sure her mind was sound. I can't imagine anyone taking advantage of her. Then I was in Coffee Joe's the other morning, and I saw a woman who reminded me of her. It jarred my memory. It's probably nothing, but it reminded me that I'd seen Edie in the coffee shop with a man I didn't recognize. This couple looked so similar, it was like having a flashback. I'd never seen the man Edie was with before. If I remember correctly, I'd guess he was a bit younger than her. He had brownish hair. Dressed in coveralls. I never saw him again. It's probably nothing."

"If he was dressed in coveralls, he doesn't sound like a salesman, does he?"

"No. He looked like he'd come in off the farm, more likely. As I say, it was probably nothing of any importance. I'd never seen her with a strange man before."

"Interesting. I don't know if it fits into my puzzle, but I'll add it to my facts. I believe that the twelve sewing machines at the high school were anonymously donated by Aunt Edie. But twelve are still missing. I've looked everywhere and followed almost every possible lead, and they seem to have vanished—if she actually received twenty-four machines, since she paid for twenty-four. I'm not sure what company she bought them from, but the phone number is disconnected, and the post office box is no longer valid. I do have a few more ideas. I just hope one of them pans out."

"I hope so too, for your peace of mind. But I can't imagine anyone cheating Edie Summers. She was too sharp for that, but she also had a way of always bringing out the best in people. I'm sure if she felt cheated, she would have tracked them down and made them reimburse her or produce the machines."

"Mildred said the same thing. I can't imagine it, myself. That's what makes this such a puzzle. I feel compelled to find those machines."

After she said good-bye, Anne thought about her aunt meeting a strange man at Coffee Joe's. Aunt Edie had seemed perfectly content with her single status. Had she met someone she was attracted to in her elder years? Edie was a lovely, intelligent, vibrant woman. The surprising fact was that there hadn't been more men pursuing her over the years. And Reverend Tom only saw the man the one time. It seemed a far stretch that Edie had been on a date. So who was the man in the coveralls? Could it have been someone after Edie's money?

* * *

Anne left Bella in charge of the library Monday afternoon while she went to pick up office supplies for the library. She allowed herself enough time for a side trip and pulled her silver Impala to a stop in front of Manny's Pawn Shop. This time there were two cars parked in front and the lights were on inside. A man nearly bumped into her as she entered the building. He muttered something and stepped aside, then went out and let the door bang shut.

A slender man with thinning hair stood behind the counter, arguing with a customer. Anne went right to the sewing machine. It was a Bernina, the same model as the ones Aunt Edie purchased, but it was only one machine. She checked the price tag. $649.99.

As Anne studied the machine, she tried not to eavesdrop, but she couldn't help overhearing. The shop owner was questioning where the customer got a collection of coins. The young woman said it was hers and she was an adult. He asked her for identification. She countered that she'd left it at home. He told her to go get it and not come back without it, and the woman turned in a huff and stomped out, her western boots clicking on the concrete floor.

"Kids," he said as he approached her. "They think I was born yesterday. Ha." He shook his head. Then his demeanor changed. He smiled. "Are you familiar with the Bernina brand machines? That is one fine sewing machine. You won't find a better price."

"Do you have more than one?"

"Nope. Berninas don't come up for sale often. People buy them and keep them."

"Have you had it for long?"

"A while. I don't get much foot traffic here. Most of my sales are online anyway. I intend to put the Bernina up on the Internet, but I haven't gotten around to it. Your luck. If I put it online, the price goes up." He gave her a questioning smile. "But you could take it home with you today."

"Much as I'd like a new sewing machine, this one is out of my price range, even at this price. Actually, I was hoping you might be able to help me with something. I'm missing some Berninas, this exact model. I heard you had some trouble with a boy trying to sell some stolen goods a little over a year ago. I got to thinking, how could you know something was stolen if it hadn't been reported to the police? Maybe this could be one of the missing sewing machines…"

Manny's expression transformed into a scowl. "Look. I don't know what you might be getting at. I make every effort never to buy stolen property. I get ID and keep records of everything I purchase. I often work with the police when there's been a robbery, keeping an eye out for stolen property. When I buy something, it sits in the back room for a good long time, just in case someone comes in looking for it."

Anne held up placating hands. "I'm sorry. I didn't mean to imply…"

Manny's expression softened a little. "If you want, I can show you the paperwork on the Bernina here."

"If you don't mind," Anne said.

Manny took a file box out from under the front counter, set it on the glass top, and started pawing through it. As he looked, he muttered to himself, but Anne couldn't understand what he was saying. After a few minutes, he pulled out a piece of paper. "Here it is." He slapped it down on the counter.

Anne looked at the form. It had a long list of items, mainly household appliances and collectibles. Manny strategically put his hand over the prices paid. "See there. I bought these off a lady's estate. Her daughter brought them in. Whole truckload of stuff. There's the sewing machine. See that serial number? You can check it. It matches." He picked up the paper and turned it over. Stapled to the top was a newspaper clipping. He showed it to her. "There's the lady's obituary. I keep track of the obits. I get lots of merchandise from estates."

Anne had wondered as she entered the pawnshop if Manny might deal in stolen items. His shop had a disheveled, mismanaged, overstocked look about it. It might be easy to slip in items that no one would even notice without looking closely. But after talking with him, she realized that it was more organized than it appeared at first glance. Organized chaos. It gave the impression that great deals hid amongst the stacks of stuff. It was a bargain hunter's dream.

"Thank you for explaining to me. I had no idea."

"No problem. You sure you don't want the sewing machine? I can give you a super deal."

"It's tempting, but no, thanks. It's a nice machine, but somewhere, I have a dozen of them."

* * *

Remi came in earlier than usual Wednesday so that Anne could attend a special assembly at the elementary school. After giving Remi a few instructions, Anne headed out for the school and made her way to the gymnasium. She sat on the bottom row of bleachers, and soon the kindergarten class filed by. Liddie stepped out of line to give her a hug, and a few other children also ran to hug their parents. Miss Reed gently herded them back in line. Anne appreciated the young teacher's patience. If the other children were as energetic as Liddie, and it seemed they were, their teacher had her hands full.

Each teacher recognized several students that they had nominated as exemplary in various projects or deportment. Liddie beamed when her name was called. Miss Reed recognized Liddie's kindness to others for initiating a coat drive. She was given a certificate and a coupon for an ice cream cone at the soda fountain at Thrifty Drugstore. Anne realized at that moment how important it was to Liddie to take a coat to the school, even though she already had worked hard to collect coats through the library to take to church. In her young mind, the school collection was different. Separate. But it was still part of her mission, and she was directly involved.

After the assembly, Anne puzzled over how to help Liddie. She could go out and buy another coat, but that seemed too easy. Liddie's generosity came from her heart, not her mother's pocketbook. Liddie had prayed for an answer. As much as Anne wanted to make sure God answered Liddie's prayer, she could not step in and answer for Him. As she started her car, she said her own prayer. "Lord, please give me wisdom and patience. And please answer Liddie's prayer for a coat."

Before returning to the library, Anne drove over to Elm Street. The package she'd seen still sat on the porch of the red brick house. She parked by the curb and walked up to the front door. No sign of life. She rang the doorbell and knocked on the door. No answer.

The wind whipped her jacket open, hitting her with a blast of frigid air as she returned to her car. She glanced up. Steel gray clouds covered the sky. The weatherman was predicting snow, but Anne wasn't ready for that.

As she got back into her car, she realized the cross street was Laurel Lane. Mildred's street. Mildred knew almost everyone in town. She had mentioned seeing Victoria and Vince's aunt in town.

Anne stopped across the street from Mildred's house and went to her door. Mildred wasn't home either. She started back to her car, then saw Coraline Watson looking out the window next door, waving. She went over to see if she wanted something.

"How nice of you to stop for a visit," Coraline said, opening the front door as Anne approached the steps. "Come in. I was just about to make tea."

Anne gave a discreet peek at her watch. A visit with Coraline could take a long time. The widow loved to chat. But she also made a point of knowing what was happening in the neighborhood. Would that include Elm Street?

"Thank you, but I can't stay long. I was on my way back to the library."

"Of course. Mildred left an hour ago. She isn't usually gone more than an hour, so it's likely she'll be back soon. Let me take your jacket and purse."

"I'll just set them here by the door," Anne said, taking off her jacket. "How are you doing?"

"Fine, thank you for asking."

Coraline loved to share her knowledge. Anne knew from previous visits that all she had to do was ask. "Maybe you can help me. Have you ever heard of a company called A Able Surplus Sales?"

Coraline's brow wrinkled as she thought. "No. Something about the name seems familiar, but I can't think what. Are they local?"

"I think so. They might be out of business. My aunt bought something from them, and I wanted to talk to them."

"Good luck with that. Companies come and go so fast, you can't get good service."

"Sounds like you've had a bad experience," Anne said. "By chance, have you had someone come by selling water filters or air filtration systems recently?"

"No. Is that who you're looking for? I wouldn't have thought Edie Summers would fall for a sales pitch like that. Not that filtration systems are bad, mind you. My nephew is a plumber, and he installs systems with filters, but he told me there are lots of scams." Coraline looked toward her kitchen. "I have a pitcher that filters all the water I need. I'm making our tea with filtered water. I prefer the taste. But it's not like the city water isn't safe to drink. They have to test it regularly, you know."

"I haven't had anyone come by either," Anne assured her. "I heard of a woman who bought a system recently, so I just wondered. Do you by chance know the Douglases who live on Elm Street?"

The teakettle whistled. Coraline went into the kitchen to turn it off. A few minutes later, she came out with a tray of tea and cookies. "Here's your tea. Take a cookie too." She handed Anne a cup of steaming tea. "They didn't buy one, did they?"

It took Anne a second to realize that Coraline was asking if the Douglases had purchased a filter system. "Not that I know of."

"Oh, good. I'm assuming you mean Vince and Victoria Parker's relatives?"

"Yes. Did you know the Parkers?"

"Oh yes. Vince mowed my lawn one summer. Mildred recommended him, plus I knew he worked for your aunt, and I saw him working at the egg farm out past Dillon's Auto Parts. I used to buy eggs from them. He did a good job, but he unnerved me."

"Really? Why is that?" Anne took a sip of tea. It tasted like some kind of tropical fruit.

"He kept to himself, didn't talk much. I tried to be friendly, but he just scowled all the time, like he was upset about something. Brooding. You know? Like a pot of boiling potatoes, almost ready to boil over. Now, his sister—she was a sweetheart. Always had a kind word for everyone."

"What about the Douglases? I went by their house and it looks deserted, but there's a package sitting on the porch."

"Such a shame. The husband might not make it, you know."

"What's wrong?"

"He was working on his roof and fell. No one to help them since Vince took off. After all they tried to do to help him... It's a shame, if you ask me. They're getting up there—in their late sixties at least. The paramedics came and took him to the hospital in an ambulance. I heard he was in a coma. His wife is probably at the hospital."

"Oh dear." Anne's heart went out to the older couple. "I wonder if there's some way to help them. Do you know them well?"

"Oh no." Coraline's green eyes widened in surprise. "I've never even met them."

* * *

When Anne was able to make a polite exit from Coraline's house, she checked in with Remi at the library. Things were quiet, so Anne made a trip to the hospital in Deshler.

At the information desk, a woman in a volunteer uniform looked up over the top of her glasses and smiled. "Can I help you?"

"I'm looking for Mr. Douglas. I understand he had an accident and fell off a roof. Do you have his room number?"

She looked at her computer screen. "He is in room 210. Do you know the way?"

"Yes, thank you. Is he in intensive care?"

The woman looked again. "No. He's in a regular room."

"Oh, good. Thank you." If he wasn't in ICU, he must not be too serious.

Anne walked down to the elevator, then went up to the second floor. The scent of disinfectant hit her as she got off the elevator. The door to Mr. Douglas's room was cracked open several inches. Anne tapped on the door.

"Come in."

Anne stepped inside and found an older woman sitting in a chair next to the bed. A man lay still, covered by a neat white blanket to his chin. He had an oxygen mask over his mouth and nose, plus IV tubes and monitors. He appeared to be asleep. "Mrs. Douglas?"

"Yes?"

"I'm Anne Gibson, Edie Summers's niece."

"Oh, hello. I was sorry to hear your aunt passed away. Edie was a nice lady."

"Thank you. I miss her a lot. I heard about your husband's accident. How is he doing?"

Mrs. Douglas shook her head. Anne could see the distress and fatigue in her eyes. "He just sleeps."

"Could I buy you a cup of coffee or tea?"

Mrs. Douglas looked at the bed, then nodded and got up. "That would be nice. I could use something to drink."

They went downstairs to the cafeteria. It was lunchtime, and Anne talked Mrs. Douglas into getting a sandwich. They found a small table.

"Would you mind if I say a prayer, Mrs. Douglas?" Anne asked. She bowed her head and thanked God for their lunches, then asked the Lord to heal Mr. Douglas. When she looked up, Mrs. Douglas had tears in her eyes. "I'm so sorry. I didn't mean to distress you."

"No, it's all right. Thank you. I've been praying, but I'm not very good at it. The doctors don't know if George has permanent brain damage or even if he will wake up. He has a head injury and broken ribs and a broken wrist, so they are keeping him sedated to keep him quiet and let his head and bones rest and heal. Otherwise, they said we just have to wait." She dabbed at her eyes with a tissue. "I'm afraid he'll never wake up."

"I'm sorry." Anne didn't know what else to say to comfort her. "What can I do? How can I help you?"

"I don't know. I don't need anything."

"There's a package on your front porch. I went by there. Do you want me to give it to a neighbor until you go home? Or I could bring it to you here."

"You're as nice as your aunt. I can call a neighbor. My name is Mae, by the way. No one else has come to see George or me."

"Maybe people don't know about his accident." Anne thought it odd that their neighbors hadn't come to see them or inquire if they needed help. "Have you contacted your niece and nephew?"

"No. I don't want to bother them."

"I think they'd want to know. After all, didn't they stay with you while they lived in Blue Hill?"

"Vince stayed with us. Victoria had her own place. I'm sure it sounds odd, but I'm not sure where they are. There was some trouble with the young men Vince was hanging around with. Trouble with the law, you see. Vince said he wasn't involved, and I believe him. He's a good boy. But I couldn't help wondering if they were putting pressure on him when he took off before graduation. He only had a few days and he would have stood up with his class to get his diploma, but he said he couldn't wait. Then Victoria left. As soon as her classes were over, she went to find him. She said she was going to Philadelphia. That's where he'd said he wanted to live. I got one postcard from her a few months later, but it was from West Virginia, not Philadelphia." She shook her head. "I can't imagine those children going back to their father. He's the reason they came here in the first place. Since my sister passed, he's alienated everyone with his temper. He was hardest on Vince."

Anne wondered if her letter to the Philadelphia address had reached the brother and sister or if they had moved on. "Do you have an address in West Virginia?"

"I have the address where they lived before my sister died. I don't know if it's still good. It's at home in my address book. Do you need it?"

Anne didn't want to bother Mae while she had so much on her mind. "Not right now. Maybe I can get it from you later. I got a Philadelphia address from the high school and sent Victoria and Vince a letter. I'll see if I get a response."

"Oh, I hope so. I do worry about them. Vince was so angry about life, and Victoria was so innocent, like my sister. She sees good in everyone and just wants to help people."

"That's the impression I've gotten from everyone who knew her. Do you have any other family I can contact for you?"

"No. It's just George and me."

Anne recognized the lonely resignation in Mae's slumped posture and sad eyes. She had felt that way after Eric died, and yet she had Ben and Liddie to keep her going and her parents and other relatives for support. Everyone at their church in Brooklyn had stepped up to help, and the people at Blue Hill Community Church had opened their arms and accepted her and the children. "Do you have a pastor who will come pray with you?"

"No. We haven't joined a church here. We went with Victoria a few times."

"She went to my church with Aunt Edie. Would it be all right if I ask Reverend Tom to come see you?"

"That would be nice. Thank you."

"You're welcome. Here's my phone number if there's any way I can help." Anne wrote her cell phone number on a library business card and handed it to Mae.

When she got back to the library, she called Reverend Tom and told him about George and Mae. She still had learned nothing about the fate of the missing sewing machines. Could Vince have taken them to Philadelphia to sell and finance a new start? They'd be easier to sell in a large city. Mae had enough distress without adding the possibility that her nephew and possibly her niece might have cheated their friend Edie.

It occurred to Anne that her aunt might have known the extra twelve machines had disappeared. If Vince took them, and Victoria followed him, trying to get them back, Aunt Edie might have decided not to press charges, for Victoria's sake. Or if Vince had been innocent but implicated by his friends, she might have tried to shield him. Anne couldn't imagine her aunt allowing Vince to get away with a crime though. She would have tried to influence the troubled young man to mend his ways. How disappointing for her if her efforts to help had failed.

CHAPTER THIRTEEN

"We received a couple more coats today," Anne told Liddie and Ben after she closed the library Wednesday evening. "Let's take them upstairs and look them over."

"I'll carry them," Ben said.

"Me. I want to," Liddie said.

"You can both carry one. Put them on the table in the sewing room and we'll check them over."

Liddie picked up the woman's jacket and Ben took the man's coat and they hurried up the stairs.

"What's for dinner?" Ben asked. "It sure smells good, and I'm starving."

"Me too," Liddie said.

"Wash up and set the table. I made Crock-Pot chicken stew."

"With dumplings?" Ben asked.

"As a matter of fact, yes."

"Yum!" Both kids hurried to wash up.

After dinner, Ben went to his room to work on homework while Anne and Liddie cleaned up the dishes.

"Can we look at the coats now?" Liddie asked when they'd finished.

"Yes." They went into the sewing room, and Anne picked up the man's coat. "You can check the pockets while I look for rips or holes." She turned it, looking at every seam. "This one's in good shape."

"Mommy, look! I found a whole bunch of money."

Anne looked up as Liddie placed a wad of bills and a small business card on the sewing machine table. Anne picked it up and counted ninety-five dollars. The business card said *Reliable Health Systems. Stanley Fulton.* It also had a phone number. Could it be the Stanley who sold Uncle Walter's friend a filtration system? She knew he wasn't the donor of this coat. Denise Brown was. She'd seen Denise come in with her youngest children plus several of her daycare kids. She'd been carrying two coats, and she dropped them into the bin before going up to the Children's Room. Anne knew the young mother's finances were tight, so she especially admired that Denise wanted to help others.

"We can use the money to buy coats that I can take to school," Liddie declared, beaming.

"No, we have to return the money to the person who donated the coat," Anne said.

"But, Mommy, they donated it."

"They donated the coats. They might not have checked the contents of the pockets. We've found all kinds of things in pockets, haven't we?"

"Buttons and shells and hair thingies. We didn't give them back." Liddie's lower lip pooched out.

"But they didn't have any value. This money doesn't belong to us. I know you want to take a coat to school to donate, but this isn't the way to do it."

"But it wouldn't be for us. It's for someone who needs a coat." Liddie wasn't a whiner, but she was getting close.

"That's up to the person the money belongs to. This is like if we went to the store and the clerk gave us too much change. We would return the extra to the clerk."

"Okay." Liddie's lower lip protruded farther.

Anne put her arm around Liddie's shoulders. She stiffened for a moment, then melted against her mother and hugged her tight. Anne put her finger under Liddie's chin and gently raised it. Liddie's big blue eyes filled with tears. "We'll go take it back tomorrow. Okay?"

Liddie nodded.

Anne knew Liddie's heart wasn't in her concession, but she would see her mother doing the right thing and learn from it. "Now, how about you go get ready for bed, and I'll come read you a story?"

"Okay." Liddie gave her a hug, then trudged to her room, her feet shuffling along.

Anne checked the ladies' jacket to make sure it didn't need any repairs. The jacket was quilted in slightly faded shades of purple, orange, and green. It had seen better days, but it was still in good shape. She hoped it would bless someone and bless its giver. She knew Denise could use a blessing. But then, who couldn't?

* * *

After picking up the kids from school on Thursday, Anne drove across town to an older neighborhood that had been built during the railroad's heyday in Blue Hill. Most of the neatly maintained, one-and-a-half-story homes looked similar, with covered front porches and two dormer windows. The homes had been built to attract skilled railroad workers in the early twentieth century.

Denise was expecting them. Anne had called ahead but didn't tell Denise the reason for their visit. Ben and Liddie followed her to the door, but Anne could see by the way Liddie held back, trailing her brother, that she did not want to be there. A teenage boy answered the door and invited them inside.

They stood in the living room. Signs of children were everywhere. A baby was sitting in a bouncy chair, shaking a rattle and bobbing up and down. The room held a playpen, a doll buggy, and assorted toys. A dining room table occupied the far end of the L-shaped room. A chubby toddler sat in a high chair, eating fish-shaped crackers.

"Mom, they're here," the boy shouted. "You can wait in here," he told them. Then he dashed upstairs.

"Hi. I'm sorry. He shouldn't have left you standing here. Please, sit down." Denise entered the room and moved a blanket and a pile of folded laundry off of the couch. The baby in the bouncy chair started fussing. Denise checked her diaper, then gave her a bottle that was sitting on top of a side table.

"You've really got your hands full," Anne said. She sat on the couch with Ben on one side and Liddie on the other. She was holding Denise's multicolored jacket.

"Yes. Their parents will be here in about an hour. Then it gets almost quiet with just the six of us." She laughed. "If you can believe that." She pushed a loose strand of long blonde hair behind her ear and plopped down in a chair across from them. She gave Anne a quizzical look. "That's my jacket. I donated it to the coat drive. Is there something wrong with it?"

"Oh no. We really appreciate it. I just wanted to make certain it had come from you."

"Why?"

Anne looked down at Liddie, who was clutching a clear plastic sandwich bag with money inside. Liddie looked up at her, then stood and walked across the room to hand it to Denise as Anne explained.

"We always go through the pockets, to make sure someone didn't forget something. Liddie found this in the pocket."

Denise took the bag and stared at it. "Oh, wow." She looked up at Liddie. "Thank you so much. I thought for sure I'd lost this. I thought it was in my purse, but when I got to the utility company to pay my bill, it wasn't there. I've been so worried. I was just a little short this month." She reached out and clasped Liddie's hand. "Thank you for being so honest and bringing it to me."

"You're welcome," Liddie said. Then she smiled and went back to stand by her mother.

"Well, that's our errand. We'll let you get back to all your charges," Anne said, standing. "Oh, I did have a question." She fished into her pocket and took out the business card. "This card was in the pocket too. It's for a company called Reliable Health Solutions. Do you need it?"

"No. It was a guy selling water filter systems. He said I need one with a daycare in my home. He even offered to test my water. He said one of my neighbors is having a problem and bought his system." Denise grimaced. "As if I need to spend more money."

"Do you mind if keep the card?"

"I don't mind, but I think the whole thing's a scam. Don't let him sell you something without checking him out."

"I won't."

As soon as they got into the car, Liddie gave her mother a thoughtful look. "Mommy, Mrs. Brown really needed the money, just like you said."

"Now aren't you glad we took it back?"

"Yes. But I still have to get a coat to take to school."

Anne had to admire Liddie's determination.

* * *

"Thanks for minding the library while I was gone," Anne told Betty Bultman.

"You're welcome. Call on me anytime."

"Has it been busy?"

"Yes, but nothing I couldn't handle. I'm glad to see the high school students coming here to work on homework. I had to shush them a couple of times. There's a table full of kids up in the Reference Room. Oh, and a new volunteer. He said his name is Jason."

"Oh yes. Miss Latham at the high school asked me to take on an intern. Jason will be with us on Thursday evenings for a couple of months. Where is he?"

"He's in the Nonfiction Room, dusting and collecting books that have been left out. I didn't know what else to have him do."

"That's great. I'll go and talk to him. I'll be here now if you need to leave."

"Thanks. I've just got time to get home and get dinner on the stove. The mayor is such a creature of habit. He wants his dinner at six thirty sharp. Not that he always gets his way, mind you, but I try."

Betty got her coat and purse from the workroom and left. Then Anne went to the Nonfiction Room. Jason was standing on a stepstool, dusting a top shelf.

"Hello, Jason. I see Mrs. Bultman put you to work."

He looked down from his perch. "Hi, Mrs. Gibson." He got down. "Is there something else you want me to do?"

"I'd like to go over your assignment with you so we can figure out how best to use your time here. Let's go to the checkout desk. You can learn how to check materials in and out and we can talk between patrons."

"All right. I'll put this away first and wash up."

Anne was impressed. She needed to talk to Jason's mother and learn how she instilled such good habits in her son. She heard a heavy thump overhead and laughter. "I need to check upstairs, then I'll meet you at the desk."

Anne went upstairs. A heavy chair had tipped over backward with a teenage boy in it. She hurried over.

"Are you all right?" she asked the boy who was staring up at her with a chagrined look on his face.

"Yeah, I'm fine." He got up and rubbed the back of his head. "Guess I leaned back too far."

Several teenagers sat at the table, grinning or trying to look busy doing homework. She talked to the kids, giving them a stern but gentle warning, then she went back downstairs. Jason was waiting for her behind the desk.

Several people came up to the desk to check out. The first woman stepped up and set two books on the counter.

"Watch the process," Anne told Jason. "Then you can do the rest of them." He stood next to her. Anne turned to the woman. "Good afternoon. Do you have your library card?"

The woman took a card from her purse and handed it to her. Anne scanned it and checked out the books. The woman took the books and left while the next person in line stepped up to the counter and set one book down.

Anne stepped aside. "Go ahead and take care of these folks, Jason."

Jason was a little slow, but he managed to check out three patrons. When the counter cleared, Anne smiled at him.

"Good job. Now let's take a look at your assignment."

Jason handed Anne a piece of paper. "I'm supposed to keep a journal of what I do and what I learn." He showed her a spiral-bound steno notebook.

Anne looked over his assignment and nodded. "All right. This covers all the basics. On a college level, an internship would require ten to twelve hours a week and you'd be so busy, you wouldn't have time for your own research. I would like you to put in two to three hours a week, and I'll give you one hour of that for research. For the rest of tonight, begin to look through all the bookshelves and get an idea of what we offer. For the journaling that Miss Latham assigned, I think she'd like to see title, catalog information, and a brief description of at least one book off each shelf. You can work at it for half an hour every Thursday, so it may take several weeks to complete. You are welcome to come in any time on your own to work on anything."

"Okay." He headed toward the books.

"Wait. I want to hear about your research project first. You told me it's about the railroad era in Blue Hill. Do you know where to start on it?"

"Yes. My plan is to research the Blue Hill railroad. When it was built, how it affected the town, why it closed, and what happened to the town when it left. From that I will draw conclusions about the importance of transportation on commerce."

"That's a big project. Have you looked at our local history section?"

"Yes. There are some great books on the railroad."

Anne nodded. "We're fortunate. You also have access through our computer system to all kinds of resources."

"Cool. Well, I'd better get to work." He held up his notebook, then went into the Nonfiction Room to start perusing the shelves of books.

Anne watched him for a moment. He gave full attention to his task. She couldn't imagine Jason goofing around upstairs with the group of teenagers who were more interested in having fun with their friends than doing any homework assignments. She had a feeling his research paper would be thorough and interesting.

* * *

Friday afternoon, Anne drove out to find the egg farm where Vince had worked. She didn't know what she hoped to find, but any insight into the young man might give her a clue as to his whereabouts or his activities around Blue Hill.

She hadn't been out to the old farm road in years. Just beyond Dillon's Auto Parts, the road narrowed, becoming more of a lane than a road. She pulled close to the gravel shoulder as a tractor came toward her. It moved over to hug the other shoulder so she could get by. She passed a dairy farm and a farm advertising hay and honey. She didn't see a sign for eggs. She was beginning to wonder if she'd missed it when finally she rounded a bend and saw the sign.

Eggs for sale. The faded sign had half fallen off the fence post, and the fence was badly in need of repair. A plank with the name Tandy hung from the top of a tall post ranch gate over the driveway. Anne pulled into the farmyard. Old, rusty equipment littered the area. A tiller. A swather. An old hay wagon. The two-story farmhouse had once been white, but most of the paint had peeled off. A dusty tan compact car was parked near the house. A middle-aged woman in a blue checkered apron came out the side door when Anne pulled up.

"If you're looking for eggs, we don't sell them anymore."

"Oh. No, I'm not. I'm looking for the farm where Vince Parker used to work."

"Don't know. You'd have to ask my father. It's his farm. He's out in the shop."

"Thank you. I'll go talk to him, if that's all right."

"Suit yourself." The woman turned and went back inside the house.

Anne looked past the house and saw a large barn and a one-story building with a large sliding door for vehicles and a regular door beside it. An old blue pickup truck was parked between the buildings. She walked back to the smaller building and knocked on the door. When no one answered, she opened the door and peered inside.

Two rows of lightbulbs attached to metal pie pans on the ceiling illuminated the room, which smelled like old engine oil. Shelves full of boxes and tools and all kinds of odds and ends lined the walls. More unidentifiable stuff was stacked on the concrete floor with narrow pathways between the piles. In the center of the room, a white-haired man in grease-stained overalls was bent over, working on an old tractor.

"Hello! Mr. Tandy?" Anne called out. The man looked up with a start and turned toward her. He raised his bushy eyebrows, then turned off an air compressor and removed stained work gloves that came halfway up his forearms.

"Howdy, Miss. What can I do for you?" He approached her, his shoulders stooped.

"Hello. I'm Anne Gibson, the librarian in Blue Hill."

"Nice to meet you, Ms. Gibson. I'd shake your hand, but mine's a mite greasy." He wiped his hand on his denim overalls.

Anne smiled. "That's all right. I was wondering if you once employed Vince Parker? I heard he used to work on an egg farm out here."

"Vince, you say?" He removed a ball cap and scratched his head. "Maybe. Had two boys working for me a year or two back. Vinny — that might be your Vince. And Stan. He was the older one, but that didn't account for much when it came to working. Vinny was a worker. Stan was a talker. He had a talent for talking Vinny into doing his work for him. Good boy, that Vinny. If you're looking for a worker, I'd recommend him, but I heard he moved away."

"How long ago did he work for you?"

"Well, let's see. I hurt my back a little over a year ago. That's when I had to retire, and my daughter insisted on coming to live with me." He gave Anne a wry smile. "Don't tell her, but I don't need a caretaker."

Anne glanced around at all the possible snares that might trip and injure a person. With all the equipment and junk lying around, the building looked as if it was booby-trapped. The yard had looked nearly as cluttered. "I'm sure she's concerned about you. It's a long way to town if anything were to happen."

"Yup." He put his hat back on. "That's what she says."

"Could Stan be Stanley Fulton?"

"Dunno. Might be. To me they were Stan and Vinny."

"What kind of work did they do?"

"This and that. Some farming. Pickup and deliveries. Fixing and cleaning stuff. Guess you might say I'm a collector. All this stuff . . ." He swept his arm back to encompass the room. "I used to buy and sell and trade things. If you need anything, I can find it for you at a bargain."

At a glance, nothing looked usable. "You don't do that anymore?"

"Had to quit. Not supposed to lift more than twenty pounds now. My daughter wants me to have a big farm sale and get rid of everything."

"That's a good idea." She felt sorry for his daughter. The man appeared to be a hoarder. If so, he might not want to part with his treasures. He had a lot of stuff piled up in what looked like chaos. She doubted he even knew all the things he had.

"Do you want to take a look around while you're here? I can sell you a nice juicer or a dehydrator or a vintage typewriter. I've got a pristine green IBM Selectric. It'd look beautiful on display at the library or in your office. It still works."

Anne was almost tempted to look at it, but she resisted. Another thought occurred to her. "Do you have any sewing machines among your...inventory?"

He scratched his head again, then shook his head. "That's probably the only thing I don't have out here." The smile appeared again for a moment.

"Well, I hope you have great success with your, uh, farm sale, Mr. Tandy. Thanks for the information about Vince and Stan."

"You're welcome. If you find Vinny, tell him hello for me. Nice kid. I predict he'll do all right in life."

"If I see him, I'll tell him."

As she drove back to town, she wondered about Vinny and Stan. She was pretty sure Vinny was Vince Parker. Stan could be

Stanley, the water filter salesman. Mr. Tandy had confirmed some of the other reports she'd heard about Vince. A troubled young man with anger issues, but he was a hard worker and generally liked despite his demeanor. Stan, according to his former employer, was lazy and glib tongued and an opportunist. That fit the character of a con man.

Something told Anne that finding Stanley might shed light on what had happened with Vince and Victoria.

Chapter Fourteen

Bella was checking out a stack of books at the counter when Anne got back from her trip to the farm and picking up the children from school. She waited until the patron left.

"Has it been busy this afternoon?"

"Not really. I finished shelving all the returns and new books."

"Great. That helps a lot. It's beautiful outside. The colors must be near their height for the season, and it's warm. Do you have plans for the weekend?"

"Yes. There's a football game at the college tonight, then a bonfire afterward. Tomorrow we're going canoeing at the reservoir out at Bald Eagle State Park. And somewhere in there I've got to do my homework."

"Sounds like a busy weekend. You can go whenever you're ready. I can close up."

"Thanks! I hope you have a great weekend." Bella got her backpack and hoodie from the kitchen workroom. "Oh, a package came for Liddie and Ben. I put it in the kitchen."

"Thanks." Anne went to see what had come. It was from her mother, addressed to the kids. After she locked up the library, she carried the box upstairs. It was light for its size. She shook it, but couldn't guess what was inside.

The children were watching a movie. She carried the package to the dining room table. "Ben. Liddie. There's a package for you."

The sound stopped. The children came running. "For me?" Liddie said.

"Me too?" Ben said. "What is it?" He looked at the return address. "From Grandma."

"Let's open it and see." Anne got a knife and slipped it through the tape around the edges. Ben pulled back the box flaps.

"It's a...blue plastic bag," Liddie said, pulling out a bag taped closed over something fluffy. "Maybe it's a dog or a bear."

"That one has Ben's name on it. There's one for you underneath it." Anne pulled out a red plastic bag that looked equally fluffy and handed it to Liddie.

Both children ripped into the bags.

"It's a coat," Ben said. He held it up. "But it's too big for me."

"I got a coat too." Liddie held up a red down-filled jacket. "Mine's too big for me too."

Anne took a note out of the box. She handed it to Ben. "She wrote you a note."

Ben looked at it, then smiled. "How did she know?"

"Know what? Read it to me," Liddie said.

"Okay," Ben said. "It says, 'Dear Ben and Liddie. Grandpa and I don't need these jackets down here in Florida. Maybe you can figure out what to do with them. They're really warm. I know they are too big for you, but there must be someone who needs them. Love, Grandma and Grandpa.'" Ben looked up at his sister and grinned. "We can take them to school, Liddie."

"Yes!" Liddie pumped her fist in the air. "Now I have a coat to take to school, and it didn't cost anything."

"I'd say you got an answer to your prayer, Liddie. Sometimes God uses other people to send us His answers."

"Oh yes! Thank you, God! Can I call Grandma?"

"Yes. You can both call and thank Grandma and Grandpa." She handed Ben her cell phone. "Then wash up and come help me with dinner."

"All right." The movie, which Ben had paused, was forgotten. Ben hit the speed dial number for Anne's parents. A moment later, he put the phone on speaker and he and Liddie talked excitedly with their grandma and grandpa.

Anne knew her mom had gotten the idea the last time they'd talked. The package had surprised her as much as the children though. She doubted the coats came out of her parents' closet. Her mom had gotten rid of all traces of winter when they moved south. Besides that, the coats looked brand new. From the sounds coming from her children, they were thrilled to have one more coat to give away.

* * *

Sunday morning, Liddie came screaming, running into Anne's bedroom. Blood dripped down Liddie's chin onto her white turtleneck sweater. Anne rushed her into the bathroom and grabbed a washcloth.

"What happened, honey? What did you do?" Her lip wasn't bleeding. Anne tried to look inside her mouth.

"Ben," Liddie said between sobs.

"Ben?" Anne called to her son. "What happened?"

Ben appeared in the bathroom doorway, grinning. He held up a tiny, bloody tooth. "She lost a baby tooth, Mom. I helped her. When it came out, she yelled. Then she saw all the blood and started screaming."

"Oh dear. It's all right, Liddie." Anne turned to her daughter, then to her son. "But next time, Ben, let's let it come out on its own. Okay?" She dampened a cotton ball, then pressed it into the empty tooth socket in Liddie's mouth. "There. Hold that in place for a minute, and it will stop bleeding."

"You can put it under your pillow for the tooth fairy," Ben said, grinning at his sister.

Liddie's tears dried up and her eyes filled with wonder. "I wost my toof," she mumbled. "Give it to me," she said, holding out her hand toward Ben.

"I'll take it," Anne said. "Ben, you wash up. Oh dear, you have blood on your shirt too. Go change." Anne took the tooth, then noticed blood on her own blouse. "Looks like I have to change too."

Anne washed the tooth and wrapped it in a tissue.

"Can I put it under my pillow now, please?" Liddie asked. Anne handed the tooth to her daughter, who ran into her bedroom and put it under her pillow.

Liddie picked out a red top, in case her gum started bleeding again. Anne helped her change, then went to change her own shirt.

By the time they were ready and Anne had put their stained shirts into a tub of cold water to soak, they were almost late for church.

The three of them carried armfuls of coats and winter clothes into the church and deposited them in the donation box. The library bin had been full again.

After the congregation finished singing, Reverend Tom gave announcements.

"Friends, I am overjoyed to share what your outpouring of love has meant to Blue Hill. We have supplied warm winter clothing to the county's Youth Emergency Services, for children in dire need. We have donated outerwear to the Community Health and Wellness Program, for area residents in need. We have worked alongside the Community Action Association and Senior Care. We have literally blanketed our area with warmth for the winter. I know everyone has participated. I want to particularly thank our children, who took it upon themselves to fill the box. Liddie Gibson was the first to step up, and she was determined to fill the box by herself. I've asked Liddie to come up and tell you about her experience the last three weeks."

Liddie stood and marched up front, to Anne's amazement. Liddie hadn't said a word to her. Neither had Ben or Reverend Tom. She wondered what her daughter was about to share.

"Liddie, tell us about your coat drive," Reverend Tom said, holding the microphone down so she could be heard.

"Well…" Liddie clasped her hands together, then flipped her wrists so her palms were extended outward. She took a deep breath. "When we had story time in church and you told us we needed to fill the donation box. I felt bad, 'cause I just gave my coat away. But then I thought I wanted to do it by myself 'cause I have lots of clothes." As she talked, Liddie's voice rose, and she rocked up on her tiptoes, then down onto her heels. "When we got home, my mom helped us go through our clothes, and we didn't have very much after all. She said we gave it away before we moved here."

"So you had already filled a donation box in New York?"

"I guess so. But I wanted to fill this box." She pointed to the foyer. "So Mom told me to call our friends and ask for clothes. And they brought lots of clothes." She threw her hands up in the air.

"So were you able to fill the donation box?"

"Yes."

"What did you learn?"

Liddie looked up at him as if she had no idea what he was talking about. She thought for a minute. "I learned it takes lots of coats to fill the box 'cause it's so big."

The congregation laughed. Liddie looked startled. Then she giggled.

"Thank you, Liddie. I don't know if you realize it, but you organized a coat drive. Lots of people came together to help fill the box."

"Yeah." Liddie grinned, showing the gap where she'd lost a tooth, and she rocked on her heels and toes again.

"Thank you, Liddie. You can sit down now."

Liddie ran down the aisle and plopped down on the pew next to Anne.

"Phew," she said. "I'm glad that's over."

Someone in front of them chuckled. Anne patted Liddie's hand and smiled down at her. It was a good thing she didn't have to speak. There was a big lump in her throat and her heart was overflowing with pride and joy.

"Two reasons Jesus encouraged us to meet together," Reverend Tom said, "are so we can help take care of each other and so we can reach out to help others and spread God's love. You have all been so generous, we have an abundance. So we will be sending warm coats and clothing to a mission that we support here in the United States, in a very poor area. To help with that, we will extend our coat drive another week. Next Sunday we will have a special program and a potluck after church. Look around and see what you can find to bring. And also bring a covered dish to share. Something with an international flavor to commemorate missions."

Liddie tugged on Anne's sleeve. When Anne looked down, Liddie whispered, "Mommy, I have to take grandma's coat to school. Then I won't have anything else to give."

"It's all right, honey. Maybe we'll get some more at the library."

"Okay."

That seemed to satisfy Liddie. She had seen God provide this week through her grandparents. Liddie seemed willing to accept that somehow, God would work things out. Such simple faith. Anne wished her own faith were as uncomplicated.

* * *

Discovering what happened to twelve sewing machines shouldn't be so difficult, but Anne still had no idea where they could be. If she hadn't personally seen twelve of them, she would doubt they existed. Stringing together connections, she had Aunt Edie, who was connected to Victoria, who was connected to Vince, and Anne was almost certain that twelve of the machines had ended up at the high school. Vince was connected to the Tandy egg farm, and through the farm, he was connected to Stan. Anne felt more certain than ever that Stanley Fulton was part of the puzzle.

She was staring at Stanley's business card when Alex brought Liddie and Ben home after school Monday. He came in while Ben and Ryan went to look up some more local information for their history project.

Alex leaned his elbow on the counter across from her and smiled. "Busy?"

"Not really. It should pick up for the last two hours, since school is out." She showed him the card. "Is this the Stanley with the bad reputation?"

"Health Solutions? That's a new one. It's got to be the same guy though. Stanley Fulton. He's done roofing, fencing, concrete finish. Jack-of-all-trades, master of none. He has worked for just about every contractor in town at one time or another, but he doesn't last. I hired him once, before I knew about him. He would show up when he felt like it, then not put in a full day. Or he wouldn't show up at all. I tried to talk to him, but he just gave me lame excuses. So I fired him."

That fit with Mr. Tandy's description of the Stan who'd worked for him, Anne thought. "How old is Stanley?"

"Maybe in his mid-twenties. He's still pretty young, so maybe he'll learn and straighten out. Contractors won't use him as a sub, so he works on his own. Unfortunately, he'll underbid a job, so people hire him. I've had to go in and redo a couple of his jobs. Then the homeowner ends up paying double."

"He tried to sell Denise Brown a water filtration system. She wasn't having it. I'm guessing he's the one who installed a system for Uncle Walter's friend Ruby too. I found out he used to work with Vince Parker out at Tandy's egg farm."

"Really? That's interesting. He could have been one of Vince's bad influences."

"That's what I was thinking. I wonder if Stanley Fulton has any idea what happened to Vince Parker, or the missing sewing machines, for that matter."

"How are you going to find out?"

"For starters, I think I might need a water filter. This is an old house. The pipes might be rusty and full of contaminates."

"Your pipes are in great shape," Alex said, frowning.

"I know that, and you know that, but Stanley doesn't know that."

Alex gave her a dubious look. "I wouldn't be too sure about that. He might not be a good worker, but I doubt he'd be fooled."

"I don't intend to take him to the basement," Anne said. "The faucet in the old kitchen is at least sixty years old."

"And it still works well," Alex said. "I want to be here when he comes. I don't trust him."

"That would scare him away. Don't worry, Alex. I'll be fine."

Anne had to talk to Stanley. Right now, he seemed to be her only hope for finding out what happened to Edie's other twelve sewing machines.

CHAPTER FIFTEEN

Tuesday morning, Anne thought about Stanley Fulton's water filters. She doubted if approaching him and asking questions would yield any helpful results. She needed to meet him on his terms and get him to talk to her. Remembering her college science lab, she decided to conduct an experiment. First she needed a baseline control. She logged on to the Internet and looked up the county health department for instructions.

After lunch, Betty Bultman came in and offered to staff the library if Anne needed her.

"I appreciate your coming in. I need to make a trip to Deshler this afternoon," Anne told her.

"I can be here until it's time for school to get out."

"Great. It's been slow today. We got in a new shipment. I checked them in, so they're ready to shelve. Maybe you could look through the books and arrange some of them on display."

Betty's eyes lit up. She loved getting a first look at new books. "I'd be delighted to do that."

"I know you keep up with what's going on around Blue Hill, so have you heard about someone selling water filtration systems in the area?" Anne asked. She knew Betty took her position as the mayor's wife very seriously.

Betty looked surprised. "My next-door neighbor had a system installed several months ago. I told her it wasn't necessary, but she said she needed to do it for her health. She has lots of issues. I don't know if it has helped her, but I told her our water is perfectly good." She sniffed. "The health department makes the city test its water regularly, you know."

"Do you have her phone number? I'd like to talk to her."

Betty frowned. "You're not thinking about getting a system for the library, are you?"

"Oh no. I'm doing a research project on the subject." Which was true. She hoped Betty didn't find out how far she intended to take her research.

"I'm sure she'd be happy to help with research. Here, I'll write down her number. Just tell her I told you to call her." Betty jotted a name and phone number on a notepad on the counter, then removed the paper and handed it to Anne.

"Thank you. I'll call her later. I'm off to Deshler now. I have my cell phone if you need me."

It took Anne twenty minutes to get to Deshler. She found the County Health Department in a one-story brick building behind the County Courthouse. It only took a few minutes to find the right office and pick up a water test kit. She returned to the library with just enough time to collect the sample then take it back to Deshler and drop it off while Betty was minding the library.

Anne carried the sample kit to the old library kitchen, then got out the instructions. She unscrewed the aerator on the end of the faucet, then burned off any residue on the end of the faucet with a match. She let the water run, timing it for five minutes before she filled the sample container. Then she sealed it and filled out the paperwork to turn in with the sample.

"I need to run back over to Deshler. Will you be able to stay until I get back?" Anne asked.

Betty was manning the checkout desk. "Yes, I can stay. We have a couple of interlibrary requests from the Deshler Library. Could you pick them up while you're there?"

"I'll be happy to." Anne got the information, then made the trip back to Deshler. After dropping off the water sample with the county health department, she stopped at the library.

Kim Olivett, the Deshler librarian, was behind the counter. She looked up from the computer when Anne approached.

"May I help you? Oh, Anne. How nice to see you. How are things at the Blue Hill Library?"

"Hello, Kim. It's going well. I believe one of my staff called you. We have two interlibrary requests. I was in the area, so I thought I'd pick them up if they're ready."

"Yes. I have one of the books here. Let me check to see if we've found the other book. It may have been mis-shelved."

Anne glanced at her watch. "I'll step outside and make a phone call while you check." There was a bench just outside the front door. Anne went over to it and called Wendy.

"Hey, girl. What's up?" Wendy answered.

"I'm down in Deshler. Could you pick up Ben and Liddie for me?" asked Anne.

"Happy to. How long will you be? Shall I take them home with me?"

"I should get back to the library by the time you pick them up."

"Okay. I'll see you then."

Anne went back inside.

"I found it," Kim said, coming to the counter with a slim volume. "Someone put it on the wrong shelf."

"We have the same challenge. But it keeps us busy. Thanks for the books."

Anne reached home and had just gotten out of the car when Wendy pulled up. Ben and Liddie jumped out of the car and headed for the back door.

"Hi, Mom." Ben ran past her.

"Mommy!" Liddie gave her a hug, then ran on toward the door.

Anne shook her head, then went over to talk to Wendy. She leaned in through the open window. "Thanks for bringing them home."

"No problem. What have you been up to?"

"I took a sample of water to the health department. Then I had to stop at the Deshler library."

"Is something wrong with your water?"

"No. At least, I don't think so. But you never know."

"The city tests it all the time. But Chad put one of those under-the-sink filters in our kitchen. We just use it for drinking and making coffee and tea. I don't notice a big difference, but it didn't cost much. He could install one for you if you want."

"Thanks. I'll keep that in mind." She didn't tell Wendy about Stanley. Until she had proof, she didn't want to malign the man, although from what Alex said, he had tarnished his own reputation.

"When will you find out the test results?"

"I should have them by Thursday."

"That's fast. Let me know what you find out. See you later."

Wendy waved and drove off. Anne went inside to relieve Betty.

"Here are the books."

"Good. I'll call to let the patron know the books are in before I go home."

"Has it been busy?"

"Fairly. A couple of homeschool families came in and spent most of the afternoon here. I intended to shelve the books they returned, but I haven't had time." She indicated a large stack of books. "Then they checked out at least that many more."

"I'll take care of the shelving, Betty. Thank you for helping out."

"Always a pleasure." She got her purse and jacket and a copy of a new novel Anne had entered into the library inventory earlier that morning. Anne smiled. Anne read fast, but Betty was a voracious reader. And that was fine with Anne. She was happy to let the volunteers have the first look at the new books. It gave them a reward for helping out, and they loved recommending books to other patrons.

Anne checked on the children, then went down to the checkout desk. At the moment, only two patrons occupied the library. Anne went to the workroom to call Betty's neighbor, keeping the door open so she could see if anyone came to the desk looking for help.

"Hello, this is Anne Gibson, from the library. Is this Norma?"

"Yes it is," a gravelly-sounding voice responded.

"Your neighbor, Betty Bultman, gave me your name. She said you recently purchased a water filtration system. Could I ask you a few questions about your system?"

"Yes, but let me tell you, it isn't working right, and I can't get that man to come fix it. He won't return my phone calls."

"I'm sorry to hear that. Is his name Stanley?"

"Yes, that's him. I left him a message, threatening to report him to the Better Business Bureau, but he still hasn't called me back."

"What is wrong with the system?" Anne asked.

"It's supposed to take all the impurities out of my water. He told me it would help my arthritis and bursitis and keep me from getting pneumonia. I felt better for about a month, but then I got pneumonia and the doctor said now I have COPD. And my arthritis is worse." Norma's voice rose as she spoke, until she suddenly had a coughing fit. After a minute, she said, "I have to hang up. Can't stop coughing."

The line went dead.

Norma was not a happy customer. Anne had a feeling there were others around town with similar stories. Another good reason to find this Stanley.

* * *

Anne had planned to wait for the county report on her water test before she met with Stanley, but she hated the thought that he might take advantage of another unsuspecting resident of Blue Hill like he had Betty's neighbor. She took the small white business card out of her pocket and stared at it.

Was she right about Stanley? It appeared that he was cheating people, but was he actually breaking the law? Alex said he had a poor reputation with the local contractors, but what he did was unethical, not necessarily illegal. Ruby's son thought she'd been bilked. And Betty Bultman's neighbor was unhappy with her water filter. Stanley had worked with Vince. Had that given him access to the sewing machines? Was there any connection?

She punched his number into her cell phone and hit Send. It rang several times, then a deep voice instructed her to leave a message.

"Hi, I'm trying to reach Reliable Health Solutions. I spoke with Ruby—I can't remember her last name—but you installed a water filtration system for her and she was very impressed with it. I might want one. My water doesn't taste right. Please call me back." She left her name and number, then hung up.

There. She'd done it. Now she just had to wait.

What if he suspected? But how could he? He didn't even know her. What if he didn't call her back?

She set her cell phone on vibrate and put it in her pocket. For the next hour, she checked in the stack of books that had been returned, loaded them onto a rolling cart, then put them out on the shelves. She was almost finished when her phone began to vibrate. She stepped out to her desk and answered.

"Hello, this is Anne Gibson."

"This is Stanley Fulton, from Reliable Health Solutions. I'm returning your call."

The moment she'd been waiting for was here. Anne's heart raced, but she willed herself to be calm. "Oh yes. Thank you for calling me back. I'd like to talk to you about a water filter system. I understand that's what you do."

"I have water purifiers and filtration systems and air filter systems to remove contaminants from your home that cause allergies, viral and bacterial infections, and exposure to dangerous metals and chemicals. I can come by tomorrow and give you a free analysis of your water and air." He sounded confident and knowledgeable. It was easy for Anne to see how people might be taken in by his smooth phone presentation.

"That would be good. Can you make it around noon?"

"Let me check my calendar." There was a pause. "Yes, I should be able to do that. What is your address?"

She gave him the address, then said good-bye and disconnected the phone. Making sure she'd turned it off, she put it in her pocket. She couldn't wait. She wanted to expose Stanley Fulton if he was scamming people, but meeting him offered her what felt like her only chance to get some answers about Vince Parker too.

CHAPTER SIXTEEN

Bella was at the checkout counter with Anne when Stanley arrived at the library. He opened the front door, then stood in the doorway and stared, letting in a gust of cold air.

Bella looked up at him, then turned to Anne. "I wonder what he's doing here," she muttered.

"Who is he?" Anne asked.

"Stanley Fulton," she said under her breath. "He does not like to read."

"Oh." Anne looked at the hesitating young man. The sun was hitting him, outlining him, but obscuring his features. "You know him?"

"Yeah. He was a few years ahead of me in high school."

"Actually, he's here to see me." Anne went around the counter and approached him. His jeans and black sweatshirt looked clean. He had on a red, white, and blue baseball hat with the word *Phillies* on the front. Not professional, but presentable.

"Are you Stanley, with Reliable Health Solutions?"

He gave her a quizzical look. "Yeah. Are you Anne? Am I at the right place?"

"Yes. Come in."

"You didn't tell me this was a business. I don't do commercial work."

"Oh, it's not. It's a library. A nonprofit, you know. But it's also my home. Follow me."

"A-all right."

As they walked past the checkout counter, he did a double take. "Hey, Bella. How's it going?"

"Good, Stan. And you?"

"Great. Business is good."

Anne opened the door to the old kitchen. "In here. As you can see, this is a very old house."

He looked around. The kitchen had old cabinets and appliances and a table in the center of the room, which was covered with books and plastic covers and tape. She'd had the public rooms remodeled, but the kitchen showed the age of the house. The library used it as a general work area for the staff and occasional meetings.

"Here's the sink." She indicated a deep, chipped white porcelain sink with a tall faucet with two pipes coming up and across like a bridge with two knobs that looked like wheels with spokes. It joined together with a curved center spigot coming up and out over the sink. The discolored brass faucet had been top quality in its day.

"I've never seen anything that old," he said.

"I'm concerned there might be sediment or rust or other problems with the old plumbing and fixtures. My family drinks this water, but so do people coming into the library. Sometimes when we have a reception or a book club, refreshments are prepared or served from here, so I need to make sure it's safe."

She could almost hear the wheels in his mind turning as he looked around the kitchen. She would call it dated, but it was perfectly functional. Anne thought it had been remodeled in the 1950s, though the house was much older. To a young man, it must look ancient. She envisioned remodeling it someday, but that was way down her list of library projects.

"I can run a test, to see if the water is safe."

"Please do. I'd feel much better knowing."

"All right." He hitched up his jeans, then set a small metal toolbox on the counter and opened it. Inside, he had brochures and test kits in plastic bags. He took one out. It had a clear plastic cup and lid. He opened it, then held it under the faucet and turned on the cold water. It spurted out, splashing some water out of the cup. He shut it off quickly and popped the lid on, snapping it in place. Then he shook it and held it up to the light from the window over the sink.

"There. You see how cloudy it is?"

It looked almost murky. "I didn't realize how dirty it is. Is that rust?"

"Might be, but there are many possibilities. I can run some of the tests right here." He set the cup of water on the counter, then took a small black case out of his toolbox and set it on the counter. Inside was an electronic reader about the size of a cell phone and eight small plastic containers the size of pill bottles. He opened the electronic device and rinsed the top of it, then took an eyedropper and put some of the sample water from the jar into the top of it. He added a test strip from one of the white bottles and pushed a button. It took about twenty seconds and the machine displayed results. He wrote the results on a sheet of paper, then repeated the test with a different test strip. He repeated the test with a strip from each small container. By the time he finished, he had a page filled with names and numbers. He put away his equipment, then stood for a few moments, studying the piece of paper with the results.

"Whoa," he said, then let out a shrill whistle. "This is worse than I've ever seen. Your water is acidic. That's rare. You have high concentrations of bromine, calcium, iron, copper, ozone, permanganate, nitrate and nitrite, chromium hexavalent and cyanuric acid. I'll have to take the sample with me to test for coliform bacteria. That will take two days."

"That sounds bad."

"It's not good. I have a system that will filter out and neutralize all the particulates. It's not cheap, but compared to replacing all your plumbing, it's a bargain."

"How much will it cost?"

"You need the deluxe system, since you serve the public. I'll include a bid with my report."

"Well, I don't see that I have a choice. How soon could you install it?"

"It will take a few days to get the system. I keep my prices low by taking prepaid orders, so I'll need cash up front."

"Oh dear. I don't have that kind of cash. I get all of our funds through the estate trustee, so it will take me a few days. When you get the results of the organism test, send me a copy and I'll submit it."

"I don't think that's a good idea. I don't deal with trustees. I told you I don't do commercial business."

"I know. But this is my residence. I live upstairs. I'm sure there won't be any problem getting the funds to go ahead. After all, the health of the public is of utmost importance. We can't have people getting sick from the water here."

"All right. I'll bring you the report. Meanwhile, I recommend you buy bottled water."

"Yes, that's a good idea. I can make a copy of this report now," she said, whisking the paper up off the counter. She went out to the front and ran it through the copier. "There." She kept the original and returned the copy to him.

"It was so nice of you to come right over. I've been concerned. Did you grow up in Blue Hill? You know Bella Miller."

"Yes, I've lived here most of my life. I know a lot of people in town." He placed her sample in a plastic bag and wrote her name on the bag.

"I'm sure you do. I like doing business with local firms. I suppose you went to school with Vince Parker too, then? He used to do work for my aunt. This was her house."

He looked up at her. "I know Vince, but I was out of school when I met him."

"My aunt was very fond of him. You wouldn't happen to know where he moved to? We've lost track of him."

"Nope. 'Fraid I don't. I'd guess New York or some big city. He hated living in a small town. Said he couldn't wait to get out and see the world. But I do know someone who might know his whereabouts. I worked for a farmer outside of town. Vince worked for him too. He might know."

"Really? So you worked with Vince? What a small world." Anne crossed her arms and leaned back against the counter. "If you're a friend of Vince, that's all the recommendation I need."

"Yeah, me and Vince spent a lot of time together." Anne resisted the urge to correct his grammar, and he went on. "He was kind of like a younger brother to me. I watched out for him, you know? He planned to go into business with me, but he had to move. Family obligations."

"Maybe you can help me then; did you ever help Vince deliver a truckload of sewing machines to my aunt, who lived here?" Anne held her breath and watched Stanley for a reaction, hoping her question wouldn't scare him away.

"Sewing machines?" Stanley looked at her, then started packing up his test kit. "I don't remember any sewing machines."

She'd expected some reaction, but there was nothing. "They were still in boxes. They would have said Bernina on the boxes. Some of them went to the high school."

He shrugged. "I might have helped load them. We made lots of deliveries for old Abe. I never came here or delivered to the high school though."

Anne's antenna went up. "Who did you say? Old Abe. Who is that?"

"Abe? He was the old guy we worked for at the egg farm. We didn't make much. Not even minimum wage, but it was a job until I could get my business going."

"Abe Tandy?" Anne's mind was clicking. Abe, as in Able, as in A Able Surplus Sales? Was Abe, or Able, Tandy the man who sold sewing machines to Aunt Edie? Could he have been running a scam and pulled Vince and Stanley in? Anne quickly dismissed the notion, though the names seemed too close to be coincidental.

"Yeah. That was our boss. You know him?"

"I met him once." It seemed odd to Anne that Stanley didn't remember a delivery of twenty-four sewing machines. Unless he hadn't been involved. Or he had, and he was good at covering up his reactions. "I'd love to get in touch with Vince if you happen to find out where he is," Anne said.

"I'll keep my ears open."

Anne accompanied him to the door. "Thanks. And please hurry with your report on my water. I'm pretty worried about it."

Anne watched him walk down the sidewalk and get into a shiny black pickup truck.

"Are you going to buy something from Stan?" Bella asked when Anne went back to the counter.

"I don't know. Why?"

"I probably shouldn't say anything, but I don't think I'd trust him."

"Really? Why not? He seems nice."

"He never got caught, but rumors said he was mixed up in things that weren't right. Some of his friends even went to prison."

"I see. But he was never charged with a crime?"

"Well, no. But I don't want to see you get cheated."

"I'll be careful. I guess Stanley was pretty good friends with Vince Parker?"

She shrugged. "I think so, maybe."

"You don't happen to know where Vince and Miss Parker went when they moved, do you?"

She shook her head. "They just left. I think Vince left before school got out. I remember because he wasn't part of graduation. Then the day after school got out, Miss Parker was gone too."

* * *

"I don't have any more coats, Mommy." Liddie stood in front of Anne with hands on hips.

"Sweetheart, you've given lots of coats and warm clothing to the church donation box. You've given your own and gotten donations from friends and neighbors and people at school and even your grandparents. At some point, you've gathered all there are to collect."

"But Reverend Tom said we need to bring more."

"Yes, but he knows you've exhausted all your sources."

"I have money in my piggy bank. Can we go buy a coat?" Liddie's big, brown eyes held hope and expectation.

Reverend Tom had issued a challenge and given the church a goal to help with a mission. How could Anne refuse to let Liddie carry out her own mission to the very end? "Let's see how much you have."

"Okay. I'll go get it." Liddie ran to her room and returned with a brightly painted ceramic pig. Anne removed the plug on the bottom, and Liddie shook the coins out on the table. Anne recognized the two Sacagawea gold dollar coins she'd placed under Liddie's pillow for her first baby tooth. The rest were nickels, pennies, dimes, and quarters. Most of the money Liddie had earned for doing various chores around the house and yard.

"Help me count it, Mommy."

It took a while, with Anne helping Liddie figure out what coins she had and how much they were worth. Anne totaled the figures. "You have $7.46. That's impressive, Liddie. You've been saving for a long time."

"I was going to buy a bracelet kit, but I don't need it."

Anne remembered seeing the bracelet kit in the store with Liddie. It had beads and charms in every imaginable color. She could understand why Liddie wanted it.

"Are you sure you want to spend your money on a coat?"

"Please, Mommy? Can we go to the store?"

"Yes, we can go tomorrow after school. I'll find someone to work in the library, so I can leave. I need to run an errand in Deshler, anyway."

"Okay! Thank you, Mommy." Liddie hugged her around the neck. Anne gave her a sandwich bag for her coins and told her to put them in her purse until tomorrow. Liddie skipped to her room, singing a song.

Ben came out of his room and stood next to the table where she was working on a library order. "Mom?"

"Yes, Ben?" He looked worried.

"Do I have to spend my savings on a coat to donate?"

"No, honey. You don't have to donate another coat. You've already given a lot."

"But Liddie is giving up her money."

"God puts different things on each of our hearts. For Liddie right now, it's the coat mission. This has touched her in a deeply personal way. That doesn't mean you have to have the same mission."

"But how do you know when God is telling you to do something?"

Anne thought about it. That wasn't a simple question to answer. What had compelled her to move her children to Blue Hill to take on Aunt Edie's dream of opening a library? They could have stayed in New York. She could have found work there. And why did she feel so driven to find out what happened to Aunt Edie's sewing machines? "I think you feel an urging inside here," she said, putting her hand over her heart. "Something inside tells you it's the right thing to do. For Liddie, I think it started when she felt a strong compassion for her classmate who didn't have a coat."

"But when is it enough? I gave a coat and some other clothes and grandpa's coat. Is that enough?"

"You also helped your sister reach all the neighbors and the people who come into the library."

"Yeah. So, is it enough?"

"The truth is, Ben, we can never give enough. There will always be more need in the world. But we can't fix that either, no matter how much we try. Only God can do that. And for now, He does that by touching our hearts to make us want to help. Before we left New York, and when we first moved here, you helped me more than you'll ever know by watching out for your sister." She reached up and put her hand on his head, smoothing back his thick brown hair. "I'm proud of you, and your dad would be too. And you don't have to give another coat."

"Thanks, Mom." Ben gave her a hug, then went back to his room.

* * *

After Wendy arrived for her volunteer shift at the library, Anne felt confident it was well staffed for the afternoon. Wendy suggested that she watch Ben as well, so he didn't have to tag along on Liddie's shopping expedition. Anne helped Liddie fasten her seat belt in the backseat, and they set off for Deshler. They made their first stop at the County Health Department to pick up Anne's water report. As she'd expected, her water showed no signs of coliform bacteria. Chlorine levels were within the normal range, as were other metals and trace minerals. She tucked the report into the glove compartment, then took Liddie to the mall.

Finding a coat for $7.46 seemed an impossible task. Anne didn't want to pay the extra, though she could. This was Liddie's sacrifice, and Anne said a silent prayer that it would be enough. Liddie went through racks and racks of coats and jackets. They trudged through all the department stores. Anne was searching her mind for an alternative as they left a large department store. Right at the lower level entrance was a large table with closeout items. Piles of all kinds of merchandise were stacked on the table.

"Let's go through these and see if there's anything here," Anne said.

Liddie had to stand on tiptoe to reach the top of the table. She dug through a stack of towels. There, beneath the towels was a bracelet kit. She grabbed it and held it up. Anne saw it, and her heart dropped. The very thing Liddie had saved to buy. Just then, Anne spotted a fuzzy pink baby sleeper with covered feet and hands and a hood. It zipped up the front to go over lighter clothes. She looked at the price tag. $4.99. That seemed too good to be true. She'd seen similar buntings for $45.00. She examined it and found the reason for the lower price. The zipper was coming undone on one side, but it would be simple to repair. She found no other flaws. Liddie was staring at the bracelet kit. Anne saw her distress as she put the kit down and moved to look through another stack.

Anne held the baby bunting out to Liddie, whose eyes lit up when she saw it. She rushed over and grabbed it from Anne's hands.

"Oh, Mommy! Do I have enough money for this?"

"Yes, you do. With $2.47 left over."

Liddie's eyes grew big. She walked around the table to the bracelet kit. "How much is this, Mommy?"

Anne looked at the price. It was marked down to $1.99, probably because the box was crushed in on one side and a corner of the plastic had been taped. They couldn't sell it as new.

"Is that less than $2.47?"

"Yes it is. You have enough money to buy them both."

Liddie squealed with joy. She took both items and they went to find a sales register.

When it was their turn in line, Liddie put the two items on the counter and took out all her money.

The clerk rang up the sale. Anne began helping Liddie count out her coins, who proudly handed them to the woman at the cash register. She started to take it, and then stopped abruptly. "Wait! The bracelet kit is an additional fifty percent off." She retotaled Liddie's purchase and handed Liddie one of the Sacagawea dollars back, along with a few more small coins.

Liddie's windfall wasn't a grand miracle, but it was miraculous nonetheless.

Liddie beamed as she carried her prizes to the car.

They stopped on the way to pick up some take-out fried chicken, mashed potatoes and gravy, and biscuits. When they got back to the library, it was nearly dark out, but Wendy's kids and Ben were playing keep-away outside on the lawn under the back porch light. Anne took the sack of chicken dinner upstairs, then went downstairs to relieve Wendy. Liddie followed, carrying her shopping bag.

"Good timing. I need to get home and fix dinner," Wendy said.

"Thanks for all your help."

"You bet. Your intern is in the History Room. He seems to be pretty self-sufficient. I didn't have to tell him anything."

"I'm glad to hear that. He has his assignment."

"So" — Wendy turned to look at Liddie, who was waiting patiently, holding her shopping bag — "was your shopping trip a success?"

"Beyond our dreams," Anne said, looking at Liddie and winking.

"It was the best," Liddie said, lifting up her bag.

Anne told Wendy what had happened with Liddie's purchase.

"Wow. That's amazing," Wendy said. "Oh, and this came for you." She handed Anne an envelope. "It's from Stanley Fulton. He didn't want to leave it, but I promised him I'd give it to you, sealed." She gave Anne a look of curiosity, her eyebrows raised.

"Interesting." Anne smiled and put it under the counter in a safe place.

"You're not going to tell me about Stanley Fulton and the mysterious sealed envelope, I take it?" Wendy said in a hushed tone.

"I'll tell you all about it later," Anne said quietly, looking around to make sure they weren't overheard. Until she proved Stanley was guilty of fraud, she didn't want anyone—even Wendy—to find out what she was doing.

CHAPTER SEVENTEEN

A ll right." Wendy got her coat and purse. "I'll be waiting to hear this story, and I bet it'll a good one. But now I'll get my gang and go home."

"Thanks again for stepping in for me," Anne said. "I know you're busy, and I really do appreciate it."

Wendy brushed aside her thanks. "No problem. You know I'm happy to help out. I'll see you later."

Wendy went down to the back door.

"Mommy, can we go eat dinner now?" Liddie asked.

"In a few minutes. You can go upstairs. I need to talk to Jason, my intern, and let him know where I'm going first."

Liddie carried her bag to the stairs and went up. Anne went into the History Room, where Jason had a book open in front of him at a table, writing information in his notebook. Anne went over and sat next to him.

"Good evening, Jason. How are you doing?"

Jason looked up, startled. "Hi, Mrs. Gibson. I was just adding this book to my list, but it looks like one I want to read. Can I check it out to take home?"

"Absolutely. If you can take a break from going through the shelves, could you watch the checkout desk for me for a little while? I'd like to go upstairs and have dinner with my children."

He closed the book and his notebook and stood. "I'll do it right now."

"Thank you. Did you bring something with you for dinner?"

"Yes. My mom sent me something to heat in the microwave. Is that all right?"

"Yes, that's fine. You're welcome to use the refrigerator too. Just put your name on anything you leave here. I won't take too long, so you can have your dinner when I get back downstairs."

"No hurry." Jason went behind the counter and sat on a stool. "I'll just check out my book while I'm here."

Liddie had left her shopping bag in the living room. She was in the kitchen, setting the table. Anne took out their food and put the mashed potatoes and gravy in a bowl and put them in the microwave to reheat.

"Thank you, sweetheart. Would you go call your brother to dinner?"

"Sure, Mommy." Liddie went upstairs and pounded on his bedroom door. A minute later they both came running down.

They sat at the table, and Anne said a blessing before they dug in.

"I saw your bag in the living room, Liddie. What did you get?" Ben asked.

"Can I show him, Mommy?"

"Not until you finish eating and wash your hands."

Liddie licked her fingers. They were greasy from eating a chicken drumstick. She giggled. "Okay." She gobbled down her chicken, then got up. "All done," she announced. She washed her hands, then retrieved her bag, which she carried to the table.

Liddie pulled out the pink bunting and the bracelet kit, which she proudly displayed.

"Way cool! Did Mom buy you that?"

"No, silly. I bought it with my own money."

"No way!"

"Way!"

"They were on sale," Anne said. "Wasn't that amazing? Liddie even ended up with a dollar left over. God provided in a really amazing way."

Ben looked closely at the box. He looked up at his mother. She winked at him.

"I'll say. You did good, Liddie. You're a super shopper."

Liddie beamed at her brother's praise.

"Want to know what I did?" Ben asked.

Anne raised her eyebrows. "Yes. What did you do?"

"Mrs. Pyle made copies of our coat drive fliers, and we went downtown and put a bunch up in the stores. Maybe we'll get some more coats for Sunday."

"Good for you." Anne hoped they got a few, but there were only two more days left to collect them.

"Can you help me make a bracelet tonight, Mommy?"

"Not tonight. I have to go back down to the library. It's Thursday night. We're open until eight."

"Oh yeah, I forgot."

"I've got math homework," Ben said. He carried his plate to the kitchen, scraped the bones into the trash, rinsed his dish and put it into the dishwasher.

"Do you have homework too, Liddie?"

"Miss Reed gave us a page to practice doing numbers. Can you help me?"

"Why don't you give it a try on your own? Then I'll check it before you go to bed."

"Okay." Liddie took her dish to the kitchen and did as her big brother had done. Anne was grateful that Ben was being such a good example for his sister. It helped her a lot.

"All right. I'll see you later. At eight, get ready for bed."

"Okay Mommy." Liddie took her bag and disappeared up the stairs to her room.

Anne put away the food, then went back down to the library. She sent Jason to the kitchen to eat his dinner as she sat behind the counter. There were a few people in the various rooms, but the library wasn't very busy. Anne was tempted to open the envelope from Stanley, but she resisted. She would wait until later when she was alone.

The evening seemed to drag. Finally, it was time to close. Jason's mother came to get him, but she waited outside in the car. He was the last one to leave the library.

"I'll see you next Thursday, Mrs. Gibson."

"Good night, Jason. Thanks for helping out tonight. Have a good week."

"I will."

Anne waited until he got into the car, then she shut off the outside lights and locked the library door.

Anne retrieved Stanley's letter, then went through the library, shutting off lights. It was almost eight thirty when she set the envelope in the living room, then went upstairs to say good night to the children.

She entered Liddie's room first. Liddie was curled up on her bed, clutching Raggedy Ann, sound asleep. Anne gently pulled the bedspread out from under her, then covered her up. Liddie sighed but didn't wake up. Anne smiled down on her precious daughter, then leaned over and kissed her cheek. Liddie had had a busy day. Shopping was hard work. Not to mention, running a coat drive was hard work for an adult, let alone a five-year-old. Liddie was exhausted.

Anne looked at the page of numbers Liddie had copied. She'd done a pretty good job. *Sweet dreams, baby girl*, Anne thought as she turned out the light and softly closed the door.

Ben was sitting on his bed in his pajamas, reading, when Anne opened his door and looked in.

"Time to turn the lights out."

"Okay, Mom. I'm almost to the end of the chapter."

He cast a pleading glance her way, and she nodded. "Okay. Just to the end of the chapter. Did you help Liddie with her numbers tonight?"

He glanced up from the book and shook his head. "No. She insisted she could do them by herself."

"She did a fine job too. Did you finish your homework?"

"Yeah."

"Good," Anne said. "Can I see your homework before you finish your chapter?"

"Here it is." He handed her his math workbook.

"Brush your teeth while I look it over. You can read to the end of your chapter when you're done." She started looking through his calculations while he went to the bathroom. She heard the water running. He was back before she finished.

"You did well. I see one mistake." She showed him an error in a fraction.

"Duh," he chastised himself. He bent over the page as he erased his answer and reworked the problem.

"Yes, that's better," Anne encouraged him.

She sat on the side of the bed while he said his prayers. Then she kissed him good night and shut the door, leaving the soft glow of his bedside lamp to peek into the hallway.

Anne made a cup of herbal tea and carried it to the living room. She sat down and picked up Stanley Fulton's report.

She had to admit, it looked professional. A sealed nine-by-six manila envelope with a printed label held the report. She opened it and removed two pieces of paper. One had a printed report of her water sample. Besides the list he'd compiled using the test strips in the library kitchen, showing high percentages of the various contaminants, the report listed the presence of coliform bacteria. The second sheet was a bid for a whole-house filtration system with ultraviolet light to kill bacteria and other filters to get rid of metals and chemicals. The cost was five thousand dollars cash up front, less a discount of 10 percent. Anne nearly choked. She'd searched for filtration systems on the Internet, and she knew she could get an ultraviolet system installed for less than half that amount.

Price gouging aside, the water contaminant report was false. Had Stanley put something inside the cup before he took her water sample? She'd watched him test it, right in front of her. She needed to compare it to the county test, but she'd left it in the car. It could wait until morning.

* * *

Anne sat outside the elementary school after dropping off Liddie and Ben on Friday morning. She had forty-five minutes until the library opened. She debated what to do. Stanley Fulton's water report, compared to the county report, was concrete proof of fraud. She hadn't found proof that he'd been involved in the disappearance of twelve sewing machines, and she still hadn't found Vince or Victoria Parker, but she felt certain she had enough evidence to stop Stanley's scams. She took out her cell phone and called her friends Jennifer and Michael Banks.

Jen answered. "Anne, how are you? What's up so early in the morning?"

"Hi, Jennifer. I'm sorry to call this early. Is Michael still at home?"

"He just dropped the kids off at school for me. Is something wrong?"

"Sort of. I need to talk to him about a legal matter."

"He always goes over to Coffee Joe's before work. You can catch him there if you hurry."

"Thanks. I'll try that."

Anne hung up, then drove away. The coffee shop was only a few blocks from the school, right across the street from the police station. She parked and went inside. The strong aroma of coffee and the sugary smell of fresh sweet rolls greeted her. Michael Banks sat with three other policemen, drinking coffee and eating donuts. Anne looked around to make sure there wasn't anyone she knew there—especially Stanley Fulton. Reassured, she went up to the group, instantly drawing their attention.

"Hey, Anne." Michael stood. "What's up?"

"Can I talk to you for a minute?"

"Sure." He picked up his coffee and donut and followed her to a table in the back corner. "Can I get you something?" he asked.

"No, thanks. You go ahead though."

"So what's the problem? You and the kids all right?"

"Yes, we're fine. Michael, I think I've uncovered a scam that takes money under false pretenses from some local residents. I know of at least two for sure. And I have proof here." She took the two envelopes out of her purse. One from the county and one from Stanley.

"Here's how it works. Stanley Fulton goes into a home and runs a water sample. It comes back full of contaminants and even bacteria. Then he sells the unsuspecting homeowner an expensive water filtration system. Evidently he does the same with air filtration, but I can only prove the water. I took a sample of water from the library kitchen to the county. Then he came in and tested my water. Here are the two samples."

Michael looked over the two reports. "Whoa. Big difference. Same water source? Sure looks like a scam." He peered at her. "You haven't given him any money?"

"Not yet. But there is one woman at the retirement center who bought air and water filters from him, and the mayor's neighbor is very unhappy with a system she bought."

"I think the chief should see this. But we need to catch our crook in the act of selling a system. Can you carry it through?"

"You mean, give him money?"

"Yes. The chief will make the arrangements. And you'll have backup. I'll request to be part of it. Can you take these over to the precinct to show the chief?"

"I suppose so, but I don't want to be seen. I'm sure Stanley will show up sometime today wanting to close the deal."

"I can run them over, if you don't mind letting me take them. It'll take a few minutes."

"I need to go open the library. Can I meet you back here in a half hour? Do you know who Stanley is?"

"Sure do. He has managed to skirt the law for years but just barely. It'll be nice to catch him in the act. I'll meet you here in half an hour. I'll make sure he isn't around when I come back over."

"Thanks, Michael."

Anne drove up the hill to the library. She got there ten minutes before time to open.

The waiting made Anne edgy. When would Stanley call her? Or would he just show up? Or did he expect her to call him?

When the library phone rang, she jumped. "Blue Hill Library. Anne speaking. How may I help you?"

"Anne, it's Remi." Anne heard a raspy fit of coughing. "Sorry. I'm sick. Bella is coming in to take my place, but she'll be late."

"How late?"

"She has a test this morning, so it will be about ten. I hope that's all right."

"Yes, that's fine. Thanks for calling. I hope you feel better soon."

"Thanks. Me too."

Anne was supposed to meet Michael in fifteen minutes. She picked up the phone and called Wendy.

"Hello?"

"Wendy, it's Anne. Any chance you could fill in for me for an hour? Bella will be in by then. I've got some errands to run this morning, and they're important."

"I've got the twins. They'll be all right though. I'll set them up with an art project. I'll be right over."

Anne didn't know what kind of art project Wendy had in mind, but her ideas could get messy. She hoped it wasn't anything too wild. She was relieved, ten minutes later, when Wendy arrived and set her four-year-old twins up at the old kitchen table with coloring books that used paint brushes and water to reveal their pictures.

"So what's going on this morning?" Wendy asked.

"I'll fill you in later. Okay?"

"*Ooh!* More mystery. Now you really have my curiosity up. If I'm gone, you call me. Promise?"

"I promise."

Anne parked behind Coffee Joe's and went in through the back door. Several tables were filled with people drinking coffee and eating. She didn't see Michael, and she didn't want to chance seeing Stanley, so she took a back table and sat with her back to the front door. The rich scent of bacon and fried eggs made Anne's stomach growl, but she wasn't there to eat.

"Good morning. Can I get you a cup of coffee?"

The waitress startled Anne, coming up behind her. The woman was middle-aged and had an apron on over jeans and a long-sleeved tee shirt. Anne didn't know her name, but she remembered seeing her working at the coffee shop for a long time.

"Yes, I'd like a cup of coffee. Thanks. You've worked here a long time, haven't you?"

"Eight years."

"Did you by chance know Edie Summers?" Anne asked.

"Sure did. She came in at least once or twice a week. Always had a smile and a word of encouragement."

"Yes, she was like that. I'm her niece, Anne."

"I know. You're the one who opened the library in Edie's old house. Nice to meet you, Anne. I'm sorry for your loss. I miss her too. She was a nice lady."

"Thanks. Do you remember seeing her in here with a man maybe twenty months ago? He was wearing coveralls, like a farmer."

"Yeah. Once. She had coffee with Able Tandy. He used to come in once in a while. Haven't seen him in ages. I remember 'cause Edie usually came in with Mildred Farley. It surprised me, and I wondered if Edie had got herself a boyfriend. There weren't too many eligible men around here that were near her age. I think he was a few years younger. But I only saw them together the one time, so I guess not."

"Able Tandy?"

"Yeah. He's got a place outside of town somewhere. So were they more than friends?"

Anne must have given her a startled look, as the waitress said, "Sorry. Don't mean to be nosy. I was just curious. I liked your aunt."

"That's all right. You know, I think I'd like a crumb donut with my coffee."

"Sure. I'll get it for you." The waitress hurried away.

Perhaps Aunt Edie met with Able to talk about getting sewing machines. He must be the man Reverend Tom saw with her aunt.

Anne's order came just as Michael entered the cafe. He spotted her and came to join her. When he sat down across from her, Anne forgot about Aunt Edie and Able Tandy as she realized she was about to get involved in a sting operation.

"Here are your papers," Michael said. "The chief made copies, but he'll need the originals when this is over. Anne, this is a big deal. We've had complaints about Stanley Fulton, but no proof of actual fraud. This is it. Here's what you need to do if you're willing. Set up a time to meet Stanley somewhere public today and let us know when. At the bank would be ideal. We'll be there waiting, but we'll stay out of sight. We'll get the money to you. When you hand it to him, we'll step in and arrest him. You won't be in any danger, I promise."

"I'm not worried about that. He'd be stupid to carry any kind of weapon and I don't think he's stupid."

"Can you do this?"

"I think so. I need to talk to Eldon Martin, the bank president. He's on the library board. I can imagine what he'd think of me handing someone that kind of cash."

"The chief will make sure he's okay with this. In fact, Eldon would be the perfect one to give you the cash."

"All right. I'll do it. Today, I hope."

"I'll be there. Don't worry."

"I won't. But there's one more thing."

"Sure. What's that?"

"Stanley might be involved or know something about twelve missing sewing machines that my aunt purchased. She bought twenty-four. I believe that I found twelve, which she may have donated anonymously to the high school. The rest are missing. Vince Parker was involved in delivering the twelve to the high school, and he worked with Stanley."

"I remember Vince. He got into trouble with a stolen bike. He claimed he didn't steal it, but he was convicted of possession of stolen property and did community service. The kid had problems, but I liked him. He had potential. Wouldn't surprise me if Stanley got him mixed up in trouble though. I'll question Stanley myself."

CHAPTER EIGHTEEN

When Anne got back to the library, Bella was there and Wendy had gone home.

"Mrs. Pyle left you a note," Bella said, handing her a folded piece of paper.

"Thanks." Anne took the paper and went upstairs to her living quarters where she could have privacy.

Anne unfolded Wendy's note.

You had a call from Stanley Fulton. Remember, you're going to tell me about him. Call me. Wendy.

Wendy and her curiosity would have to wait. Anne used her cell phone to call Stanley back. She got a recorded message and left her phone number. She puttered in the kitchen for a few minutes, hoping he would call right back. When he didn't call in fifteen minutes, she started downstairs. She'd reached the second floor landing when her phone rang. She stopped and answered it.

"Hello?"

"Anne Gibson?"

"This is Anne." She recognized the voice and started back up the stairs.

"Stanley Fulton. Did you get my report and estimate?"

"Yes, I did. Are you certain my water contains coliform bacteria?"

"Positive. I can bring the test culture if you want to see it."

"No, I believe you. It's just a shock. How soon can you install the filtration system?" she asked.

"Like I told you, it will take a few days after I order the system. I can order it as soon as I have your payment."

"I can get it today. Can you meet me at the bank?"

"I'd rather not. Is there somewhere else?"

She'd expected his resistance. "I have to go to the bank to get the money. I don't keep that kind of cash around. Then I have an appointment downtown, so that's the best place. I don't want to be carrying that much cash."

She heard a sound somewhere between a grunt and a sigh. Was he going to turn her down? Where else could she meet him? Anne mentally crossed her fingers. She couldn't imagine him opting to meet her where the police hung out or on the street in plain sight of anyone who might be passing by.

"All right. I guess I can meet you at the bank. What time? I may need to rearrange my schedule."

"Can you meet me about one o'clock? I'll make sure the funds are ready."

"One o'clock. That'll work."

Anne let out her breath and hoped he didn't hear her relief. "Good. I'll see you then."

Anne's hand was shaking by the time she disconnected the call. She held it up in front of her and wondered at her reaction. She felt no fear. Anger, perhaps, at Stanley's audacity and lies?

Adrenaline at her own fibs to catch him in the act? She needed to calm down before she faced him in the bank, or he would know something was wrong.

* * *

Anne pulled up in front of the gray granite bank building. Anne loved the old building with the wide steps and stone pillars across the front. A polished stone by the entrance had the date 1892, built four years before Aunt Edie's house. She looked around. No police cars, and she didn't see Stanley's pickup truck. She went inside.

She could see Eldon Martin at his desk through the glass window that looked out at the bank foyer and teller cages. She approached his office. Seeing her, the distinguished man stood and motioned her inside.

"Hello, Anne. How are you?"

"Very nervous," she said.

"So am I, and I'm not the one confronting our suspect. I've never done this before," he said, indicating she should sit down.

"Neither have I." She sat down, then held up her hand. It trembled slightly.

"You look composed. Don't worry, you'll do fine," he said. "And it looks like our suspect has just entered the bank."

Anne turned to look over her shoulder. Stanley was standing in the foyer, scowling as he looked around, his arms crossed. Obviously, he was not happy to be there. "So what shall I do? Do I take the money out to him?"

"That's the instruction I received. Personally, I'd make him try to cash a check, but that might scare him off."

"That's true. He told me it has to be cash."

The bank president opened a drawer in his desk and took out a stack of bills. "Here is the cash. By accepting it, he is liable."

"Can we put it in an envelope? That way he has to take it and open it."

"Good idea." Eldon took an envelope with the bank logo and put the money inside, then handed it to Anne. "Are you all right? Do you want me to go out with you?"

"No. Better not. That might make him more nervous. I'll wave for you if I need you. Thanks." She stood. "Well, here goes."

Stanley watched her walk out of the office and approach him. His scrutiny made her nervous. What if he sensed a trap? She could feel her hand shaking, and she willed it to stop as she took a deep breath.

"I was about to leave. I wondered if you'd changed your mind," he said.

"Oh no. I told you I had to get the money from the library's banker." Oops. She'd actually called him the trustee, but she hoped Stanley wouldn't notice the difference. She held up the envelope. "Here it is. I hope there is still time for you to order the filtration system today, so it can go in next week."

"There's time."

She placed the envelope in his outstretched hand. He took it, frowned, then opened the envelope and looked inside. She saw the relief on his face. "I need a receipt," she said.

"I didn't bring one with me. I'll bring it when I install the system," he said, still staring at the money.

She glanced sideways, trying to see if the police were there. She didn't see anyone in uniform. "Do you want to count it?" she asked, stalling for time.

"No. I trust you," he said, looking up at her. Just then Michael and another police officer stepped up behind Stanley. He didn't even see them coming. Anne stepped aside.

"Stanley Fulton, you are under arrest for fraud."

"What—" Stanley tried to jerk around, but Michael had his arms and clapped handcuffs on his wrists.

"You've made a big mistake. I was just conducting business with the librarian here. Tell them," he said, looking at Anne.

Anne raised her eyebrows but didn't say anything. In the aftermath, her adrenaline had crashed, leaving her feeling even shakier. Her mouth was dry. Stanley's last words stuck in her mind. *"I trust you."* Ouch. She couldn't remember a time when she'd betrayed someone's trust. But Stanley had intended to cheat her and had cheated others, she reminded herself.

As the other officer led a protesting Stanley away, Michael turned to Anne. "Are you all right?"

"Yes. I'm glad that's over."

"Not quite. We need you to come file a complaint. Do you want to walk with me to the station?"

"Sure. Let's get this over with. Do I have to face Stanley?"

"Not today, but you'll have to testify at his trial, unless he confesses. We're looking for others that he's swindled. That might convince him not to protest too much."

"Don't forget to ask him about Aunt Edie's sewing machines and Vince Parker. He told me he didn't remember any sewing machines, but he might give you a different answer."

"I won't. Edie was a special lady. I'd love to help you find them."

* * *

"I wanted to give you an update," Michael told Anne on the phone two hours later. "We've finished interrogating Stanley. He wasn't exactly cooperative, but he caved when we confronted him with three formal complaints. The mayor's neighbor was happy to give us a complaint, and the woman from the retirement center agreed to press charges when she heard about your experience. In light of your evidence, he confessed."

"That's wonderful. Any chance of restitution for the people he cheated?"

"Depends on whether or not he has any assets and what the judge imposes as a sentence. We hope to find out if he had more victims."

"I'll help any way I can."

"You've already been a big help and stopped him from cheating anyone else. I asked him if he helped Vince steal your aunt's sewing machines or if they swindled her out of her money for nonexistent machines. He insists he didn't steal any sewing machines or run a scam involving sewing machines. He remembered loading them all into Able Tandy's pickup truck. For what it's worth, I believe him. I asked him if he thought Vince had done it on his own. He laughed at that idea. He said Vince didn't have the smarts to run a scam. I'm sorry I couldn't find out more for you."

"That's all right. Thanks for asking, Michael. I appreciate it."

A call was coming in as she said good-bye. It was Wendy. "So I heard you caught Stanley Fulton trying to scam the library."

"Yes. I'm afraid I set him up." Anne explained the way Stanley gave people false reports on their water, then sold them water filters and air filters at inflated prices.

"So that's what his letter and call was about. You knew all along and you scammed the scammer. That's priceless. I'd heard rumors about him, that he wasn't very reliable, but what he did was despicable."

"I suspected after hearing about a woman he'd conned. Then Alex told me he didn't have a good reputation. Well, now he won't swindle anyone for a long time. Hopefully, he'll reform."

"That's a big hope."

"Yes." Anne let out a sigh. "I had hoped to connect Stanley to Vince and to Aunt Edie's missing sewing machines. Evidently, there's no connection. Stanley claimed he's innocent of involvement with the missing sewing machines, and he said Vince couldn't do it on his own."

"That's true. Remember, he got caught with a stolen bike, and he claimed he didn't steal it."

"He might have lied," Anne said.

"Even if he did tell the truth, it didn't help him. But Chad liked him. He believed Vince had real potential."

"What if his sister was the one who cooked up the scheme to take the missing machines?" Anne said.

"You don't really believe that, do you? If so, she fooled everyone," Wendy said. "Besides, you trust Edie's instincts."

"Yes, I do." Aunt Edie had trusted Victoria and Vince. From what she'd discovered about Victoria, she had a generous, caring heart. Her students loved her. She'd volunteered at church and in the community. Edie would have recognized her compassionate spirit, because they shared that trait. Anne had a hard time imagining the brother and sister stealing twelve sewing machines from her aunt. But who else had access to the machines? No one as far as she'd discovered. She still needed to talk to Able Tandy, now that she knew he had sold Aunt Edie the machines.

"I want to know what happened to all those beautiful Berninas," Anne said. "I can see one of them in my sewing room."

Wendy laughed. "If you find them, save one for me."

"Could you do me a favor and pick up Ben and Liddie for me today?"

"Sure. Do you want me to drop them off at home or take them to my house?"

"They'll be all right at home. Bella is here at the library. I'll ask her to keep an eye out for them. I won't be gone long. I discovered who A Able Surplus Sales is. I want to go talk to him."

"Cool. I hope you find the sewing machines. Just don't let him talk you into some crazy purchase."

Anne laughed. "I won't. I'm getting good at resisting a smooth salesman."

Chapter Nineteen

After talking to Bella, Anne made another trip out to Tandy's farm. The tan car wasn't there. She pulled up near the house and got out. She went up to the side door and knocked, and waited. No one came to the door. She tried again, knocking louder. Still no one.

Anne stood on the small porch and looked around. She could see the tail end of the pickup truck parked in between the barn and the shop, so she walked back to the shop and knocked on the door. She listened. No sound of a motor or machinery today. She opened the door and looked inside. The lights were on, but she couldn't see anyone. Then she heard a rooster crow.

The sound seemed to come from behind the barn. The space between the buildings was barely wide enough to park the truck. Being careful not to rub up against the dirty vehicle, she made her way past it. Now she heard clucking sounds and the rooster crowed again. At the rear of the buildings, she spotted a chicken pen, enclosed in chicken wire. Mr. Tandy was standing in the middle of the enclosure, raking up debris. The chickens cackled at him and the rooster paced back and forth along a board on top of the fence, agitated by the intruder in his space. Anne approached the fence. The rooster started flapping his wings and moving toward her. Mr. Tandy looked up and saw her. He raised his rake and took a swing at the rooster, missing it but scaring it away. It retreated to the other end of the fence, where it stood glaring at them.

"Sorry about that. I didn't hear you coming," he said.

"I knocked at the house and on the shop, but no one answered. Then I heard your feathered friend back here and thought I'd investigate. I don't know if you remember me. Anne Gibson, from the library."

"'Course I remember you," he said, taking off his straw hat. "What can I do you for?" He chuckled at his own wit. "Did you decide to buy that Selectric typewriter after all?"

"No sir. I have an entire attic filled with stuff I need to go through. I don't need to add to it."

He grinned. "A collector, eh? We have that in common. All right then. Do you have a family, Ms. Gibson?"

"Yes. I have two children." She didn't tell him she wasn't the collector. Most of it had belonged to her aunt.

"All right then, would you like some fresh eggs?"

"I thought... Well, your daughter told me you aren't selling eggs anymore."

"Ain't selling them. I don't have that many chickens left, but I got more eggs than she and I can eat. Besides, the doc says they aren't good for my arteries, though I think that's a bunch of baloney." He chuckled again.

"If you have eggs going to waste, I'd love to have some."

"Good. I'll gather a basketful for you. You might want to wait in the shop. Ol' Rusty there is going to object to my interference with his brood. He can get nasty."

Anne chuckled. "Yes sir. I wouldn't want to get Rusty's feathers ruffled."

"Yup." He smiled and winked at her. "You've got it."

Anne walked back to the shop and went inside. She took the time, while she waited, to look around. The stuff piled everywhere had looked like junk before. He'd said he was a collector. He'd told her he bought and sold stuff. But it had been over a year since he'd had an injury that made him stop. She saw a blender in its original box, which was dusty and torn in one corner. There were boxes of tools and small kitchen appliances and vintage toys. And signs. Gas station signs. Motor oil signs. An old drugstore sign. A red-and-white-striped barber pole. Several bicycles. Had he bought all of this? Could any of it be stolen? Vince had been caught with a stolen bicycle, but he'd refused to say where he got it. Had it come from this collection of stuff? Maybe Able didn't steal. Maybe he picked up things he thought nobody owned. Or maybe he had a psychological problem. Maybe he was a kleptomaniac. No, Anne thought. A collector. Perhaps a hoarder. But that was it.

The door opened and Mr. Tandy came inside. He had a small basket filled with eggs.

"There you are," he said. "You can take the basket and return it later. Bring a container and I'll give you some more. Now you didn't come out here to get eggs. What can I do for you?"

"There is one thing I need. I didn't think to ask you before. Are you familiar with a company called A Able Surplus Sales?" Anne asked.

Mr. Tandy chuckled. "You might say that."

Good. At least he wasn't going to deny it. "Do you know if they are still around?"

"Not no more. Forced out of business by circumstances." The man grinned at her as if he was enjoying a private joke. "The A stands for Andrew. And if I'd ever been in the phone book, I'd be the first business listing. Andrew Able Tandy, at your service, ma'am." He took a bow. "I never opened a store or incorporated, but I bought and sold just about anything you could imagine. Anything legal, that is."

At least he claimed to run a legal business, Anne thought. "That's great. I've been looking for you."

"Have you? Did you see one of my old ads? I bet you're wanting to sell some of those treasures you've collected in your attic. I wish I could help you, but I don't do business anymore. There's an auction house in Deshler that I'd recommend. They won't try to cheat you."

"I'll remember that for the future, but I'm not ready to part with anything just yet. Do you remember doing business with my great-aunt, Edie Summers? She purchased two dozen Bernina sewing machines from you. Does that ring a bell?"

"Of course I remember her," he said, as if affronted that she would question his memory. "So you're Edie's niece. Nice lady. Paid me in cash and didn't even quibble at the price. Of course I got her a super deal. Took me a long time to put that sale together."

"How did you get so many of the same machine?"

"Found a closeout at a surplus store, believe it or not. Vinny must have told his sister, because she and Miss Summers came out to see them." I got a good price on them, and I was able to sell 'em at a good price too. My equipment sales kept the farm afloat. Takes a good job to keep a farm running, you know. Selling eggs and hay don't pay the bills. Besides, it kept me busy in the off seasons."

"Do you know what my aunt did with all those machines?"

"Nope. None of my business."

"But did she get all twenty-four machines?"

"Sure did. Vinny and Stan loaded them into the back of my pickup truck and delivered them."

"Stanley helped deliver them?" Had Stanley lied to her and to Michael? Maybe he was the one who took the missing machines. With his glib tongue, who knew what story he might have concocted for Aunt Edie. If he even met her. What was truth and what were lies?

"Yeah...Well, wait. No. I don't believe he did. Can't say for sure, but I think Vinny wanted to do it by himself. Besides, those machines filled up the back and the passenger seat too."

"Well, thank you for the information. I appreciate it."

"No problem. If you hear of anyone who wants to buy a shop full of merchandise, send them my way. It's time for me to get rid of this stuff."

Anne suspected the items collecting dust in his shop would still be there after he was gone, but she didn't tell him that. She liked the man. She imagined Aunt Edie had enjoyed dealing with him. He was a trader and she imagined he loved to haggle for a great deal, but he didn't strike her as a swindler.

The picture she was forming of Vince was filled with contradictions. Troubled. Angry. Chip on his shoulder. Dependable. Hard worker. Thief. Good kid. Just who was he? And the picture of Victoria seemed totally at odds with someone who could steal from Edie Summers. Every other lead turned up empty. Where in the world were the twelve missing sewing machines? They had to be somewhere.

* * *

"Mommy, can I make a bracelet tonight?" Liddie asked. "I want to put one in the donation box, so some little girl can wear it with her coat."

Anne knew Liddie could hardly stand having the jewelry kit she'd been saving for and not be able to use it yet. Patience was not her strong suit. "I'll help you make one after dinner, all right?"

"Yes." Liddie pumped her hand in the air, like she'd seen Ben and Ryan do.

"Now, what shall we have for dinner?"

"Pizza," Ben said.

"*Hmm.* I think we can manage that." Anne took English muffins out of the freezer and got out a jar of spaghetti sauce. She opened a can of sliced black olives and took out cheese, hot dogs and pepperoni. "You get to make your own."

Liddie spread sauce on her muffin and topped it with cheese. Ben did the same, making two and adding olives and pepperoni and a sliced-up hot dog. Anne fixed a couple of minipizzas for herself, then placed them all on a cookie sheet and put them in the oven to bake. While they cooked, Anne made a Caesar salad to go with them.

As they ate, Ben seemed quieter than usual. His appetite was good though. When he finished his two English muffin pizzas, he made two more for himself and one more for Liddie. Anne caught him watching her with a serious expression a couple of times.

After dinner, when Ben started working on his math homework, Liddie brought out her new jewelry kit.

"Can you help me make a bracelet now, Mommy?"

"Sure. Let's see what you have." The top of the box showed examples of four bracelets. "Which one do you want to make?"

"I like that one." She pointed to one of the middle bracelets. She took the lid off the box and pulled out two square looms with colored slots and various colors of embroidery floss and beads.

Anne opened the directions. At first it looked complicated, but she read it out loud and helped Liddie with each step. Liddie chose pink and purple. The center strings were yellow. They cut the strings to the proper lengths and tied them together and arranged them on the loom. Anne read the directions on how to reposition the strings. Liddie moved the strings as instructed. Before tying the middle strings each time, Anne helped Liddie add beads. After turning the loom and moving the strings six times, they turned the loom over to see the results. A woven band appeared, about a half inch wide, with pink and purple stripes.

"Cool," Liddie said. "I can do it by myself now."

"Okay. I'll watch."

Liddie worked slowly but deliberately through the repetitious steps, and the bracelet grew. A couple of times, Anne had to help, but Liddie managed to complete the band. When it was long enough, Anne helped her tie the end and cut the tassel.

Triumphant, Liddie held up the finished bracelet. "Put it on me, please," she said, holding out her hand.

Anne secured it around her wrist through the double-knotted end of the bracelet. Liddie held up her hand and grinned. "It's beautiful. Can I wear it to bed?"

"I suppose so. But be careful with it if you're going to donate it. Now it's time to put on your pajamas."

"Okay!" Liddie ran to her room, leaving behind a mess all over the table.

Anne sighed. She should have mentioned putting the jewelry kit away first, but it was already later than usual. She put the loom and beads and floss back in the box, then went to check on Ben.

"How's the homework going?" Anne sat on the side of Ben's bed and watched him.

"Good. Mom?"

"Yes?"

"I heard you caught a bad guy at the bank today." He stared at her with deep concern on his face.

"Where did you hear that?"

"I just heard a couple of people talking. They didn't know I was listening. Did you?"

"Not exactly, honey. Officer Banks and another officer arrested a man who was trying to cheat people out of their money. I was there. I had found out this man cheated several people. One was a woman who is a friend of Alex's uncle. I met her when I went with Alex to the retirement home. Remember?"

"Yeah. So what did you do?"

"I pretended I was going to buy something from him, and I handed him an envelope full of money. When he accepted it, Officer Banks arrested him."

"Oh. He wasn't robbing the bank?"

"No." Anne was alarmed that a rumor like that had started. "Is that what you heard?"

Ben looked embarrassed. "Not exactly. But I thought..." He looked at his mother with such concern and relief, she thought he might start crying.

"Honey, I would never put myself in a dangerous position. I would never do anything that could jeopardize my being here for you and Liddie. And the police would never allow me or anyone else to do something dangerous, like confronting a criminal or a bank robber. But I couldn't let this man keep cheating people when I could report him and help the police get the evidence they need to convict him."

Ben's lower lip trembled slightly. He raised his chin. "I was worried about you. That's all. Dad isn't around to protect you and Liddie. I can't let anything bad happen to you."

"Oh, Ben." Anne reached over and hugged her son, who was growing up so fast and trying to take on so much responsibility. "You do not have to fill your father's shoes. He wouldn't want you to think that. But I promise I'll be careful. Okay?"

Ben hugged her back a bit stiffly, like a boy who was too old to cuddle with his mother. "Okay," he said. He backed away and wiped his eyes.

"I'm done with my homework, so I guess I'll play a game and then turn in."

"All right. Why don't you get ready for bed now and we'll pray. Then you can turn out the light when you're finished. I'll go tuck Liddie in while you get changed."

Anne was deeply moved, as she prayed with Liddie and then with Ben, at how her children were developing into such caring, concerned people. She wished Eric were there to see them. How proud he would be. She knew there were bumps in the road ahead, as her children grew and developed and made their own way in life, but she had a feeling they were going to be terrific adults someday. Probably way too soon for her liking.

CHAPTER TWENTY

Mildred arrived at the library first thing Saturday morning with a sign-up sheet for her knitting class and three knit stocking caps.

"If you'll put these out where they can be seen, maybe people will sign up for the class," she said, handing a red, a yellow, and a green hat to Anne.

"These are great, Mildred. So colorful. I'll tack them up on the bulletin board."

"Good. I made these for the donation bin." She took two hats out of her large purse. "I'll leave them here so Liddie and Ben can take them to the church."

"Thank you. That's very thoughtful of you."

"So what are you taking to the potluck after the special service tomorrow?"

"Someone gave me some fresh eggs yesterday, so I'm thinking of making Chinese fried rice with chicken. Ben and Liddie love it, so I know the children will eat something besides desserts. What are you taking?"

"I'm making a *tres leches* cake. Everyone likes desserts."

"Yum. That's one of my favorite cakes, and it will be a hit with my kids, for sure. We'll have to get in line early to make sure we get a piece."

"I'm making an extra large one."

Mildred checked out a couple of books, then left. Anne got the mail, and as she glanced through the stack, a familiar envelope caught her eye. It had the Blue Hill Library logo and return address on it. She stopped and stared at it.

It was her letter to Victoria and Vince. Returned. Someone had scrawled a forwarding address. An APO address. Army Post Office. One of them had gone into the military service. *Most likely Vince*, Anne thought. She couldn't wait to pursue that line of possibility. But she couldn't take time now.

Wendy and her five youngest children came in with three storybooks that she'd picked out to read for Story Time. Each of her children had a garment for the donation bins.

"My mother-in-law sent us a care package of clothes she'd found at yard sales. Trouble is, she doesn't pay attention to sizes. She figures we have a kid to fit any size." Wendy shook her head. "She means well."

"Someone will be happy to have the clothes," Anne said.

"Christian is going to help me with Story Time today. Does Ben want to help too?"

"You can ask him."

Christian was talking to Ben by the entrance where Ben and Liddie were minding the donation bins. Ben and Liddie left their posts and started up the stairs to the Children's Room.

"I guess that answered that question," Wendy said. "See you later."

"Have fun," Anne said.

Wendy looked over her shoulder at Anne and grinned. "I always do."

As the day wore on, the donation bins filled up. Some people came for books or Story Time, but many came just to drop off clothing.

Just before one o'clock, parents collected their children from the Children's Room and Wendy came downstairs with her children and Liddie.

"You had quite a group today," Anne said.

"Fourteen, besides my kids and yours."

"Miss Wendy, look at all the clothes!" Liddie said, pointing to the overflowing donation bin.

"Wow, that's wonderful," Wendy said. "I think the signs you kids put up downtown worked."

"Can we take them to the church now, Mommy?" Liddie asked.

"That's a good idea. I'll have food to carry in tomorrow and it's supposed to rain. But first we need to go through the clothes."

"I can help you do that right now," Wendy said.

"All right."

It took thirty minutes to sort through and check pockets with Wendy and all the children helping. Fortunately, the clothes were clean and none needed mending.

"Can Ben come home with us?" Christian asked. He was a year older than Ben.

"Sure. Liddie can come too. Is that all right?" Wendy asked.

"I want to go with Mommy to take the clothes to church," Liddie said.

"All right. Ben, I'll pick you up about four," Anne said.

"Come on, kids, let's help put these clothes in Mrs. Gibson's car," Wendy said.

Ben put on his jacket. Wendy and Anne and each of the children carried an armful of clothing to the trunk of Anne's Impala. Hershey bounced along with them, running circles around them as they piled the clothes in the trunk. The sky was overcast, and Anne felt a few drops of rain.

"Mom? Will you put Hershey back inside, please?" Ben asked his mother.

"All right."

"Can we go now?" Liddie asked as Ben left with Wendy.

"Yes, as soon as I put Hershey inside and lock up."

It was nearly two as Anne drove down the hill and stopped at the stop sign. She waited for an older model van to drive by, then she turned onto the street behind it. They went in the direction of the church. Several blocks down, the van turned into the left turn lane and stopped at the light. Anne pulled up next to it. She hadn't seen the van around town before. She glanced over. A young woman with long dark hair sat next to an older woman in the front seat. An older man was driving. The young woman looked familiar, and Anne tried to remember where she'd seen her before. The light changed, and the van moved forward. As the van turned, Anne proceeded through the intersection. Suddenly, she recalled where she'd seen the woman. She looked just like the picture of the teacher, Victoria Parker, from the high school yearbook! Could it be? But why would she be in Blue Hill? Then Anne thought about Victoria's uncle in the hospital. Anne hadn't been back to the hospital. She wondered if Reverend Tom had found Victoria, and if the uncle had improved or gotten worse.

Anne made a left turn at the next street and drove around the next block to find the van.

"Mommy, where are you going? The church is that way," Liddie said, pointing from her child seat in the back.

"I know. I need to see something first. We'll go to the church in a few minutes."

At the next intersection, she looked down the street to the right and spotted the van a couple of blocks ahead. She hurried to follow it, hoping she wouldn't lose the van. This was her chance to learn what happened to Aunt Edie's sewing machines.

The van turned up ahead of them. Anne followed, turning on the same street.

"Mommy," Liddie whined. "We have to go to the church."

"Patience, Liddie."

Anne watched in disbelief as the van pulled into the driveway of the church parsonage, where Reverend Tom and his wife Maggie lived. They were only a few blocks from the church. She saw the van driver's door open as the man got out. Just then it started drizzling. Anne pulled over to the curb past the driveway as the man hurried around the van and opened the passenger door.

She knew where the van was parked. It wouldn't take long to deliver the clothing. Maybe they could get the clothing unloaded before it rained harder. "All right." Anne drove off, fully intending to return. She had questions that needed answers.

Carrying all the clothes into the church with only Liddie's help took many trips between the car and the foyer. Drops of rain sprinkled on them, but not enough to get them really wet. Anne wished she's taken the time to load everything into plastic bags. A couple of times, she dropped a piece of clothing and had to make an extra trip. Liddie only carried one small armload at a time.

"Look, Mommy. The box is full," Liddie said on their fourth trip.

"Yes, and we have more. We'll have to pile it high." Anne took time to fold the clothing, so the box would hold more.

A half hour passed before Anne strapped Liddie in her booster seat and drove back to the parsonage. The van was gone. It was now raining steadily. Anne parked in the driveway and unhooked Liddie, then they ran to the front door. Anne wasn't in the habit of making impromptu home visits to the pastor's home, but today she wanted answers. Surely a friendly visit to see if she could help with boxing up the clothing or cleaning up after the potluck lunch gave her enough excuse for the visit.

She rang the doorbell and waited a full minute, listening for footsteps coming to the door. Hearing none, she rang again. After waiting a few minutes and ringing the bell once more, she gave up. No one was at home. In the short space of a half hour, Victoria had eluded her. Anne realized that with the special mission program tomorrow and the dinner afterward, she might not have an opportunity to question Reverend Tom about his visitors until Monday.

As they got back into the Impala, she wondered about Victoria's uncle. Surely he was the reason Victoria was in town. Reverend Tom must have visited and then tracked down Victoria to let her know her uncle was in serious condition. Of course, they must have gone to the hospital. Perhaps Victoria would stay an extended period with her aunt. However, since Victoria was a teacher, she might visit a short while and leave immediately.

She turned around to look at Liddie. "Are you buckled in, sweetie?"

"Yes Mommy. Can we go to Miss Wendy's now? I want to play with the kids."

"Sure." Anne knew her opportunity to learn the truth could slip away from her. She made a U-turn and headed to Wendy's. At her friend's house, she helped Liddie get out of her seat and they hurried through the rain up to the house. She rang the doorbell. Christian and Ben answered it.

"Aww. Can't I stay longer?" Ben said.

"That's up to Mrs. Pyle." Anne stepped inside, followed by Liddie, who immediately ran off to find the twins. Although they were a year younger, Liddie fit right in with their rough-and-tumble games.

"Hey, Anne, come on back. I'm doing laundry," Wendy called.

Anne found her at the dining room table, which was covered with piles of folded clothes. "How do you manage to do work with so many kids running around? Especially when they're stuck inside."

Wendy laughed. "I just ignore them."

Anne knew that wasn't true. Wendy managed to keep track of what her kids were doing. "Could I impose on you a little longer?"

"Sure. Do you want to leave Liddie here too?"

"Yes, if you don't mind. I want to go up to the hospital and see how Victoria's uncle is doing. I can't be positive, but I believe I saw Victoria Parker in town. In fact, I followed her to Reverend Tom's house."

"The domestic arts teacher? Did you stop and talk to her?"

"No. I went on to the church to unload the clothes. When I went back, no one was there."

"Well, get going and find her. She couldn't have gotten far."

Anne grinned. "Thanks. I'll be back before dinner."

"Plan to eat here. I've got a big pot of stew in the Crock-Pot. And I'm making biscuits."

"Sounds wonderful. I'll be back."

Before driving all the way to the hospital in Deshler, Anne decided to check in Blue Hill first. It was raining as she drove to the Douglases' house on Elm Street. There weren't any cars parked near the house, nor in the driveway. She ran through a downpour to the front door and knocked. No one answered.

Anne made a sweep of the downtown. She didn't find them, so she headed for Deshler. When she got to the hospital, she cruised through the parking lot but didn't see the old van or Reverend Tom's car. She decided to go in to see how George was doing. She went up to his room on the second floor, and found the door open partway. She looked in and saw him in the bed. She couldn't tell if he was sleeping or still in a coma, but he was alone. Anne didn't want to bother anyone at the nurses' station with questions, so she left quietly.

By the time she got back to her car, her jacket was wet and drops of water trickled down her neck and into her brow from the rain. She used tissues to dry off the worst of it.

Just to be thorough, when she got back to Blue Hill, Anne drove past the parsonage and the church. No van. No cars. The van with Victoria Parker had disappeared. So had Reverend Tom and his wife.

Disappointed, Anne drove back to the Pyle residence.

"No luck?" Wendy asked, taking Anne's wet raincoat.

"Nope. I'm beginning to wonder if I imagined that van. It vanished."

"Very strange. But you saw it at Reverend Tom's house. You can ask him about it tomorrow. Come in and I'll give you a towel to dry off your hair. I'll hang your coat in the laundry room until you're ready to go home. Maybe it will stop raining by then."

"I hope so." Anne slipped off her shoes by the door, accepted a hand towel, and dabbed at her hair and wiped moisture off her slacks. "All that running around in the rain for nothing."

Chapter Twenty-One

A nne took the children home early enough Saturday evening to get their baths and get them in bed at a decent hour. After they said their prayers and settled down, Anne prepared the rice and put it on to simmer while she sautéed chicken breast and vegetables for the fried rice.

Forty minutes later, she sat down in front of her laptop to check e-mail. Then she remembered the returned letter. She'd put it in her purse. She got it out and sat down in front of her computer again.

She wasn't sure how to search for a member of the military. She entered the APO address in the Internet search engine. Several sites popped up that wanted her to subscribe and pay a fee to begin a search. She tried a different approach and found several references to a Vince Parker. One of them referred to a Vietnam veteran and another was a Korean War vet. She kept looking.

Most people who enlisted in the army were deployed to the Middle East at some time in their tour of duty, so she started looking for military news and lists of deployed military. She scanned for Vince Parker, then V Parker, then just Parker. That brought up a lot of leads. Following links from article to article, she found lots of reports of bravery and destruction, but no mention of Vince Parker. She yawned and leaned back in her chair. Glancing up at the time, she was shocked to see it was eleven o'clock. No wonder her eyes felt so tired. She was about to shut down the computer when a headline caught her attention. In it was the name Corporal Parker.

Sitting up straighter, she clicked on the link to another article. It told about an attack in a crowded marketplace in Afghanistan. She read down until she found his name.

Corporal Vincent Parker was critically wounded during the engagement when he took action, quickly assessing the situation, then vaulting over his fallen squadron leader to confront the enemy. His selfless actions neutralized several barricaded enemies and prevented further casualties, saving his unit and a crowded square filled with Afghan civilians, including women and school children. Corporal Parker was awarded a Purple Heart for wounds sustained and a Silver Star for conspicuous gallantry and intrepidity in action during combat operations.

Anne sat back and stared at the screen. Corporal Vincent Parker. Could it be Aunt Edie's Vince? His actions fit the good things she'd heard about him. Hard worker. Responsible. Carried through on his jobs. Had he walked, or *run*, away from bad companions and chosen a better path for his life? She couldn't help feeling a little guilty that she had almost believed he'd stolen Aunt Edie's sewing machines, but that was not the choice a hero would have considered. She wished Aunt Edie had known about his heroism. She was glad to discover it, and she couldn't wait to find out if it was the same Vince Parker. She wanted to share it with Mildred and Chad and Vince's aunt and uncle.

Perhaps Victoria already had. Anne prayed his uncle would be able to learn of it and know he had made a difference in his nephew's life.

* * *

Anne carried a box with her hot Chinese fried-rice casserole to the church kitchen a few minutes before the service on Sunday morning. Several women worked in the kitchen, taking in food and getting tables set up for the dinner.

"This needs to stay hot," Anne said, setting it on the counter. "Do you need help setting up?"

"Thanks, but we're fine. Be sure to pick up your dish before you go home today."

"I will. Thank you."

Anne went into the sanctuary and joined Ben and Liddie, who were already seated in the row behind the Pyles. The organ played the introduction to the hymn, and everyone stood and joined in. She glanced around, looking for the missionaries. She saw a couple whom she didn't recognize standing next to the pastor's wife. Could it be the couple from the van? It seemed likely, but she couldn't be certain. She hadn't gotten a good look at them, and Victoria wasn't with them now.

Anne got caught up in the music. She loved the atmosphere of praise as the worship team and congregation raised voices in harmony. Ben and Liddie sang out in their sweet, high voices. Ben read the words on the screen, but Liddie sang whatever words came to her mind and heart, making Anne smile. As the last chords faded, the congregation sat and

Reverend Tom walked up onto the platform and picked up a microphone.

"I love when missionaries visit us and we can see and hear firsthand how the Lord multiplies our humble offerings. Last week I announced that the contents of our donation box would go to a mission we support in the US. Have you seen the box? I looked at it before I came up here. It is brimming over. After all the warm clothing you've collected over the past month, I am overwhelmed by your additional generosity. I know one of our five-year-olds inspired all of us to keep digging to find more clothing to give. Because of her, the entire community has caught the spirit of giving. That's an amazing feat for a young child. It goes to show what we can accomplish when God puts a desire in our hearts.

"We have special guests today, so I won't take up much time. I just want to share how exciting it is to me to discover something unexpected. Yesterday God showed me how He has multiplied our offerings. But I'll let you discover for yourselves. Our church has supported Joseph and Gwendolyn Hartley for many years as they serve the people in the Appalachian region of West Virginia. I'll let them tell you about their work. Joseph..."

When the missionary walked up to the platform and turned to face them, Anne recognized him as the man she'd seen getting out of the van in the parsonage driveway. He was tall and slender, with thinning brown hair. He wore a dark blue suit and tie. When he smiled, Anne felt as if a humble gentleness reached out to settle over the congregation.

"I recognize a few of you from our last visit, three years ago. I'm sorry to see one of your congregation missing. Edie Summers was our hostess the last time we came, and we enjoyed her hospitality and visiting with many of you who attended a tea at her lovely home in our honor. I'm sure all of you miss her."

Anne's eyes filled with tears. Aunt Edie had influenced so many people. How blessed she was to live in her home and carry on her legacy. She could imagine the grand tea her aunt served. She loved bringing people together, and the old Victorian house made a perfect setting for such gatherings.

"I'm not going to give a long sermon," Joseph said. "I'll let our video presentation do that in a few minutes. I want to thank you for your faithful support and encourage you in your outreach endeavors. The Bible explains how God uses each of us to fulfill His purpose much better than I could explain. If you'll turn to Second Corinthians chapter nine, verses ten through fifteen, we'll read it together."

Anne opened her Bible and found the passage. She followed along as he read it out loud.

"This passage applies to anything we give to help others," the missionary said. "God supplies the seeds needed to grow the wheat that makes the bread we eat. When we sow liberally— when we are generous with the seed, He multiplies it, so we have a store of seed for the next planting. We are enriched so we can be generous, and in turn, when others are blessed, they will thank the Lord for the gifts and the givers. It's a circle. God blesses us, so we bless others out of our hearts of gratitude, and those who are blessed, praise God and ask Him to bless us in return. I can tell you how this works, but there's no example as great as love in action. Now I'm going to ask my assistant to share a video with you. If someone could dim the lights, please. I'll try to explain as the slides come up."

The lights went out. Music came through the speaker as a beautiful mountain scene appeared on the pull-down screen. The sun shone down on low-lying mist that hung over a valley. The next picture showed a white clapboard church with a green metal roof and a long meeting hall attached.

"This is our church. Three years ago, with the help of a team of workers from Blue Hill, we started adding the community center onto the church. We finally finished it six months ago. It has a kitchen and bathrooms. Before that, we had outdoor facilities, so this has been a real blessing. Especially in the winter, when the snow is deep."

That gained a few laughs. Anne couldn't imagine tromping through snow to use the restroom.

"We needed a place where the community could gather, but we had no idea how important it would become."

Another slide appeared. The room was filled with women, working at tables. Fabric covered a large work area, with several women cutting out patterns. At other tables, women sat at sewing machines, stitching garments together. Anne gasped as she watched. The sewing machines looked like Berninas. Like the ones at the high school. Like the ones in the brochure.

Aunt Edie's sewing machines.

Of course. It all made sense now. No one swindled her aunt or stole from her. Aunt Edie had hosted the Hartleys. She'd known their need. Out of her generous heart, she had filled it. Those had to be the missing sewing machines. Anne couldn't tell from the pictures how many were there, but she had a strong feeling that all twelve were in the mission in West Virginia. She couldn't wait to talk to Gwendolyn to be certain. And Victoria?

Anne turned to look in the back of the church, at the audiovisual booth. She couldn't see well, but she knew. Victoria Parker was handling the video equipment, showing the PowerPoint presentation. She had moved from Philadelphia and gone back to West Virginia to teach sewing on Aunt Edie's sewing machines.

What a relief! She'd been right all along. Victoria took the sewing machines. But with Aunt Edie's blessing. That explained why Anne couldn't reconcile what she'd learned about Victoria with a scheming swindler who would steal from a woman who welcomed her into her home. She'd already learned that Vince Parker was a war hero. She wasn't positive it was the same young man, but at least this confirmed that he had not stolen the missing sewing machines.

Anne remembered being in on some of Aunt Edie's secret missions when she was growing up. Aunt Edie would put together a meal for someone or a box of groceries, and they would sneak it to the recipient's house when no one could see them. Or she would make a handmade card and put twenty dollars in an envelope and mail it with no return address.

Sometimes she drove all the way to Deshler to mail it, so the person wouldn't know it came from Blue Hill. May Day had been a favorite day, when they would make posies and leave them on doorsteps, then ring the bell and run to hide. They would peek around a bush or the side of a building to see the smile when someone came to the door and found the flowers. Just thinking about it brought a lump to Anne's throat. How she missed her sweet, mischievous, adventurous great-aunt. She'd been such a wonderful friend.

Anne wondered how Aunt Edie had managed to keep the sewing machines a secret from her best friend. Mildred truly had not known. Evidently, Reverend Tom hadn't known either.

After the video presentation ended, Joseph invited Victoria to come join him on the platform, along with his wife.

"Since her ministry is vital to our mission, I'm going to give Gwendolyn a chance to share her thoughts with you. He turned the microphone over to his wife.

"Thank you, Joseph. It's so good to be here with you. I just want to give you a bit of background. If you haven't seen it for yourself, it's hard to understand the poverty in our area of the Appalachians. Once upon a time, the residents worked for the logging industry or the mining industry. People didn't have much, but a family could live on the meager income. Due to regulations or depletion, those industries have all but disappeared, leaving many residents out of work. Other challenges make life hard for the people. Expensive gasoline and food. Poor roads. Few medical facilities. Only the main roads are paved, so rain and snow and mud make travel a challenge.

Communication is also difficult. Few areas have cell phone coverage or Internet access. When we visited here three years ago, I shared how I was praying for job opportunities in our area. Women, especially, have difficulty finding employment. I met a young woman here that many of you recognize." She turned to the young woman standing beside her.

"Victoria came to talk to me. She grew up in a nearby area and knew the hardships and struggles we faced. She had a dream to return and help people, but she didn't know what she could do. We prayed for guidance and the Lord answered our prayers. Thanks to the generosity of one of your members and Victoria's heart to help others, we have set up a school and workshop to teach the women to sew and produce garments and quilts to sell. We set up a satellite Internet center in our community building and we take orders, sew, package, and ship from there. So you see, your generosity was multiplied many times over."

Anne heard the murmuring of the congregation and a few people looked around, as if trying to figure out who among them had been so generous. Anne knew. She imagined Mildred and Reverend Tom and Wendy knew too. All the puzzle pieces were coming together.

"I'd just like to add," Victoria said, leaning close to the microphone. "I brought samples and catalogs with me, so you can see what we make. Maybe you'll find something you'd like to order. Or you can pass a catalog along to a neighbor or friend. Gwendolyn and I are wearing dresses made by our ladies. But we definitely appreciate the coats and warm clothing. We haven't graduated to making coats yet, and most of what we make, we try to sell. The women and even some of the men show a real talent for the sewing arts. One of our men has designed and produced beautiful fiddle and guitar cases."

Anne couldn't wait to get a catalog and to talk with Victoria. She knew just how elated Reverend Tom felt, discovering Aunt Edie and Victoria had conspired to develop such a wonderful mission.

CHAPTER TWENTY-TWO

Anne filled her plate and helped Liddie take a good variety of the sumptuous feast prepared by the members of Blue Hill Community Church. Ben filled his own plate. Anne attempted to guide his choices, to no avail. There were too many in line, chatting and laughing as they dug into the assortment of dishes.

"You might as well give up," Alex said. Anne noticed his plate held similar fare to her son's and Ryan's plates. She supposed one meal wouldn't hurt him, but he had piled on pasta, bread, and Jell-O, then headed for the dessert table.

"Ben," she called out. He turned toward her. "One dessert."

He pulled a disappointed expression. She shook her head. He shrugged and turned away toward the table.

As she went through the line, then found a spot for her and Liddie to sit, she tried to keep an eye on Victoria. Instead of their guests going through the line first, they had hung back to visit with people. Mildred and Victoria were deep in conversation. Others stopped to give Victoria a hug, then moved on. Anne watched, determined to talk to her before she left, but the young woman knew so many of the congregation from her two years with them, Anne didn't want to interrupt.

Alex sat across from her. Ben and Ryan took their plates off in a corner with several other boys.

"Were the sewing machines in the video the ones you've been trying to find?" Alex asked.

"I think so, and I couldn't be more thrilled."

"I would have bet that Stanley Fulton was involved," Alex said. "I suppose Edie would have filed a police report if they'd gone missing."

"I wouldn't have discovered Stanley's scheme if not for the missing sewing machines. Finding that receipt led me on quite a wild-goose chase."

"Yes, and you caught the goose. Just not the one you expected. You saved a lot of people from his schemes. I expect he will serve a few years in prison."

"I hope he learned a lesson, so he won't go back to a life of crime when he gets out." Anne knew the chances of him reforming were slim, but it did happen. That made her think that she should pray for him.

"I hope so too, but it's hard for people to change," Alex said, voicing her thoughts.

"Unless someone cares enough to get involved and offer alternatives."

"Like Edie and Victoria and the Hartleys?"

"Exactly." But it took a combined effort. Which made her think of Liddie and the coat drive. Reverend Tom had presented a problem and Liddie had caught his vision, but it had taken the entire town to fulfill her mission and solve the problem.

"I see our boys headed back to the dessert table," Alex said, getting up. "I'll waylay them."

"Thanks."

Anne watched Victoria, hoping for a chance to talk to her. A couple of times, she caught Victoria's gaze on her, and she wondered if the young woman knew she was Edie's niece.

Wendy came over and sat next to Anne. "I heard your gasp. So I gather those were Edie's sewing machines. What a relief, huh?"

"I haven't confirmed it yet, but I believe those are the missing machines. And yes, it is a huge relief."

"We're heading home. I know you want to talk to Victoria. Can I take Liddie home with us? You can pick her up on your way home."

Anne could have hugged her friend. Wendy was a take-charge sort of person. At times like this, Anne welcomed her friend's understanding and interference. "That'd be great. Thanks, Wendy."

"Don't mention it."

Anne got a bowl of apple crisp and sat back down, toying with it, taking her time, waiting for her opportunity. The missionaries and Victoria finally went through the food line. The Hartleys sat at a table with Reverend Tom and his wife. Anne was surprised when Victoria kept walking until she reached Anne.

"Mind if I join you?"

Victoria had a soft drawl that flowed like honey. "Please do! I've been wanting to meet you."

"Reverend Tom told me you're Edie's niece. I'm so sorry." Tears welled up in Victoria's eyes. "I didn't know about Edie until he told me. I had so looked forward to seeing her again."

Her tears made Anne's eyes fill up. "Oh dear, I didn't mean to come over here and make you sad," Victoria said. "Reverend Tom told me that you're the one who alerted him to my uncle's accident. The Hartleys, bless their hearts, were kind enough to bring me along so I could see Aunt Mae and Uncle George. Thank you so much for caring enough to check on them."

Victoria reached out her hand. Anne took it and gave her hand a gentle squeeze. "You're welcome." Anne didn't want to admit she checked on them because she was hunting for Victoria and Vince. "How is your uncle? Is he improving any?"

"Oh yes. He woke up and his mind seems to be all right, although he gets confused easily. He sleeps a lot, but the doctor said that's normal for someone who had a bad concussion. We went right along to see him yesterday after we arrived. Then Reverend Tom and Maggie took us all out to supper to a new place on the road to Deshler."

"Oh." She must have just missed them. "I'm so glad he's getting better."

"So am I. I'll try to keep better track of them from now on." Victoria picked up her knife and fork and started cutting a piece of chicken. She looked up at Anne. "I told Aunt Mae she needs to get a computer or a cell phone at least, so we can stay in touch. We get pretty good cell service at the church."

"That would help. Older people can be intimidated by technology though. They could come to the library and use our computers. I can help them get e-mail addresses." It was a little thing, but she could be part of a solution, Anne thought.

"I heard you started a library in Edie's house. That's a great idea. Aunt Mae wants me to write letters, but I'm afraid I'm no good at that. I'll tell her about your offer," Victoria said with a smile. "You know, Edie talked about you a lot."

"She did?" Anne could only imagine the stories Aunt Edie could share about her.

"Yes. She was so proud of you. She talked about opening a library, but she didn't have the energy to do it by herself. Her dream was to have you help her." Victoria's expression grew sad. "She never had that chance. I miss her. I can't believe she isn't here." Victoria shook her head. "I can just imagine her smiling down from heaven, watching you carry out her dream."

"Thank you. I hope so." Anne felt as if Aunt Edie had just given her a blessing. "It looks to me like you're carrying out another of her dreams. She had such a heart for missions, and you're there, teaching women a trade. Are those some of the sewing machines Aunt Edie purchased?"

Victoria's jaw dropped, and her eyes widened.

"I found the receipt, and I saw the ones at the high school," Anne told her with a conspiratorial smile.

"Oh?" A dimple appeared in Victoria's cheek when she smiled. "So you figured out our little secret."

"I admit, after I found the receipt among her things I wondered where all those machines were."

"Edie got all excited when the Hartleys came to the church and talked about their mission. Of course, she wanted to help. She had already talked to me about the horrible shape of the sewing machines at the school. She knew that because Mildred had tried teaching on them before I got there. Edie arranged to send half of the sewing machines to George and Gwendolyn at the mission and half to the high school. When I told her I wanted to go back home to help other women, Edie told me that was my chance to help. It was a long-range goal. I couldn't afford to go back to West Virginia without a job there so I took a job in Philadelphia. I was there for six months, doing a long-term substitute position. I thought it was going to turn into a full-time job, but it didn't work out that way."

Anne nodded. "I suppose your first priority was your brother. Didn't he go to Philadelphia?"

Victoria's eyes widened again. "Yes. How did you know?"

Anne smiled. "Part of the prerequisite for being a research librarian is having an insatiable curiosity. I'm afraid I'm nosy."

Victoria laughed. Anne was relieved. She could have been offended by Anne's snooping.

Mildred came over to their table. "Mind if I join you? I didn't get enough of a visit."

Anne scooted over. "Sit down here. Victoria was just confirming what we've been trying to figure out," Anne said.

"Oh yes. I wondered. So Edie supplied all those sewing machines and didn't tell a soul. Not even me, her best friend."

Mildred shook her head. "I should have known. She did love a good secret."

"I know she didn't mean to exclude you," Anne said.

"Yes she did," Mildred responded. "What good is a secret gift if you tell someone you did it?"

Anne was relieved to see that Mildred understood and didn't feel slighted. "You're right, of course." She turned to Victoria. "Tell us about your brother. Did he go into the army?"

"Yes. You discovered that too? We went home to West Virginia to visit, so I could apply for a job teaching at the high school. I hoped Vince and Daddy would get along and maybe Vince would get a job or apply to go to community college. He and Daddy got into it the first day we were there. He stayed one more day, until I had my interview, then he took a bus back to Philadelphia and went straight to the nearest army recruiter and enlisted in the military. I was really concerned about him, but he's found purpose, which he never had before."

"Good for him," Mildred said. "At least he's away from the likes of those so-called friends he had here."

"I read about a Corporal Vince Parker saving his unit and a lot of Afghan civilians," Anne said. "Is that your Vince?"

"Yes. I'm so proud of him. Vince got injured, but he recovered and went right back to Afghanistan. He's fixin' to go to college when he gets out. One of the last things our father said to him was that he'd never amount to nothing. Vince proved him wrong. Daddy won't admit it, but I know he's proud too. Vince is a genuine hero with a great future."

"That's wonderful. I'm so glad to hear that. Aunt Edie would be thrilled." Anne was glad Mildred had joined them, so she could hear this too. "I talked to Able Tandy. He said your brother was a hard worker."

"That's good. I worried about him when he worked at the farm. There was another guy, Stan, who tried his best to get Vince in trouble. He was not a good influence. In fact, he was part of the reason we moved. I'm pretty sure he was the one who got Vince to take a stolen bike to the pawnshop. Vince didn't know it was stolen."

"You can tell Vince his old friend is about to serve time in prison for swindling a bunch of people. He finally got caught." Out of the corner of her eye, Anne caught Mildred's surprised look.

"I'll tell him."

The Hartleys and Reverend Tom and Maggie came over to their table. The Hartleys expressed their sympathy to Anne.

"I'm so glad you were able to discover your aunt's little secret," Gwendolyn told Anne. "She did want to keep it a secret and made us all promise not to tell."

"That's Edie for you," Mildred said. "She had her secrets, even from me. For all her outgoing, fun-loving ways, she was one of the most humble people I've ever known."

Anne felt like hugging Mildred. What a great friend she'd been to Aunt Edie, and vice versa.

"It's time for us to go," George said. "We have a long drive home." He turned to shake hands with Reverend Tom. Victoria hugged Anne as they said good-bye.

After they left, Reverend Tom and Maggie sat down with Anne and Mildred. Alex came over and joined them.

"Ben and Ryan are outside playing," he told Anne. So did you get a chance to find out all the details?"

"Sure did. Amazing how everything fits together. Aunt Edie's generosity is helping a lot of people. I should have known," Anne said.

"How could you have known?" Mildred said. "When Edie wanted to keep a secret, she was a master at concealment."

"Anne's curiosity put a swindler out of business," Alex said, giving her a look of pride, which made her feel good, even if that discovery was accidental.

"I only uncovered Stanley's scheme because I had doubts about my aunt's mental faculties and the sewing machine order," she said.

"Don't sell yourself short," Maggie said. "You're a talented research librarian, and you have to dig for the right answers."

"Thank you. I'm thrilled that the answers proved Aunt Edie's mental acuity and compassion. She took an interest in two young people—strangers to Blue Hill—and gave them respect and hope. I have a lot to live up to, following in Aunt Edie's footstep."

Reverend Tom shook his head. "You've passed compassion and generosity to your children. We're all amazed at what Liddie accomplished. I know she had your encouragement and help, but she mobilized the entire town to give warm clothing to the needy."

"I didn't help her much. She did all that on her own. I have a feeling I'm in for a lot more projects as she grows up. I just hope I can keep up with her."

Mildred sat back with a smile. "You're so much like Edie. I can see her in you. Look at how she rubbed off on you! You can't help but pass it on to the next generation. And we'll all be here to help you. Won't we?" Mildred looked around the table.

"Indeed we will," Reverend Tom said, and the others nodded agreement.

ABOUT THE AUTHOR

Emily Thomas is the pen name for a team of writers who have come together to create the series Secrets of the Blue Hill Library. *All Sewn Up* was written by award-winning author Sunni Jeffers. Sunni is currently setting her course for a new life adventure. After college, Sunni started her first adventure as a navy wife and mother. Ten years later, they moved to Denver to take over management of the family security business. When her children left home, she began writing books. In 1992, Sunni and her husband moved to a ranch in the Great Northwest to raise cattle, timber, and hay, and to give her the time to hone her craft and write stories about women and their struggles and victories. Now Sunni's fourth adventure has begun. After downsizing to a cottage in town, Sunni and her husband are exploring the US and Canada in their motor home. As they travel, she continues writing heartwarming stories of delightful women living out their faith in small-town America as they face challenges and adventures in everyday life.

A Conversation with the Author

Q. *Describe your writing process.*

A. I'm a plotter. I have to know my story before I sit down to write it. I spend days thinking about it. Then I write a long, detailed outline with major scenes. Once I start, I write straight through. I keep a countdown spreadsheet to keep me on target with word count and a spreadsheet of scenes and the day/date they appear. This helps when I go through revisions. These days, I write as we travel. We are full-time RVers, so I write as my husband drives our rig down the road. When we settle in one place for a while, I write at our small dinette, spending mornings writing. We'll take a break to go for a walk, a bike ride, or a sightseeing excursion, then I'm back writing for a couple of hours in the evening.

Q. *What are the challenges of collaborating with other authors on a series?*

A. Writing for a series can be more challenging than writing a stand-alone novel. Like an actor playing a part, the authors must be able to "get into character" and know how Anne or Wendy or Alex or the other characters will act and react to events. Author voice must flow seamlessly from book to book. Facts have to fit. Descriptions of people and places have to be consistent. It means constantly referring to the series guide and checking with the other authors for their details about places, people or events. I believe writing for various Guideposts Books series has helped me become a more versatile and disciplined writer.

Q. *Name the top three entries/things on your bucket list.*

A. My husband and I made bucket lists thirty-seven years ago, before the term had been invented. We called them *dream lists*. They were packed away and forgotten, until we sold our business in Denver and decided to explore America, to see where we wanted to settle. Going through things, preparing to move, we found our lists. In the eighteen years since we'd penned them, we'd accomplished all but two dreams. To own a small farm, and to live on a boat. We ended up with the farm. Now, twenty years later, we are embarking on a land cruise in our land yacht—a thirty-six-foot motor home. Time to make new bucket lists.

Q. *What advice would you give an aspiring novelist?*

A. Write. Write whether you're happy or sad. Write when you don't feel like it. When all you only have five minutes and when you have lots of time. Write stories, but also write about your hopes and dreams and trials and sorrows. Write about your adventures and misadventures, as well as the fictional stories that develop in your mind. Writing must become a habit for the long haul. Writing is great therapy and provides lots of material for future stories.

Q. *Anne Gibson likes to drink her coffee without cream or sugar. What are your coffee-shop favorites?*

A. With a Norwegian heritage, I learned early to drink my coffee black. As a hospital worker and as a navy wife, the coffee I drank was black and strong. I don't like sweet drinks, so I order mochas with half the chocolate syrup, and they come out just right. But I also have a strong English background, and I do love a good cuppa tea with cream. I love chai lattes. That's my drink of choice from a coffee stand.

Recipes from the Library Guild

Wendy's This-and-That Ranger Cookies

1 cup + 3 tablespoons
   vegetable shortening
   or butter
1 cup brown sugar, firmly
   packed, light or dark
1 cup granulated sugar
2 large eggs
2 teaspoons vanilla
1 teaspoon salt
2 cups unbleached
   all-purpose flour
½ teaspoon baking powder

1 teaspoon baking soda
1½ cups old-fashioned
   rolled oats
¾ cup shredded coconut
2½ cups crispy rice cereal,
   lightly crushed
¾ cup chocolate chips
¾ cup chopped pecans
¾ cup chopped dried
   cranberries or cherries
¾ cup white chocolate chips
   or butterscotch chips

Using a stand mixer if possible, mix the shortening/butter and sugars till blended. Then add eggs, vanilla, and salt and beat until pale yellow and fluffy. In a separate bowl, blend the flour, baking powder, and baking soda together. Gradually add the flour mixture to the shortening mixture, reserving one-half cup of the flour, and mix until well blended. Add the oats, coconut, and cereal, mixing until just blended. Stir in the rest of ingredients.

Spoon the dough into the bowl with the remaining flour and mix or knead until blended. Drop the dough by rounded teaspoonfuls onto lightly greased or parchment-lined cookie sheets. The coconut makes the dough a bit dry, so form into rounds by hand.

Bake the cookies in a preheated 350-degree oven for ten to twelve minutes or until they're golden brown. Don't overcook. If using convection oven and multiple racks, bake at 335 degrees for twelve to fourteen minutes.

Yields sixty to sixty-eight cookies.

From the Guideposts Archives

"What Prayer Can Do" by Robin O'Reilly originally appeared in Guideposts *magazine.*

I had already lined, trimmed, and finished one sleeve for my sister-in-law's wedding dress and was about to cut material for the other when I discovered the pattern was missing. I looked under my sewing machine, through all the loose fabric in my sewing box. What happened to that pattern piece?

I enlisted my children's help. The three of us scoured the house. No pattern. *I have two choices,* I thought. *I can rip apart the finished sleeve and use that as a model, or I can buy a new pattern.* I couldn't bear to dismantle the sleeve, so I drove to the fabric store, only to discover they were out of my pattern! Returning home empty-handed, I gave the house one last search before giving up.

The next morning I went into the kitchen, where I have my sewing area, ready to take apart the finished sleeve. Then it occurred to me: Robin, you have done everything but pray. I got down on my knees. *Lord, if it's your will, please help me find what's missing.*

When I opened my eyes I was staring right at the storage drawer beneath the oven. Could the pattern have fallen in there while I was fixing dinner? Sure enough, there it was. As it turned out, there had been a more important piece missing—prayer.

Read on for a sneak peek of another exciting book
in *Secrets of the Blue Hill Library*!

If Walls Could Talk

The door to the basement creaked open and Anne peered down
the dark stairwell. She stood in the kitchen, wearing fuzzy
blue slippers and a matching terrycloth robe, her hands still
slightly damp from washing the breakfast dishes.

The cavernous old basement had always spooked her as a child
and, even as an adult, she didn't relish spending time down there.
She'd been so busy fixing up the rest of the classic Victorian house
that she'd been quite happy to leave the basement alone. She'd even
contemplated moving the washer and dryer out of the basement to
avoid going down there but hadn't been able to find a better place
for them. So she tried to limit her laundry days to once a week, if
possible. The rest of the basement was used for storage and
contained Christmas decorations and an assortment of Aunt Edie's
old belongings, although it wasn't nearly as packed as the attic.

Anne reached out to flip on the light switch, not that it did
much good. The lone lightbulb in the center of the room cast a dim
glow, creating long shadows that somehow made the basement
even less inviting. It didn't help that the bushes planted in front of
the cellar windows blocked most of the sunlight from shining
through the glass.

Liddie had wanted to come down here with her to search for the terra-cotta pots that they would use to plant the seedlings they'd bought yesterday. But Anne had instructed Liddie and Ben to clean their bedrooms instead, not wanting them to dig into boxes and disrupt the layers of dust that now tickled her nose.

As she began to descend the stairs, she saw the terra-cotta pots right where she'd remembered, near the closest cellar window. Maybe she would use the creaky, cage-style elevator, which came all the way down to the basement, to take all the pots back upstairs.

Then Anne heard a sound that wasn't music to her ears: *Drip. Drip. Drip.*

She wrinkled her nose, realizing that there was water leaking somewhere inside her basement. Her first thought was the water heater, so she headed in that direction. The water heater in the apartment where she and Eric had lived in New York had rusted out at the bottom and seeped water all over the floor and even through the utility room wall into the finished, carpeted family room. They'd had to call in a carpet restoration company to suck up all the water and dry out the carpet and floors, as well as replace the water heater. It had been a mess — an *expensive* mess — and an experience she hoped never to repeat.

At least this basement had a concrete floor, she thought to herself when she reached the water heater. It stood next to the furnace and there was a covered drain on the floor only a few inches away. But the cement around the water heater was completely dry. She edged around it, looking for a leak in the back, but the floor was dry there too.

Next, she checked the washing machine, located in the right corner next to the staircase. Unlike the rest of the basement, it was well-lit. Anne rounded the worktable sitting in the center of the three-sided laundry room to inspect the washer. The hoses were all connected and there was no sign of water around the machine.

So where was the drip coming from?

Anne stood still for a moment, listening and trying to place the location. *Drip. Drip. Drip.*

The sound was coming from behind her and to the left. She headed that way, wishing she had brought a flashlight. The lightbulb flickered, indicating that it needed to be replaced soon. It was still bright enough to illuminate the boxes and crates, so she wasn't in danger of tripping. She just didn't want to run into a spiderweb.

Anne shivered at the thought. Then she looked down and saw a small rivulet of water running between her feet. She followed the trail to a large stack of crates filled with empty canning jars. No doubt they'd been used by Aunt Edie, or possibly even Aunt Edie's mother. She could see more water seeping beneath the crates and pooling in a narrow crevice in the cement before running toward the center of the basement. The sound of the dripping came from somewhere behind the crates.

With a sigh of resignation, Anne began to move the old crates that sat in front of the stone wall. She stacked them on either side of her. When she'd moved enough crates to slip behind them, she saw the problem. Part of the stone wall had caved in, spilling some dirt and rainwater onto the floor. The hole was about two feet wide and about two feet off the floor. Dark, wet dirt bulged at the remaining stones, threatening to crumble at the slightest movement. The heavy rains this past week must have put too much pressure on the old stone wall until part of it finally gave way.

"Great," Anne muttered, realizing her plans for a peaceful Saturday morning had just crumbled along with the dirt at her feet. She cleared a larger area around the wall, making sure the dripping water wasn't touching anything but the floor. Now she found herself wishing the problem had simply been the water heater. She had no idea what a repair like this would entail. But at least she knew where to start. She reached into the pocket of her robe for her cell phone, hoping Alex was already awake this morning.

* * *

"This is a terrible way to start summer vacation," Ben grumbled as he stood in the open doorway to Anne's bedroom. "Can't we at least play for a little while before we clean our rooms?"

"You and Liddie were supposed to clean your rooms last night," Anne reminded her son. "If you'd done it then, you could go out and play now."

Annoyance flashed in Ben's hazel eyes. "But I was super tired last night! We had to clean out our lockers at school and everything."

Anne smiled as she reached for a pair of small pearl earrings that had once belonged to her Aunt Edie. "If you'd spend as much time cleaning your room as you do complaining about it, you'd be done already. Besides, Ryan will be here soon and I want everything picked up and off your bedroom floor before he gets here."

"But, Mom...," Ben began to protest.

Anne turned and gave him the look that mothers had perfected for centuries. The *look* that brooked no more arguments.

Surrender flashed in his hazel eyes and he hesitated for only a moment before finally turning around and disappearing down the hallway.

Despite her insistence on cleanliness, Anne knew just how he felt. It was a beautiful Saturday morning and the last thing she wanted to do was spend it cleaning. But after taking one look at the wet basement floor, she knew she didn't have any other choice. She had called Alex and he'd promised to be over later this morning to take a look at it.

She sighed as she ran a comb through her brown hair, wondering how extensive — and expensive — the basement repair would be. She loved this old house, especially now that it also served as a town library. She just hoped the basement wall wouldn't need major construction that would require noisy tools and workmen that would disrupt the cozy, quiet atmosphere of the library. Thankfully, Wendy was filling in at the checkout desk today, so Anne could work on cleaning up the basement. She glanced at her watch, noting that the library was due to open in about an hour.

After pulling her hair into a loose ponytail, Anne took one last look in the full-length mirror, satisfied with the denim Capri pants and the light blue T-shirt she'd chosen for basement clean-up duty. She slipped her bare feet into a pair of old canvas shoes and then headed out into the hallway to check on the kids.

Anne stopped by Liddie's room first. Her five-year-old had picked up most of her toys and was now placing them in the toy box next to the closet. She'd even made her bed, although one side of the bedspread hung crookedly, with the bottom edge touching the hardwood floor and the top edge barely easing over the mattress. Her dolls were arranged neatly on her pillows, but Anne noticed that one was missing.

"Where's Cleopatra?" Anne asked Liddie.

Liddie looked up from the open lid of her toy box. "She's in a time-out." She pointed toward the small chair in the corner, where the doll sat facing the wall.

Anne couldn't help but smile. "Why does Cleopatra need a time-out?"

"Because she was naughty," Liddie said, rising to her feet and padding barefoot over to her mother. She still wore the lavender cotton nightgown that hung down to her ankles. "She wanted to wear Betsy's hat to the circus and tried to take it away from her without asking. So I put her in time-out until she tells Betsy that she's sorry."

Anne's smile widened. Betsy was a rag doll they'd found at a flea market. Her daughter loved to make up stories about her dolls, and her creativity grew every year.

"I didn't know there was a circus in town," Anne said, playing along.

"It's going to be in the backyard," Liddie clarified as she pulled a stuffed elephant out of the toy box. "I've just got to make breakfast for all of the animals first so they don't get hungry during the show."

"It sounds like you have a big day ahead of you," Anne said. "Why don't you get dressed first, and then you can go outside and set up your circus."

"Okay," Liddie replied as she pulled out a stuffed giraffe.

Anne smiled as she left the room, realizing it probably wouldn't stay clean for long. Still, it was good for the kids to learn to pick up after themselves.

When she reached Ben's room, she found him standing in the open doorway waiting for her. Hershey, Ben's chocolate Labrador retriever, lay on the end of the bed, playing innocent.

"I'm all done," Ben announced, a wide smile on his face.

She looked past him, surprised to see that his room did look clean. There were no toys or clothes on his floor and he'd made his bed. Except...There were several mysterious lumps under Ben's summer bedspread that she found suspicious.

"What's going on under here?" she asked, walking toward his bed. Hershey jumped off the bed and headed toward the door, looking eager to make his escape.

Ben raced past her and started smoothing out the strange lumps. "Nothing."

"Ben?" Anne folded her arms across her chest. "What's under the bedspread?"

He heaved a long suffering sigh and then slowly pulled the bedspread back to reveal some wadded-up clothes, his school backpack, several paper airplanes, and three toy trucks of various shapes and size.

Anne arched a brow in his direction but didn't say a word.

A guilty flush bloomed on the boy's cheeks. "It's clean, Mom. Everything is off the floor, just like you wanted."

"You know that's not what I meant," Anne told him, her voice gently chastising. She knew the transition from school to summer vacation could be a little bumpy in the first few days, but she hadn't expected it to start this early.

"But we're just going to mess it up anyway," Ben countered. "And Ryan's going to be here any minute!"

"Then you'd better get moving." Anne headed toward the door. "Because you're not leaving this room or playing with Ryan until *everything* is where it belongs."

The rumble of tires on gravel sounded through the open bedroom window. Ben flew over to it and looked outside. "They're here!"

"Start cleaning if you want to play with Ryan." Anne said from the open doorway. She stood there for a few moments as Ben moved at lightning speed. He cleared his dirty clothes off the bed and placed them in the hamper. Then he scooped up his backpack and carried it over to his desk. By the time the buzzer to the private entrance rang, he'd placed his trucks and paper airplanes into the toy box and then whirled around to face Anne. "Clean enough?" he asked, a little breathless.

"Clean enough," she agreed as they headed for the back staircase. Liddie was a few feet ahead of them, her arms full of dolls and stuffed animals. "See," Anne told him, reaching out to ruffle his hair, "that didn't really take very long once you started, did it?"

"I guess not," Ben said. He raced past both Anne and Liddie, taking the stairs two at a time until he reached the private entrance on the second floor.

When he opened it, Anne reached the landing just in time to see Ryan and Alex standing on the other side. Alex wore his work clothes, along with a leather tool belt slung across his hips. Ryan held a basketball in his hands.

"Want to shoot some hoops?" Ryan asked her son.

"Sure," Ben replied, walking outside as Alex entered the house.

Alex looked up at Anne and Liddie as they walked toward him. "So you've got a basement leak."

Anne nodded. "I sure do. It's a small mess right now, but I'm afraid it might lead to a bigger one if we don't take care of it."

"Well, let's go take a look," Alex said and then glanced down at Liddie. "Do you want to be my helper today?"

"In the basement?" She gave an exaggerated shiver and shook her head. "Uh-uh! That place is scary. Besides, I have to get ready for the circus."

Alex arched a brow in Anne's direction. "Is the circus in town?"

She chuckled. "Not quite. Liddie is going to put together a circus in the backyard."

"You can come if you want," Liddie told him, moving toward the door. "It's going to be lots of fun."

"I wish I could," Alex said, reaching out to open it for her. "But I have to work today."

"See you later," Liddie said, carrying her stuffed animals out the door and down the porch steps before heading for the backyard.

"You'll probably wish you'd picked the circus," Anne said wryly, "once you see what's down there. I'll grab a flashlight."

"I've got one," he interjected, pulling a heavy-duty flashlight from the back of his tool belt. "Lead the way."

Anne led him downstairs and into the library's kitchen. She'd left the basement door open and was grateful that there wasn't a damp or musty odor emanating from the water seepage. She flipped on the flickering light and headed down the stairs with Alex close behind her. Then she pointed out the crumbled wall.

He clicked on his flashlight, the beam illuminating the pile of crumbled stones, dirt, and rainwater at the base of the wall. "This isn't good."

Anne winced. "Not just a small repair?"

"Depends." He began to walk around the basement, slowly moving his flashlight over the length of the stone wall. "We need to know if the foundation is the problem or just that part of the wall." Every few feet he stopped and pushed against the stones.

"How does it feel?" She asked, tensing a little each time that he touched the wall.

"Strong, so far. I don't see any other water leakage areas either."

They made their way past all four walls before returning to where they started.

"Looks like this is the only problem," Alex said, running the bright flashlight beam over the hole in the wall. "Maybe we've just got a couple of brittle stones that finally crumbled."

He reached out to touch one of the remaining stones near the hole. It came loose in his hand and then more stones crumbled and fell. Dirt and water spilled onto the floor, causing both of them to step back out of the way.

"That can't be good," Anne said. She watched the beam of his flashlight move over the dirt pile in front of them.

There were some odd lumps in the soil. Anne bent down and carefully sifted her fingers through the dirt until she found one of the lumps. She picked it up and studied it, realizing it was a small piece of charred wood.

"Look at this." She handed the piece of wood to Alex.

He took it from her, studying it for a long moment. Then he bent down and picked up another piece of a small piece of glass. "I wonder if this was a dumping ground at one time."

Anne wrinkled her nose. "You mean my house was built on top of a trash pile?"

He smiled. "Maybe next to a trash pile, anyway. A very old trash pile, judging by the look of this glass."

She moved toward him for a closer look and felt something under her shoe. Anne lifted up her foot and saw what looked like a small stone. When she picked it up, she realized it was much more. "Look at this. I found an arrowhead."

Alex peered at it in the flashlight's glow. "Wow. Looks like an old one too."

Anne studied the arrowhead in her hand. It was made of dark black flint and appeared to be hand carved. She'd seen arrowheads like this before. Aunt Edie used to take her creek walking for Native American relics. They'd head to a local creek and search near the headwaters at the upper portion of the creek. The erosion of the ground unearthed all sorts of treasures. They'd found arrowheads, along with other interesting artifacts. One time Aunt Edie had even found a small primitive spear.

"I wonder what else is buried back there." Alex aimed the flashlight toward the hole in the wall, now a little larger than it had been before.

"What's that?" Alex said, taking a step forward as the flashlight illuminated the pile of dirt beyond the wall.

Anne moved next to him, carefully trying to avoid the dirt and water on the floor. "What?"

"That," he said, fixing the flashlight beam onto one spot behind the crumpled wall. "It looks like a...bone."

"A bone?" Anne echoed. "You mean some kind of animal bone?"

"I'm not sure." Alex pulled a pair of pliers from his tool belt and moved toward the hole in the wall. He used the handles of the pliers to carefully move the loose dirt around the protruding bone. As the dirt fell away, it revealed more bones and what appeared to be a ribcage.

"I don't think it's an animal." He turned to look at Anne. "I think it's a human skeleton."

A Note from the Editors

We hope you enjoy Secrets of the Blue Hill Library, created by the Books and Inspirational Media Division of Guideposts, a nonprofit organization that touches millions of lives every day through products and services that inspire, encourage, help you grow in your faith, and celebrate God's love in every aspect of your daily life.

Thank you for making a difference with your purchase of this book, which helps fund our many outreach programs to military personnel, prisons, hospitals, nursing homes, and educational institutions. To learn more, visit GuidepostsFoundation.org.

We also maintain many useful and uplifting online resources. Visit Guideposts.org to read true stories of hope and inspiration, access OurPrayer network, sign up for free newsletters, download free e-books, join our Facebook community, and follow our stimulating blogs.

To learn about other Guideposts publications, including the best-selling devotional *Daily Guideposts*, go to ShopGuideposts.org, call (800) 932-2145, or write to Guideposts, PO Box 5815, Harlan, Iowa 51593.